ARROGANT ARCHITECT

A COCKY HERO CLUB NOVEL

BY ALEXA PADGETT

Arrogant Architect is Book 2 in The Wright Family series inspired by Vi Keeland and Penelope Ward's *British Bedmate*. It is published as part of the Cocky Hero Club world, a series of original works, written by various authors, and inspired by Keeland and Ward's *New York Times* bestselling series.

To find out more about all the Cocky Hero Club World books and authors, visit: http://www.cockyheroclub.com

ISBN-978-1-945090-31-8

Editor: Deborah Nemeth
Proofreading by: Kathleen Page and Charity Chimni
Photo Credit: Volodymyr Tverdokhlib
Cover by: Chris Philpot

A sexy, new forbidden romance from USA Today bestselling author Alexa Padgett.

For the first time in years, I want…

I want Knox Wright. My best friend's brother, my boss…the man who breaks my still-shattered heart.

Knox was a college hockey legend and, now, he's one of the most successful architects in decades. I was the new hire whose desperate need to move on from *that* night drove me to succeed.

I never should have accepted the position, not once I looked into Knox Wright's eyes and felt the heat deep in my belly…but I did. Because Knox makes me feel alive. And as I fall under Knox's spell, our relationship turns intense and deep…and *secret*. When our affair runs the risk of being exposed, I face a far more intimate betrayal than I ever expected.

For Piper.

You are the best critique partner, and I'm so, so thankful to call you my friend.

Chapter One
Emmaline

"Today is going to be a life changer," I murmured into my mirror. "You are totally going to nail this interview and get offered the position."

I nodded to myself, trying to feel confident.

A text beeped through and I smiled at my friend Bridget's note:

You amaze me. I hope you're as proud of all you've accomplished in these past few years as I am.

Nurse Ratched

I laughed as I typed back a response. I'd met Bridget a few years ago under less than stellar circumstances—in the ER. She'd been my favorite nurse as I convalesced after the car accident, and I was very lucky to count her as a dear friend.

My gaze fell to the engagement ring on my finger. Right. I'd accomplished much, but I still had more to do. Like start my career…and let go of the last vestiges of my life before.

With a deep, painful breath, I slipped the ring from my finger for the first time since Sebastian had slid it on and set it on my bureau. I put my fingers on the top, remembering my happiness, my excitement, and all the love rushing through me as he kissed first the large pink diamond and then my lips.

That was my life *before*. This was now.

My future.

I'm ready, I texted Bridget. *And I can't wait until brunch Saturday to give you the details.*

She sent me back a heart emoji.

I raised my gaze and met my eyes in the mirror. I nodded.

"Today you start living again, Emmaline. It's time."

My phone beeped again. I smiled as I saw the message was from Aidy.

I'm out at The Mac—something came up—but I'm rooting for you!

I tapped back a quick response, thanking her. Aidy was my dearest friend. Crazy that I'd only known her for a few months because I already couldn't imagine my life without her. She'd boosted my confidence enough for me to finally move forward. Well, that and the fact she was one of the owners of the firm where I was interviewing.

I loved our friends Calliope and Bridget, the other two ladies in our yoga brunch sorority we'd compiled this year, but those women were nearly a decade older, more like big sisters. Aidy was a year younger than me, and we clicked on every level. Hell, her puppy had peed on me.

We were BFFs. So, no matter what happened with the interview, I knew I had a woman in my life who'd go through all my ups and downs. Though, I also knew she was rooting for me to get the position.

Energy zipped through me as I tugged at my suit jacket, trying to get the positioning right over my white silk camisole. Thanks to Aidy's endorsement, I had a good feeling about my upcoming interview at her family's architecture firm, Wright and Associates, where I'd meet the other two Wright siblings.

The brothers had brought new blood and new life to both the designs and business, making it one of the most environmentally friendly architecture firms in the Northeast corridor. Aidy was the most recent addition, but her blueprints for the Macintosh Hotel were gaining big buzz in the small, tight-knit community. My alumni email last week stated Wright and Associates would be giving a guest lecture in the capstone course next semester.

And I was interviewing for a position with the firm.

The Wright siblings were being described as modern-era Frank Lloyd Wright proteges—each of the three had a specialty that enhances designs past the point of function and beauty, but when combined, their synergistic play on texture, light, and plane proved phenomenal. I closed my eyes, imagining the newest addition to Providence's small cultural heart: the symphony/ballet hall. It had the refined distillation of purpose of Phillip Johnson but the whimsy and billowing form of Gehry's Bilboa branch of the Guggenheim Museum.

I'd stood outside the structure when it opened earlier this year, awestruck. I wanted more of *that* feeling—I wanted to be part of creating it in someone else.

I'd dressed in a fire-engine red pantsuit that my mother and I picked out together on our last shopping trip before her death—not my best color with my cream-pale skin and blacker-than-night hair, but I loved the way the long line of the pant made me feel chic and sophisticated. Professional.

My mother agreed, not even bothering to glance at the tag when she had the saleswoman ring it up. I felt powerful in it—like it was a form of armor. When I told my mother that, she'd laughed and stated that's exactly what good clothes should do. My lips tipped up at the memory even as a deep pang slammed through my chest. I missed her. I always would.

I glanced down at my sensible nude heels, and then back into the mirror where my light hazel eyes stared at me, too wide. I narrowed the corners hoping that would give me less of a bright-eyed look, but that didn't work. With a deep breath, and a touch of my mother's pearls, I headed out the door.

—— A ——

I made it to the Wright and Associates office with two minutes to spare. My dad always told me there was being on time and then there was being a minute too late. I preferred on time.

I collected my belongings in my portfolio and stepped out of the car, careful to avoid the piles of dark slushy snow. I made my way to the front of the building, enamored as always with the sweeping lines of the house the Wright brothers had turned into their offices. The windows were large and bright in the late winter sunshine. A thick set of pewter handles snuggled against the door frame.

The buzzer panel sat beside the door, under a small plaque with the Wright and Associates logo, and I pressed the intercom button.

A chirpy voice responded, "Yes?"

"Good morning. My name is Emmaline Schooler. I'm here for a nine a.m. appointment with Mr. Wright."

"Yes," said that chipper voice. "We're expecting you. Please come in."

Once the door buzzed, I opened it and stepped into the warm and inviting entry that evolved into a large reception area that flowed into the open workspace for two draftsmen and a designer.

There were three offices and a conference room that lined two of the back walls. I'd been in the conference room before and adored the dark red exposed brick that connected this building to the one next door.

I'd looked for architecture firms all up and down the Northeast corridor, sticking as close to Providence as possible, unwilling to leave the area. There were three firms in Boston I'd interviewed with, but I worried about the distance from Sebastian. I'd made him a promise, and I intended to keep it.

Deep breath in, deep breath out, just like Bridget taught me in my hospital bed all those years ago.

Now wasn't the time to think about what I'd lost because I needed to focus on building my career and a life.

I perched on the edge of one of the deep leather club chairs with a smile to the receptionist. Her name was Nanette, and she'd chattered on without seeming to take a breath. The soft buttery texture slid under my thighs, and I ran my fingers along the chair's edge as I marveled at how the space looked both masculine and inviting at the same time. No easy feat.

"Ms. Schooler?"

I rose before I turned to face a man—a tall, athletic man. A *beautiful* man. I locked my knees and straightened my spine as I took him in. He had tousled golden hair and sharp cheekbones that slid into a sturdy jaw. His broad shoulders filled out his suit coat well and his light blue dress shirt matched his eyes. He looked at me from under thick, brown brows, and I felt a flurry of emotion not just in my chest, but in my belly.

I should *not* be reacting like this to the man in front of me.

I pulled up an image of Sebastian's brown eyes, so soft and filled with love. That steadied me enough to ensure my voice was as brisk and controlled as I wished the rest of my body was.

"Mr. Wright?"

He met my gaze, a small dimple flashing in his cheek. "I'm Knox. Nico is finishing up a call, and he asked me to bring you back."

"Great," I said.

"Come on back."

I cleared my throat as discreetly as possible, and my eyes drifted over to Nannette. She gave me a double thumbs-up and a big smile. I returned her smile with a tentative one of my own, feeling a bit overwhelmed by my first impression of Knox.

He was huge—came from playing hockey in college, from what I'd read in his bio. He'd managed the star forward position and an architectural degree from Cornell—either one of those was quite a feat.

"Aidy speaks highly of you," he said over his shoulder.

Shoulders that tapered down into slim hips, and while I couldn't see his rear end, thanks to his suit coat, I bet it was spectacular. I brought my eyes back up to the back of his head, unwilling to speculate further about my potential boss. He led me to a different conference room than I'd been in before. This was larger with a beautiful table made from a solid, single plank of maple.

I couldn't help but gasp as I looked at the piece. I touched my fingers to the smooth satin of the surface. Knox settled into a chair with a chuckle.

"Yes, that was quite a find," he said. "I was on a hike when

I found this fallen tree. Couldn't believe its size or the purity of the grain. Had to haul it out with some serious-level chains. My buddy said I was crazy to even try. Best workout of my life."

I glanced up and met his gaze with my own. "You *made* this?"

He nodded, pride shining in his eyes.

"It's beautiful," I said. "One of the most beautiful pieces I've ever seen."

"Thanks. I'm proud of it." His smile widened, and his teeth flashed white and straight. I collapsed into the chair right behind me, thankful for its proximity because otherwise I'd be on my ass. This wasn't going as I expected. Of course, everyone knew the Wright brothers were handsome, well on their way to wealthy, and talented.

But their newsworthiness didn't explain my strange fascination with Knox Wright.

I'd been around good-looking men for years. My father had worked at the Naval Station Newport, which was filled with attractive, athletic young men in their prime. But none of them generated the level of excitement in my belly Knox did.

The door opened, and a darker version of Knox stepped into the room. Nico. I sighed with relief. While the eldest Wright sibling was handsome and confident, he didn't send cascades of strange sensations through my core like his brother did. I rose from my seat with a small grunt to shake Nico's hand.

"Nice to meet you," I said.

"You too, Ms. Schooler. Thank you for coming in to meet with us. As highly as Aidy speaks of you, we like to make these types of hiring decisions together."

"Totally understandable." I hesitated but then looked Nico in the eye. "And I also understand if I'm not the best candidate, regardless of Aidy's opinion. As much as I value her friendship, it shouldn't bias my chances here today."

Nico's smile warmed, and he nodded as he picked up the copy of the resume he must have brought with him into the room.

"I see you graduated at the top of your class," Nico said. "In December. Why wait until now for a job?"

I nodded—no reason to toot that scholastic horn further. "I needed the time to organize certain personal aspects of my life."

Actually, the truth was I didn't need to work. I'd completed an architectural degree at the urging of Sebastian's grandmother, Ellie. As she had pointed out, I needed something to fill my time after I refused to return to Cornell. I'd been about to start my third year in Weill Cornell Medical College, but the sight of blood... I swallowed down the fear and revulsion that licked its way up my belly.

Nope. Now was not the time to fall back into my past.

"And you interned at Collins and Miner." Knox's lips flattened and my stomach fluttered with dismay.

"I did, yes."

Nico glanced at Knox and then back at me. "Did you meet Melinda Shoals?" he asked.

I tipped my head, eyebrows scrunching together. "I did. She's a junior partner who worked on the industrial side of the business," I said, placing the stunning blonde. I shook my head. "I spent most of my time with the drafts-people. And..." I hesitated for a moment before blurting, "The few interactions I had with her proved...stilted."

Nico's lips quirked, but I couldn't read Knox's expression.

"And your time at Collins and Miner? On the whole, was it positive?"

I frowned. "Yes."

"Then why did you reject their offer for employment," Nico asked.

"Color us curious about your experience there," Knox added. His voice was now gruffer.

"Well, they're much larger, and I didn't see the same learning opportunities. They lacked interest in mentoring their new hires, which is why I'm interested in a boutique firm like yours. In addition, management didn't hold the same beliefs about environmental design I did," I said, my tone neutral. I thought of Melinda, who'd dismissed anyone who wasn't a partner—the real reason I didn't want to work at the firm.

Knox leaned back in his chair, and I wondered if I'd just lost my opportunity. I found Knox hard to read, which made me want to study him even more.

"I'm assuming Aidy explained that you'd be working mainly with her. Until we get a feel for your work, most of the tasks required will be clerical in nature, but we hope you'll fill in for some of Aidy's role when she's on maternity leave."

He wanted me to understand this position could be temporary. Why?

More of my excitement at the start of the interview fizzled.

"I understand there isn't a guarantee for a permanent position."

Knox nodded. "All right. Good. May I look at your portfolio?"

I unzipped it and slid my portfolio across the table. I'd flipped it open so that Knox could look at some of the renderings. He stopped at the third one—the building I'd like to create.

"What's this?" he asked.

"It's a prototype for soldiers or injured veterans who need medical support due to their medical or mental health conditions. At least, that was the initial idea."

"Intriguing. What was the genesis for the idea?" Knox asked. He raised his eyes enough to meet mine, and I had to squeeze my thighs together and fist my palms to keep from whimpering like a fool.

He was just a man. An extraordinarily good looking one, sure, but I'd spent my first two decades around men as muscular and attractive as Knox Wright. My response to him was out-of-control-ridiculous. I needed to get my shit together.

If I didn't get this position, I wouldn't be crushed. While I wanted to work with Aidy and for a firm of this stature, I'd be fine—more than fine—if Knox Wright hated me.

Even as I thought that, my stomach swooped. I didn't want Knox to hate me. I swiped my sweaty palms on my pants, needing to get my emotions back under control.

"My father was a physician at the Naval Station Newport. I volunteered there all through high school and the first two summers of college. During that time, I got to know quite a few of the sailors and soldiers that made it to the OR. Even I saw more than my fair share of torn up bodies and minds."

Knox swallowed, his Adam's apple dipped below the top button of his dress shirt and underneath his tie. I followed the line of motion before I managed to drag my eyes back up, but

Knox was too busy looking at the rest of my renderings to pay attention to my hopelessly growing crush.

Maybe working here was a bad idea. Sebastian deserved my loyalty. Taking off his ring today shouldn't have led me to think I was ready for anything with another man, because I *wasn't*.

Bridget had told me one of the hardest parts of living again was learning to cope with the guilt of attraction to another man. Because none of the men who talked to me, or even when I was ready to date, would be Sebastian.

"I bet you have," he said. "I've never seen any ideas like this."

Because I wasn't sure if his comments were complimentary or just to fill the space, I stared down at my clasped hands.

"Oh," Nico said, leaning over and flipping to the next page. "This one's special."

"So would you say your expertise is in the interior-exterior transition?" Knox asked, raising his gaze back to mine. Those slate blue eyes penetrated, seeing more than I wanted to share.

So different from Sebastian's sweet brown eyes.

I said, "Yes, I like it. While it's cliche, I was a huge fan of Frank Lloyd Wright's work because of his ability to merge the residence into its surroundings."

Knox chuckled. "Who isn't?"

A small smile tugged at my lips. "Exactly."

"Well, your grasp of fluidity in this design is spot-on and something one of our most persnickety clients is currently searching for."

"The Mac?" I asked.

Nico shot me a look that might cause someone else to quake, but I lifted my chin. They both knew Aidy was my friend first; I refused to pretend that relationship was any less than the closeness of sisters just to make Aidy's brothers more comfortable.

"Aidy and I discussed the problems you were having with an English-style garden in the rocky, New England soil so close to the coast. I'd already drawn a similar idea." For the seaside cottage Sebastian gifted me for my twentieth birthday. We'd made so many plans for that place, some of which I'd shared with Aidy.

But Sebastian and I were never able to fulfill any of those plans. The joy I'd found in sketching our ideas became the genesis for me transferring to Rhode Island School of Design and beginning the long painful process of moving on with my life.

Ellie even insisting on covering my school fees. I'd protested, pointing out that I might not be nearly as wealthy as she was, but I would be comfortable even if I chose not to work. She remained adamant and I gave in when she wired an excess amount to the registrar before my first semester.

"You are part of this family, Emmaline. Sebastian would want you to complete your education. I know this isn't the path you'd planned, and the final result won't look like your big dreams, but it's time. It's time to move forward."

If you'd told me five years ago I'd graduate with a degree in architecture, I would have snorted with disdain. Now, I couldn't fathom any other career. That's why I'd finally agreed after Aidy's incessant cajoling for me to interview with her brothers.

This was my best chance to keep my promises to Sebastian and Ellie.

Knox's fingertip touched the edge of the page. I dug my nails deeper into the material over my thighs.

"Chloe will drool over the garden," Nico said. "And if she loves it, she'll take it to The Mac owners."

Knox shook his head. "That would be helpful, considering we haven't yet come up with anything this seamless." His keen gaze rose to mine and I struggled not to blush once those slate-blue eyes focused on me.

"You and Aidy already discussed salary?" Nico asked. He threw out a number a few thousand dollars more than Aidy had projected. He must really like the gardens.

I nodded.

"How soon could you start?" Knox asked.

I'd thought this over, just in case it came up during this meeting.

"Next week."

Nico and Knox exchanged a look. "We'll put together our offer once I speak with HR," Nico said. He smiled. "I hope you come aboard, Ms. Schooler." He rose from his chair, so I did the same. I shook his hand.

Then, I turned to Knox. Dammit. I was trying to gain experience, build my portfolio, and create the new life I'd laid out for myself. Getting this job offer was supposed to move me closer to those goals.

But Knox...he was a temptation I hadn't expected. And did *not* want.

Knox was still flipping through my portfolio. "Mind if you give me some more background on this one?"

I settled back in the chair as Nico left. Knox had returned to the drawing of the work-life apartments for veterans. My palms grew sweaty at his interest. I had shared one of the reasons for that design, but not the only one. And I didn't plan to divulge my other, more personal reasons, for creating those plans.

"Sure."

I slid my hands under my thighs this time, trying not to think about their clamminess against my too-warm skin.

We talked about the design for another few minutes as I explained more about some of the issues I'd hoped my designs would solve, especially for the soldiers and sailors who were used to complete physical independence—their bodies no longer possessed. Knox nodded his head, brows pulled together as if lost in thought.

"I like this a lot. Would you let us incorporate some of these ideas?" His gaze met mine.

I kept my face set in a professionally neutral mask. "Depends on if I take the job," I replied.

Knox grinned and then he threw his head back with a deep belly laugh. "I think I like you, Ms. Schooler. I think you'll fit in here just fine."

I wasn't so sure.

Chapter Two
Knox

"This is your fault, Aidy," I muttered as I slammed my Sharpie down later that afternoon, unable to get Emmaline Schooler's soft scent out of my head. She smelled like vanilla but also something a bit sharper—orange maybe. It had driven me crazy from the moment I walked around the corner toward reception.

Then, I got my first look at her. She was *gorgeous*. Not simply beautiful, but heart-stoppingly gorgeous—a dark-haired Marilyn Monroe with soft, wide hazel eyes and freckles sprinkled like brown sugar over her nose and forehead.

"Dammit, Aidy. We could have gone with Forrest Cohen if you hadn't insisted we interview your friend."

Shit. I was grouching at my pregnant little sister. At least she wasn't in the room to hear my bitching.

My intercom buzzed. "Yes?" I asked.

"Would you come to my office so we can discuss hiring Emmaline?" Nico asked.

"Sure. I'll be there in a minute. Just finishing up the Davidson elevations."

I entered his office a few minutes later, no closer to completing the Davidson's exterior. I settled into a pale wood-and-leather chair, a nod to the Scandinavian aesthetic Nico surrounded himself with. He liked traditional modern with clean lines to the point of minimalism. Some people found his designs cold, even clinical. Not unlike the man. But I knew he also had a deep love for the Gothic, with three of Gaudi's Sagrada Familia prints lining his living room. He'd taken them when we traveled to Barcelona years before—before our parents' death and Nico changed.

He'd been fun, an open and affectionate big brother to both our baby sister, Aidy, and me while we grew up. But sometime between heading off to Columbia and his position at one of the elite firms in Manhattan, the Nico I remembered morphed into a tightly controlled, ruthless man.

I settled into my chair, restless. Nico steepled his fingers, elbows on his chair arms. "You have that look—the pregame focus look."

"I do not," I said.

"Do you miss it?"

I frowned. "Why are you asking me this now? I thought you wanted to talk about the new hire."

I was careful not to use her name. *Emmaline*. I didn't want Nico to pick up on my awareness. He would—he was sharp.

"We'll get to that. I was flipping through the channels and saw one of the guys you went to college with on ESPN. He's been traded."

"Ah. Lance Henney, yeah."

"It kind of brought it all home, and I realized I'd never really talked to you about what you gave up. I'd never really thanked you for sticking it out with me."

"Lucky for you I managed both the rigors of a Division I hockey program and my studies."

He smiled. "Yes. That was lucky for me."

I sighed, remembering. "That's mostly due to Dad's continued argument that life could change in an instant."

Nico hesitated. "Do you ever wonder if he knew? Do you think on some level he understood he'd take out their sailboat on a sunny afternoon for a tour of Narragansett and never return?"

I picked at a spot on the cuff of my shirt. "Dunno."

Some days, I was shocked by how little I missed playing hockey. Others, I'd give anything to be back on the ice. Those days were fading, though I still made a point to play in the local league, and we were kicking ass this season.

"Let's talk about Emmaline Schooler. She's smart, talented, capable. Everything Aidy promised," I said, choosing my words with care. I left off beautiful, which she was.

Nico raised an eyebrow. "Definitely."

I stretched out my legs even as my stomach curdled. Emmaline was talented. She was motivated. She got along well with Aidy. She was by far the best candidate, which meant I needed to ignore her beauty and how intriguing I found her hesitation regarding her intriguing designs. And they were fabulous. On par with the work we'd used to be featured in industry magazines.

And I definitely needed to get over how good she smelled.

Nico had removed his suit jacket and loosened his tie as well as his top button. Now, he went so far as to roll up his shirt sleeves. Never say Nico didn't know how to decompress.

"Melinda will be listed as a full partner soon now that she's engaged to John Miner," Nico said.

Melinda Schoals managed to land a junior partnership five years ago—when she brought them our designs for a large-scale work/live complex to help reduce Providence's skyrocketing housing prices.

"You noted that Emmaline interned with Collins and Miner. What did you think about her answer?" I asked.

He raised his dark eyebrows. "If I remember correctly, she said she didn't feel the management there held the same beliefs about environmental design she did, and that some of the management lacked interest in mentoring their new hires, which was why she was interested in a boutique firm like ours."

I narrowed my eyes. "She didn't like Melinda much."

"Nobody actually *likes* Melinda," Nico shot back.

I couldn't argue with that statement. But I heard the underlying implication: Would hiring Emmaline be a repeat of the Melinda Incident?

"We both know workplace romances don't work out," I said.

"They cause a lot of problems." Nico's tone turned caustic; his features pinched. This was as close as he ever alluded to the situation in his past that turned my quick-to-smile brother into this stone-cold man.

"Emmaline's our best candidate. And Aidy really likes her. They've clicked, which, as Aidy said, will make it easier for her to hand off some of the details for The Mac project."

I never expected to end up as Emmaline's cheerleader. From the get-go, I'd been dead set against hiring her, mostly because she was Aidy's friend. That felt like crossing a line. But something changed when I met Emmaline. She fascinated me, and few women elicited much of a reaction from me at all these days.

I paused, trying to decide if I should push him to talk about his past—since we were all up in mine. What was it the grief counselor had told us? *Keeping the emotions bottled up would cause an explosion later.* Nico was the most bottled up of any of us.

"Your reaction now has something to do with Amanda, doesn't it?"

Nico's jaw clenched as his eyes shuttered. I didn't know much about the woman, just that Nico lived with her briefly before our parents died, and he returned to Providence to take over our father's firm and ensure our younger sister, Aidy, made it through high school—and never mentioned his live-in girlfriend again.

The ensuing years proved tense and Nico's rage went beyond the loss of our parents. Something went down with the petite brunette.

"Amanda used my feelings to get what she wanted—mainly a promotion at our firm." His lips twisted. "Not unlike Melinda."

"She used your designs," I surmised. I'd been in the same situation, more publicly, with Melinda. We'd been able to fight back—and win—thanks to the nondisclosure agreement Nico insisted everyone at the firm sign. But the legal fees proved steeper than we'd expected, nearly taking us under.

We'd learned a valuable lesson: sometimes being right and getting that proven wasn't worth fighting a much larger firm.

Nico's eyes flared with a pain he typically kept buried deep. "After she fucked me over and very nearly cost me my career."

I winced, hating how similar our pasts were. Except Melinda waited until she had a junior partnership agreement before she made her move from our internship program to Collins and Miner. Not bad for a recent college graduate. And as far as I knew, she hadn't started her relationship with John Miner until she'd decided she needed to make full partner—at the ripe old age of twenty-seven. I'd only had one betrayal and it was enough to teach me to be gun shy.

"I'm sorry, man."

Nico rose from his chair.

"I'm not. Better to know her ambition always outweighed her emotion. But it caused distress among our colleagues and rampant rumors. We're running toward something bigger here than we anticipated, Knox. I know you don't make the same huge salary you could have as a professional hockey player, but we do well—better than I imagined. Our designs are proving our value, landing us clients my former Manhattan firm, and Collins and Miner, all covet. I hope you feel like you made the right choice because I'm glad you're here."

He strode from his office, door slamming against the frame with an eye-watering crash.

And I realized my brother was much more damaged by Amanda's betrayal than he wanted anyone to know. I'd been angry with Melinda, hurt at how easily she used me to access the designs that would win her the coveted spot at a well-known firm. But I hadn't hooked up with our intern because I loved her.

I'd analyzed my former girlfriends—and I used the term loosely—after my conversation with Aidy the other night, and I'd concluded I was capable of affection. But never once had I felt the kind of love my father talked about when he spoke of our mother. Or that turned Nico into a cold shell of his former self.

I stared at his closed office door and wondered if that wasn't a good thing. He'd left me in his office, which gave me a better indication of how much he was still hurting after. And then there was Aidy: she'd been engaged to the guy who knocked her up and then kicked her out once he found out he'd have more responsibility than he'd planned on. Us Wrights didn't have the best track record with love or relationships. I shouldn't forget that.

The problem was Emmaline Schooler awoke something much more fundamental than lust: she lit my desire to protect. *Wanting* her was expected; wanting to shelter her was not.

And I wasn't honest with Nico, which he knew, and that set him off tonight. But telling my brother Emmaline was my every fantasy articulated in person would ensure she went to another firm. I couldn't allow that. She was talented and we deserved that talent.

If I burned feverishly to explore her mouth and body, well, I'd just have to repress it. It wasn't fair to her either. I was her boss, for fuck's sake, and I wasn't going to be one of those men who made a woman feel uncomfortable in the workplace. Such behavior showed both lack of respect for women and lack of confidence in self. I had both.

Wright and Associates' trajectory was for greatness. Emmaline Schooler's designs could help get us there. I could do professional. I *was* a professional.

Chapter Three
Emmaline

I rang the bell and stepped back. Joshua Giovanni opened the door with a beaming smile and open arms.

"Good to see you, Emmaline."

I rushed forward into his embrace. "You too, Josh."

He was so solid, I struggled to remember he wore a thigh-high prosthesis on his left leg.

"How's Sebastian?" I asked, pulling back.

Josh grimaced before he managed to smooth out this reaction. He tugged me deeper into the large, two-story foyer, shutting the door.

"One of these days, you're going to come here to see me, not my brother," Josh said.

"I did come to see you—and Sebastian."

He chuckled.

I rummaged around in my purse and pulled out an old jewelry box I'd found. I'd tucked my engagement ring inside. I pressed it into Joshua's hand.

"What's this?"

I hesitated, my gaze on the box. Sadness pressed against me as I reminded myself I wouldn't have that life with Sebastian. But I'd taken it off, and the same day, my belly fluttered with attraction for another man. I bit my lip, hating how much everything had changed these past few years.

"My engagement ring. I figured you'd want it back, and—"

Joshua pressed the box back into my hand, closing my fingers around it and holding onto my fist. He shook his head.

"No, Emmaline. This is yours. It will *always* be yours. You had Seb's best years." He dropped my hands and pinched my chin between his thumb and forefinger. "I couldn't have asked for a more perfect partner for my brother. You're as much a part of our family as you would have been if you and Seb did tie the knot."

I winced, remembering how close I'd come to my dreams—the white dress, waltzing in Sebastian's arms, cradling our first child as he held us both.

Dreams that would never occur.

"Want a drink before you head up to his room?"

My heart sank. "He's not up and around?"

"The headaches are more frequent," Josh said, his voice quiet. He hesitated for a moment, clearly debating what to say next. "They're getting worse."

I squeezed the ring box so tightly, my fingers numbed. I managed to drop it back into my purse as I strode up the staircase and toward Sebastian's suite. While we'd dated, I'd been in his room maybe a handful of times. Since he returned home from the hospital, I'd spent more time in his room than my own.

I knocked softly on his door and pushed it open. The room remained dim, no doubt to limit the piercing pain in his head.

Even in the shadows, Sebastian's gorgeous brown eyes lit up.

"Emmy," he cried. He winced, the slight amount of color in his face fading.

I stepped into the room; my footfalls muffled on the thick carpet. His face slid in and out of shadow as I neared the deep club chair where he rested. I leaned down and pressed a kiss to his forehead.

"How are you feeling?" I asked, laying my hand on his cheek.

He took my hand in his. "My head hurts."

"You're medication—"

"I will always have headaches. The doctor said I am lucky to speak. Lucky to be able to see you and Josh and Nana."

His words were slower and more slurred today. My heart sank. Now, I understood Joshua's expression. I swallowed but managed to keep from pushing further. I settled onto the side of the ottoman.

"I missed you."

"I missed you, too," he said.

Joshua moved back home after the accident, wanting to help. We'd all held out such hope when he'd awakened from the coma, but the initial Glasgow Coma Score of a four was its own proclamation—one we should have heeded. Sebastian had severe brain trauma, and he'd never be the vibrant, witty, athletic man we'd known before.

That Sebastian no longer existed.

"What did you do today?" I asked, pulling myself back into the present.

He pouted. "PT."

He couldn't manage to say words like "physical therapy."

"Nana said I have to do it."

I tried to smile. Tears burned in my eyes, but I blinked them back. This time was better than none. So much better than losing him as I'd lost my parents.

Still, these visits caused my heart to ache. Sometimes, I swore they broke it all over again.

"You like to exercise with Manny." Manny was Sebastian's private therapist. He was a big, bald man of mixed heritage and the softest heart of anyone I'd ever met.

"I do." Sebastian smiled, and it was guileless, much like that of a young child. "Manny said I could try yoga. You like yoga, Emmy. Maybe we could do it together."

"I do like yoga," I said, careful not to commit to something without Manny's blessing.

The ache in my chest expanded. Sebastian once played soccer and rowed for Yale's team. Now he struggled to grip a pencil and do jumping jacks, thanks to his withered muscle tone, poor eyesight, and unstable balance.

And that was on a good day.

"Nana wants me to do lessons," he said.

"Lessons are important. Remember, I worked on my lessons to get my degree."

"But you're going to build stuff, and I had to do add-i-tion. It's dumb."

My heart squeezed again, more painfully. A few years before, Sebastian was reading advanced calculus textbooks the way most people read novels.

"And did you finish your lessons?" I asked.

"No. They made my head hurt." He closed his eyes and leaned his head back. When he spoke again, his cadence was so similar to the Sebastian I knew before, that my heart stuttered.

"I miss being smart, Emmy," he said.

"You have a traumatic brain injury," I said, my tone gentle.

His face crumpled and tears burned in his eyes. "I lost you."

I gripped his clammy hands. They remained limp in my clasp—so unlike the warm, capable hands I'd taken for granted during the years we'd been together. What I wouldn't give to have Sebastian hold me like he used to.

"I'm right here, sitting next to you."

As quickly as the sadness came, it faded. These mood swings still shocked me. Sebastian *Before* had been easy-going, always quick to smile. Sebastian *Now* was quick to anger, quick to tears, and quick to forget what he was doing or saying.

"I'm glad you visit me, Emmy. I'm glad we're friends."

I cupped his cheek in my palm, my heart aching as I remembered all the times he'd done that to my cheek. He continued to look at me, eyes soft once again.

"We'll always be friends," I whispered. That was all we could be—even though it hurt. I'd promised myself to no longer wish for more than that. I smiled a little and dropped my hand.

"Would you like me to rub your head?"

"Yes. I like your head rubs the best."

The doctors told us the swelling from the accident caused damage in most portions of his brain. He'd remained in a coma for almost two months, none of us sure if his body would be able to heal from the trauma.

When he'd awakened and smiled at us, I'd been elated. But then came the cold, crushing reality.

I rose and stood behind him, rubbing his temples in a slow, steady rhythm. I continued even after my fingers cramped, happy to give Sebastian a small respite from the near-constant pain.

Josh popped his head in and tipped his head toward the door. I continued to rub for another moment until I was convinced Sebastian slept. Then I headed out the door and met Joshua and Ellie in the kitchen.

"How is he feeling?" Ellie asked.

"He said his head hurts. And he didn't realize it was me until I was almost at his chair," I said. I chewed the inside of my lower lip—a bad habit that worsened after the accident. "He's getting worse, isn't he?" I asked.

Ellie glanced over at Josh and Erika, the night nurse who had arrived through the back door as I spoke.

None of them met my eyes.

"I'll go up and sit with him," Erika murmured. She darted out of the space.

Ellie pulled out the lasagna from the oven and set the oven mitts on the counter.

"Yes," Ellie said as she settled into the chair next to me. "We don't know how much more he'll deteriorate."

She choked on the last word.

I nodded, my throat clogged with emotions. The silence grew. I took a deep breath. "Remember how I told you I met a nice woman, Aidy, a few weeks ago at my yoga class? Bridget, the ER nurse, goes to the same studio. She introduced us."

Josh nodded, but Ellie was still distracted.

"Well, I interviewed for the second time at her firm today. Wright and Associates," I said.

"Oh?" Joshua said. "We've contracted with them to remodel the Martha's Vineyard property."

"Nice," I said.

"When do you find out about the job?" Ellie asked. Her face lit up with excitement. Discussing Sebastian's injuries caused Ellie to sink into her own morass of guilt and grief, which was why Joshua and I tried to focus on positive topics.

Ellie dished up plates as I extolled them with details about my interview and my chats with Aidy. We settled in together at the table, the three of us where there used to be many more faces. I told myself I hardly missed the reassuring weight of Sebastian's hand on my thigh.

After dinner, I insisted on cleaning the dishes, though both Joshua and Ellie told me the housekeeper would do them in the morning. I dried my hands on a dishtowel and headed toward the parlor, where Ellie and Joshua sat.

My steps faltered when I heard my name. I held my breath, straining to catch more of their conversation.

"I want Emmaline to be happy," Joshua said. "And coming here multiple times each week, devoting so much of her time to Sebastian isn't leaving her time to explore her interests or create new friendships."

"The one with the girl architect sounds promising," Ellie murmured. "I like how Emmaline's face lights up when she talks about architecture. Oh, I hope she gets the position."

"Emmaline wouldn't want you to interfere," Joshua warned.

"Don't start with me, young man. I'm not going to interfere with anything or anyone. That never works as one hopes, anyhow."

"Right, Nana. You never interfere."

Clearly Ellie wasn't listening because she said, "Perhaps she'll fall for one of those handsome young Wright brothers. She could most certainly do worse."

"She could also do better. Knox is a notorious flirt and lady's man. That's not what we want for Emmaline."

"No. I suppose it isn't."

Chapter Four
Emmaline

I spent Saturday morning at Calliope's yoga studio, just as I did every week. She, Aidy, Bridget, and I shared an early lunch at a little bistro after the last morning class.

"Oh, I needed this," Bridget said. She shifted her weight. "I also need these babies to behave in there."

"You're getting close to your due date," Calliope said.

"I'm starting to think I've made it as close as I can." She winced. "At least one of these two is quite active."

"Not a shocker, knowing their father. Speaking of, how's Simon behaving?" Calliope asked.

Bridget grumbled, but I noted the bright sheen in her eyes.

"He's bossy. And worried about everything I do."

"Good man," Aidy said.

She looked down at her plate, but I caught a momentary sadness there.

"I'm looking forward to starting work Monday," I said.

Aidy shot me a glance filled with thanks as the topic shifted to work.

— A —

Monday arrived quickly, and nerves danced through my belly. I pressed my hand there as I grabbed my purse. It was a fantastic thrift-store find—a luxury brand past its prime but still sturdy, even if it were a season or two from current. No doubt that was the reason the original owner ditched it, and I'd collected it for a fraction of the cost. My mother and I used to shop thrift stores, trolling aisles for great deals. I missed doing that with her.

This time, I'd shopped with Bridget. She was fun and I enjoyed the time, but it wasn't the same as shopping with my mom. She'd made everything an adventure.

I faced the mirror.

My first day of work had arrived.

I was going to prove to myself and to Wright and Associates they made the correct decision, choosing me.

I patted my professional chignon before touching the small, gold hoop earrings I'd inherited from my mother. My nicest white blouse was tucked into my black skirt. I smoothed down the sides of my lavender cardigan as I took one more deep breath and exited my room.

I toasted an English muffin while I sipped on my cup of coffee, staring out the window. My thoughts were as jumbled—scattered—as they'd been since dinner at the Ellie Giovanni's last week.

Joshua and Ellie were correct about one thing: I didn't want to stay stuck in this exact rut, and I didn't want to stay in this house any longer. I'd spoken to Bridget and Aidy about moving at our weekly brunch. Bridget wanted me to move closer to Simon and her, while Aidy suggested I find a place in her condo so we could commute together and hang out more often.

I munched on my English muffin, weighing the benefit of being close to Aidy. I'd like to spend more time with her and her baby. Being in the same building would make that simpler.

I smiled when my phone rang. "Hey, Aidy. I was just thinking of you."

She laughed. "Good to hear. So, I have to head back over to The Mac. Lidia ran into some issues with the suite interiors. The electrical boxes on the entire floor were roughed in incorrectly, and we're missing three per room."

"That sounds like a nightmare."

"It is. I swear, Jericho screwed us over big time on this project. If I didn't like my current staff so much, I'd give them all the boot."

She wouldn't, but Aidy was right to be annoyed. The former foreman was a jerk who'd gone out of his way to prove he was in charge.

"You'll get it worked out. You always think of something."

"I'm glad you have faith in me," she muttered. "Hey…I was wondering if you wanted to get together tomorrow night to celebrate your job working with awesome-me."

I chuckled. "Rain check? I'm going to visit Sebastian tomorrow."

"Of course. How about Wednesday?"

"Do you think I should mention my connection to Sebastian Giovanni to your brothers?" I asked. My stomach knotted at the idea of bringing up such a traumatic topic.

"Nope. It's not relevant to your work, and if you do, Nico will just try to figure out how to use the connection. He's all about business and getting more of it." A hint of frustration crept into her voice. "I've arrived on site. Why don't I call you later?" she said.

"Perfect. Good luck."

"I'm going to need it."

Much as I loved spending time with girlfriends, specifically Bridget and Aidy, I'd changed because of the accident, too. I liked my alone time much more. In fact, the only place I felt at home was by the ocean, which was why I planned to start renovating my tiny inlet cottage soon. It may not be an ideal long-term home due to its size, but it was something I could create into my vision—something I could control and take pride in the outcome.

Plus, I needed a change from this place. It was part of the reason I'd stagnated.

Decision made, I cleaned up my mess, brushed my teeth, and collected my purse and briefcase.

I arrived at Wright and Associates a few minutes early. The parking lot held only two other cars: a newish European sedan and a mud-splattered crossover. I exited my vehicle and walked to the door.

I pressed the intercom, but no one answered.

I pressed it again.

"Those men don't ever answer the door," Nannette, the receptionist, said from behind me. She was out of breath and carrying a few white baker boxes. "Hold these, and I'll get the door."

"What's this?" I asked.

"Hopefully your problem from now on," she said. "The guys like pastries for their morning client meetings. Come in and set those boxes on my desk. I'll show you where the platters are so that we can get the conference room set up." Nannette's round brown eyes reminded me of a puppy as did her wiggly, happy personality.

"Happy to help," I said.

She beamed. "Great."

We set up the conference room and she showed me where the restrooms were and gave me a basic breakdown of a typical day.

"That's to say there's no such thing. Knox is the one who normally does the on-site visits and Nico prefers to work with the clients. Aidy's been out at The Mac or working from home some of the time. So, no day is the same."

"Good to know."

Nannette winked. "Guarantee you won't be bored."

My smile broadened. "Who are we meeting with today?"

"Oh, you'll love her! An eccentric rich lady. Her name is Eleanor Giovanni."

"I know her," I said.

Nannette's eyes popped.

"Are you some rich girl dabbling in a career?"

I shook my head with a laugh, but if Nannette wasn't careful her questions could offend. "My father was on the board for her charity. He was a doctor at the Naval Station."

"Oh. Well, I guess that's all right. We can still be friends," Nannette said.

"And we couldn't if I were a rich girl?" I asked, mostly amused.

"Well, we wouldn't have much in common," Nannette said, her brows puckering at the bridge of her nose. "I grew up about as far from the beach as you can get in Providence, and I love a good sale at Nordstrom Rack."

My smile widened. "Who doesn't love that store?"

Relief swept over Nannette's face. "Right?"

"Back to Mrs. Giovanni."

"She's interested in a second beach home," Nannette said.

That must be the one on Martha's Vineyard that Joshua had mentioned the other night. Admitting I knew about the place might not be my smartest move—at least not around Nannette.

"What's wrong with the first vacation home?" I asked.

"We didn't design it; therefore, it lacks perfection," Knox said from behind me.

I startled as I turned around. He raised an eyebrow. "Right, Em? We strive for perfection—and giving our clients *everything* they desire."

His voice deepened, and my breath shattered. I took a moment to collect myself before I met his gaze. What surprised me was the vague look of consternation settling over his features.

"Yes, Mr. Wright. I'm looking forward to seeing Ell…er, Mrs. G. again and I'm excited to see how you and the other Mr. Wright develop a profoundly personal space."

"Again?" he asked. He mumbled something under his breath. "Never mind. I just bet you are, Em. And call me Knox. That 'other Mr. Wright' is going to get old fast."

Nannette giggled as he turned back toward his office. I sighed.

"They are potent," Nannette whispered. "And silent. Probably deadly to many women's dreams."

"Extremely," I murmured. "How do you keep from…"

Nannette widened her already round eyes. "Wanting them? Honey, you couldn't if you tried. But you can give yourself a shot of immunity with a hunky gent all your own."

"I'll have to get on that," I muttered, knowing full well I had no intention of doing so. Sebastian's beautiful eyes flashed through my mind. He'd loved to sail, and we used to spend many

Saturdays out on the water…with him in skimpy swim trunks…
when he wore anything at all.

That was a lifetime ago—happening to a different woman. I
was no longer the starry-eyed girl I'd been then, sure my every
wish would come true.

Too many of my dreams shattered for me to ever believe in a
fairy tale ending.

"Best medicine I've found is to have your guy bang you good
and hard before the start of work," Nannette said.

I sputtered out a laugh even as I shook my head. Yep, Knox
Wright was too potent, but Nannette was too much.

I made a note to never reveal my history with the Giovannis
to her—she wouldn't understand that their lifestyle wasn't mine.

I settled at my desk and pulled out my phone. After a brief
debate, I typed a message to Ellie.

*I really want to achieve my goals on my own, and I'm concerned
there may be bias if the siblings find out my history with Sebastian.*

Not all the siblings. Thanks to our weekly yoga lady brunch
dates, Aidy had a pretty good overview of my life.

I gnawed on the inside of my lower lip, wondering if I'd made
the correct choice. Though, part of me couldn't stomach a look
of consternation and disgust from Nannette. I really wanted to fit
in—to make friends. To feel like part of something.

The three dots formed, and I tried not to stare. I blew out a
breath when I received Ellie's response.

*Whatever you deem best, my dear. But, please, do not ask me to
pretend I don't know you. I simply couldn't stomach such a world.*

I smiled and assured her I wouldn't want to live in that world either. I slid my phone back into my purse and put both inside one of the drawers in my desk. For the first time in years, I felt as if I were standing upright and on my own—as if my past no longer owned me.

I smiled as I pulled up the CAD software the company used to build three-D models, feeling more fulfilled than I had in ages—even as I glanced at Knox from under my lashes. He'd stopped at Clint's desk, speaking to the older man about some changes he needed to a design. Like Morris, Clint was one of the draftsmen who rendered some of the drawings once Nick, Knox, or Aidy had confirmed a sketch.

I'd read the employee handbook and understood any kind of relationship outside a professional one would lead to my termination. Considering how coveted a position at Wright and Associates was, I had no plans to change my employment status. But that didn't mean I couldn't look at Knox's male beauty and enjoy the view.

Chapter Five
Knox

"I want a schematic of both the south and west elevations," I said.

Clint nodded, causing the thinning hair on his head to shift and giving me a better view of the large, pink spot at the crown of his head. Clint was recently divorced—so recently that his ring finger still held the faint pale line where he'd worn his wedding band. He continued to put in his hours, but his heart didn't seem in his work.

I felt for the bastard, I really did, but if he didn't get his act together soon, Nico and I wouldn't have a choice but to let him go. We'd told him as much last Friday.

"I'll get those to you before lunch," Clint said.

His pale hazel eyes were rimmed with red eyelids and sparse lashes. He'd shaved the few-days-old scruff and put on a newish long-sleeved dress shirt and a darker blue tie.

"Thanks, Clint. I'd appreciate that. I want to put together a proposal for the client before the end of the week."

"You got it," he said with more enthusiasm than I'd heard from him in months. Maybe Nico was correct, and Clint had been in a funk. A little shakeup of his world managed to give him the purpose he'd needed to reinvigorate his work.

Emmaline glanced up at me from beneath her lashes, a slight smile brightening her face. Damn if I didn't like how those soft, pink lips glistened, beckoning me to settle mine over hers. Her vanilla-and-citrus scent clung to the air, making my blood heat.

I had no intention of pursuing Emmaline—she was my employee and deserved my respect, but that didn't mean I could stop myself from daydreaming about unbuttoning her prim blouse and feasting on her lush, pale flesh right here in the middle of our office. I shifted, needing to ease the ache in my groin and the sudden tightness in my pants.

I gritted my teeth as I thought about Melinda's betrayal, which cooled my lust. Melinda liked to flash her big blue eyes and toss her long blonde hair. She was curved in all the right places and knew how to use her body to her advantage—just as shrewd with dishing out sexual favors as she was in stealing important documents.

Melinda taught me it was all kinds of wrong to get involved with an employee. I'd made a mistake with her, but now, being older and wiser, I wouldn't let anything get in the way of our reputation. That meant keeping Emmaline at arm's length. Considering we'd hired Emmaline to support Aidy during her last few weeks in the office before maternity leave, that shouldn't be hard. At least not for a while. And by then my ardor and interest would dissipate.

Women simply weren't worth the effort. Melinda taught me that—but so did a string of others before her.

I headed back to my office and settled at my drafting table. Nanette alerted me to Mrs. Giovanni's arrival at ten-thirty.

Nannette's blonde head popped into my office. "She's here,"

she whispered, wide-eyed. "I set her up with a coffee and a Pellegrino, but she didn't want a pastry."

Nannette wasn't the coolest cucumber, but she was efficient and managed our clients with a happy demeanor.

I headed toward the conference room. One didn't keep Eleanor Giovanni waiting—not if one wanted her business and to keep all the metaphorical skin on one's back. Mrs. Giovanni turned seventy-six last month—I know this because she told me—and she needed something new.

That something new was a five-thousand-square-foot home on one of the prime lots in Martha's Vineyard. The residence there currently was a measly three-thousand-square-foot "rustic mess," as Mrs. Giovanni said. "Which you will work around, making it something worth staying in."

I pushed open the door, a ready smile on my lips, only to find her seated at the table with Emmaline, who was laughing.

"I'm...I'm..." I stuttered, unsure how to correct Emmaline's faux pas. Nico would have her head when he entered, and the thought of firing the poor young woman now, on her first day, in front of one of the wealthiest women in the country, caused my skin to feel clammy.

"Knox, you hired such a treasure," Mrs. Giovanni said, her voice warm.

I shook my head, feeling both dazed and slightly ill. Nico growled behind me, but I stood my ground, not allowing him into the space until I better understood the situation before me. Nico might be my height, but I had forty pounds of muscle on him.

"So, you...ah...know Emmaline?" I asked, my tone careful.

"For years."

"How's your grandson?" Emmaline asked.

"Which one?" Mrs. Giovanni asked, a bit of bite in her voice.

Emmaline reached forward and covered the older woman's clasped hands with hers. "Both."

Mrs. Giovanni sighed. I moved forward with cautious steps. They had a rapport, and Nico wouldn't be willing to upset the silver-haired billionaire.

Nico entered the room with his blueprints, his gaze landing immediately on where Mrs. Giovanni patted Emmaline's hand. For a brief second, he squinted.

"Sebastian is...well. Joshua is being fitted for his newest pros-thesis today," Mrs. Giovanni said.

"Oh, right. Last time we talked, he said the current one chafed when he ran. I hope he likes the new one better."

"That chafing drives him crazy," Mrs. Giovanni said with a curl to her lip. "These young men, so many of them, injured and left to fend for themselves. I hate how we've turned our back on them." She shook her head, her gaze turning far away. "Reminds me of how my Bill was treated when he came home from Vietnam."

"Emmaline created drawings for veteran's housing," I said.

Mrs. Giovanni's eyebrows rose, and Emmaline looked down at the table, her face redder than the Casas das Artes in Portugal.

Nico took his seat at the head of the table, next to Mrs. Giovanni. Since Emmaline was seated on her other side, I sat across from them. From this angle, I made out more of Emmaline's face and she seemed upset. By my comment?

"She clearly put a lot of thought into the design," I said.

"Yes." Mrs. Giovanni drew out the word. "I'll have to look at it, especially after you spoke so highly of it."

Emmaline tipped her head further down, and her hair caught the sheen of sunlight from the transom windows, turning it an even richer raven sparkling with blue. She darted a quick look at me, then at Nico.

"Today's my first day, Mrs. G., and I—"

"You know I insist you call me Ellie, dear." She glanced over at Nico, lips pursed. "I supposed I should extend that courtesy to your employers as well."

Emmaline cleared her throat. "Thank you, Ellie, but I'm not sure I should be put in any type of position. I literally started mere hours ago."

Mrs. Giovanni turned to glower at Nico. "I like her," she said.

"I'll bear that in mind," Nico replied his tone dry.

Mrs. Giovanni raised an eyebrow so that it nearly touched her hairline. I wondered, again, if the woman dyed her hair to get it that perfect, rich shade of pure white threaded with silver.

"See that you do. And I want to see those renderings Knox mentioned." She turned to Emmaline. "Do you have those drawings?" she asked.

Emmaline rubbed her lower lip with her teeth. I watched the back and forth, back and forth. I would have thought Emmaline would want to show her designs to as many people as possible—especially the wealthy philanthropist like Eleanor Giovanni who was well known for her lavish aid to veteran causes.

Eventually, Emmaline nodded.

"Good," Mrs. Giovanni said. "May I take them with me? I'll have Joshua or a courier return them."

Emmaline held the older woman's gaze. "You can have the set, Ellie. I'd planned to give them to you at dinner on Friday. I thought Sebastian might enjoy them."

As she spoke, Emmaline shot me an annoyed glance, and I startled. Knowing the Giovanni family well enough to have dinner with them was a different level of personal.

Emmaline Schooler was turning into quite the contradiction, and I was intrigued. Until I realized I'd ruined her present. Guilt flooded my system.

"Then I'll wait until Friday," Mrs. Giovanni said. "Now, I must see what you've put together for that monstrosity Joshua talked me into buying." Mrs. Giovanni's tone was imperious.

Nico unrolled the first of the drawings and Emmaline rose from her chair with a faint *excuse me*. No doubt she'd caught the whiff of frustration drifting off Nico.

Mrs. Giovanni reached out and gripped Emmaline's wrist. "Sit by me, dear. I like to keep a room balanced." She lifted her gaze to mine, hers twinkling with good humor. "Actually, I prefer to tip the balance in my favor, but this will do for now. And I'm sure your employers will be happy to accommodate this old woman."

Emmaline licked her lower lips, eyes wide, as she focused on Nico. He dipped his head toward the chair.

Well, well, Emmaline's stock rose today. Nico must be thinking about all the contacts he could make if he received an invitation to the Giovanni Foundation's annual gala, whereas I began to day-dream about Emmaline Schooler in formal wear. I liked the image my mind conjured, very much. Especially when I decided her dress should be basically backless. She must have a flawless back—long and elegant. I loved the curve of a woman's spine as it flared into her hips. It was my favorite part of the female anatomy, more than lush tits and a plump ass.

I shifted in my chair, trying again to ease the tightness in my crotch as I forced my head back into the meeting. After another fifteen minutes, I sighed with relief as Nico began rolling up the plans.

"Give us a couple of days to work through these design changes," Nico said. "We'll be sure to be in touch with you as soon as we have what we feel is our best option for that garden and the outdoor entertaining space."

"I look forward to those designs. As this is my money, and I'm now well into my widowhood and considered elderly to boot, I must insist on something understatedly flashy."

"Absolutely," I said with a smile, making sure my dimples popped out. I knew Mrs. Giovanni liked them because she'd told me so at our meeting a few weeks ago. Still, I barely resisted the urge to roll my eyes at her request. Because Emmaline moved behind Mrs. Giovanni to assist with the older woman's exit, she didn't have the same problem and my lips tilted up at her subtle head shake that accompanied the eye-roll.

"I know you don't understand," Mrs. Giovanni said breezily as she collected her handbag and her suit jacket, which she draped over her arm. "But I don't really care if you approve of my eccentricities as long as you bring them to fruition so Joshua can complain about my proclivities and spend my money to fix the property in ten to fifteen years."

Such renovations were what kept us in business. They weren't always as much fun to draft and create as the small homes for the veterans or the streamlined symphony hall, but they were a large and important part of our revenue stream.

Mrs. Giovanni offered me her hand, much as a queen would bestow her rings to be kissed. I helped the spry woman to her feet and bent my head in close.

Emmaline opened the door to the conference room, and I walked with small steps to ensure Mrs. Giovanni's pace.

"You're a dear boy," she said. "When are you going to settle down?"

My mind flashed to Emmaline, as it had continually since that first interview. I managed an indulgent smile and dropped my gaze to Mrs. Giovanni instead of the raven-haired beauty walking behind us.

"Never. I couldn't meet all the lovely ladies if I was married."

Mrs. Giovanni also frowned. "Pity. Both you and Nico really should settle down and stop all the single ladies a-twittering. It gets tiresome to listen to. But, thankfully, my Joshua is deeply in love, so I don't hear about how attractive so-and-so is anymore."

I wanted to ask about her other grandson, but then I remembered the story I'd read about him a couple of years ago—he'd been in a near-fatal car accident and required constant care.

I shuddered. Losing my hockey career threw me into a tailspin. I couldn't imagine how tough it would be to lose my independence and suffer from long-term ailments in addition.

I glanced back once more at Emmaline, but she'd moved off and was settling at her desk. She didn't glance up even when I returned from walking Mrs. Giovanni to her vehicle.

For some reason, her unwillingness to acknowledge me caused my chest to ache.

Chapter Six
Emmaline

Nannette stopped by my desk just before one that afternoon. She tapped me on the shoulder, interrupting my concentration as I went over the outdoor renderings for The Mac Aidy had asked me to help her with. I pulled out my earbuds.

"I'm taking you to lunch. It's a tradition," she said.

"Since when?" I asked, amused.

"Since now. Let's go."

I grabbed my keys from the drawer and trotted out after her, ignoring Clint and Morris's stares. Morris was a squat man with thick glasses. He seemed nice and didn't speak much.

"Do you go out often?" I asked once we were on the street.

"Nope. Normally I eat with Clint and Morris. Half the time either Aidy or Knox will join us in the break room."

"Not Nico?"

She snorted. "Panera okay? Not much else is over here."

"Sure."

"No, Nico doesn't eat with us. I'm not sure he does eat. For such a pretty man, he sure does have a grumbly personality."

"What's his deal?" I asked.

Nannette shrugged. "No idea. He's been like that since I started working for the firm."

I grabbed the door and held it open, allowing her to enter. Once we'd placed our orders, we settled at a table near the back of the restaurant. She propped her chin on her hands and studied me.

"Tomorrow, when Aidy's back in the office, we'll finally have an even ratio."

"I love Aidy," I said.

Nannette's gaze widened. "Wait. How do you know Aidy?"

I laughed. "I met her at yoga. We hit it off. She's the reason I'm here in the first place."

Nannette's face cleared and a sunny smile split her face. "Well, Aidy's got the best taste of anyone I know."

"She really does," I said.

Nannette purse her lips. "What's that look for?"

"They aren't going to need me when Aidy comes back," I said. I pinched at the edge of my napkin, forming crimps into the paper.

"Like Nico would let you leave after Mrs. Giovanni gushed over you." Nannette side-eyed me, causing her cat-eye-lined eyes to appear even more authentic. "You have a gravy-train ticket with that connection, girl. Not sure if I should love you or hate you."

The idea of Nannette knowing what happened with Sebastian, feeling sorry for me, had my stomach in knots.

"I'm just me," I murmured.

"I nearly had a heart attack when she pulled you in for a hug. I thought at first she was going to headbutt you."

I giggled at the image and Nannette joined in. We talked and ate and enjoyed each other's company. I didn't feel like the girl who'd lost her family or even the young professional who'd just

started a new job. I felt like a woman getting to know a
new friend.

I loved the difference.

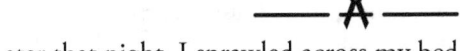

Later that night, I sprawled across my bed and groaned from
exhaustion. I'd made a good call not to wear the stilettos I'd
purchased for my first day of work—my feet might have fallen off
if I tried.

With a groan, I kicked off my pumps and traded out my work
skirt for a pair of comfy gray flannel pants. I ditched my blouse
in exchange for a long-sleeved RISD shirt. One too many washes
had shrunk the material, and I would never consider wearing it
out of the house. But it was softer than any of my other shirts
and had long been a favorite—even if it were indecently tight
across my breasts.

I padded downstairs and into the kitchen. I opened the fridge
and pulled out the bottle of champagne Joshua gave to me a few
days ago when I told him I'd been offered the position. I held it in
my hand, then sighed. I didn't like the idea of drinking champagne
alone. Maybe I could call Bridget. Nope, she would be home with
her sexy British doctor. Hmm…maybe Josh and Will…

The doorbell rang and I set the bottle on the counter before
I headed toward the front door. I made an effort to smooth my
hair and moaned internally at my choice of clothing when I saw
Knox Wright through the glass.

I opened the door a crack. "Hi," I said, my tone uncertain.

His dimples popped out and he grinned wider at my confused
look. "I brought you this." He lifted up my purse.

"Oh!" I opened the door wider and stared at it, horrified. "I can't believe I left that at work."

"Well, I'm guessing you're not used to carrying a briefcase, too…yet. So I figured you didn't notice. I also assumed you'd like to have your wallet and license when you drove around town."

My cheeks burned. "Y-yes," I stammered. "I'd grabbed my keys at lunch, and they must still be in the pocket of my cardigan. I appreciate you bringing it by, but I feel so bad you had to. You must think I'm a scatterbrain. Um, so anyway, thanks."

"I don't think that, and your place isn't too far from mine." He pointed with his thumb over his shoulder. "I'm about three blocks that way. On Ash."

I blew out a breath and offered him a smile. "Well, then, thanks, neighbor."

He winked, and it warmed my belly.

"No problem."

That damn wink made me stupid. "Would you like to come in for a drink?" I blurted. My face felt hot enough to fry an egg. "I mean, if you have time. I have a bottle of champagne—you know, to celebrate my new job—but I don't want to drink it alone…"

My voice trailed off as I realized how my comments could be construed. Like I was hitting on my boss. *Really professional, there, Em.*

Em?

I'd never called myself that before. In fact, Knox was the only person who did call me that.

I bit my lip, half willing Knox to say no. He studied me for a long moment, his large frame shifting slightly.

"Sure," he replied in that easy tone of his. Sebastian had it—rather, he posessed it before the accident. Joshua did, too, but his came over time, once he'd gone through West Point, something Ellie suggested, because before that, Joshua had been indecisive and awkward in most social situations.

I'd begun to realize that the confidence of facing any situation came from ease of self—knowing what your body and mind were capable of.

I'd never managed that level of confidence. Some might call it arrogance. What worried me most was how attractive I found the quality. I'd been drawn to it in Sebastian, and once again with Knox.

I gestured Knox inside. After I set my purse next to the sofa, I rubbed my clammy palms on my thighs and took a deep breath. Knox was attractive, sure, but he was no different from any of the sailors I'd met through my father over the course of my life. He paused in the entry to the kitchen, and I brushed past him. Fine, he was different because my body said he was.

He frowned as if something about my place bothered him. Then, I saw the family photos and the decor my mother chose when she and my father moved into this house thirty-something years ago.

I chuckled. "My mom chose all the furniture. I moved back home a few years ago. I'd been attending Cornell before."

He nodded. "What made you leave Ithaca?"

I hesitated and started to slide back into the day of the car accident that changed my life so dramatically.

"I was in a car accident."

Knox stood still, waiting. I licked my lips.

"It was...bad." My voice cracked.

That so didn't encapsulate the many long, painful moments I'd been locked in the flipped SUV with Sebastian. I opened my eyes wider, unwilling to close them and relive that scene—I relived it too often in my nightmares.

I must have spoken the last bit aloud because his clear, slate-colored eyes rose to mine.

"I'm sorry you had to go through that," he murmured.

"I missed hugs," I said without stopping to think. I blushed. "No one could touch me for weeks because of my injuries."

"Weeks? I can't imagine."

I hadn't realized how much I craved touch until I couldn't have it from the people I most needed to hold me. "I recovered."

He made a soft noise deep in his throat. "I miss my mom's hugs, too." He side-eyed me before he said, "My parents went out to sail in the bay one day. They never returned, so we assume they drowned."

I pulled myself from my own grief-laden history to focus on him.

"Aidy told me. So unexpected," I said. "That must have been terribly painful."

"Still hurts a lot of the time," he said, his eyes distant as if reliving a memory.

"I understand."

He studied me before nodding. "You know what I miss most? Besides just seeing them, being near them?"

I waited, standing close but not touching. We didn't know each other well enough for that yet, and part of me was surprised by his willingness to discuss his past.

"I miss getting up with my dad, having him drive me to the ice rink at five a.m. every day. Once I was in junior high, and national team scouts showed interest in me, my dad sat me down. I was this thirteen-year-old kid who had to make a huge life choice: did I want to focus on hockey and attempt to make the cut for the national team, for the NHL, or did I want to keep playing and skating for a local club."

I swallowed down the emotions snarling my throat.

"My dad loved hockey—watching it—but he was like a wobbly new colt once he strapped on the blades." Knox's smile was filled with humor but tinged with nostalgia.

I understood. This time, I reached for his hand and squeezed. He glanced down at where my palm snuggled against his but made no effort to return the action.

"My dad was a stubborn cuss, and he learned to skate, just so we could spend that time together. Five to seven-thirty for the next four-and-a-half years. He was my best coach, my toughest defender, my best a-man."

At my obvious confusion, Knox smirked as he casually let my hand drop.

"Assists. He did that for me, with me, because that was my passion. He had something like that with each of us. For a while, with Aidy, it was sailing. Our mother enjoyed it more than Aidy did, though, so he started taking her. If he'd taken Aidy that day, too..." Knox shuddered. He cleared his throat. "That's what I miss most."

The kitchen turned silent as I realized Knox had given me a piece of himself to keep me from sinking into my past. This man I didn't really know had understood my pattern, perhaps better than I did, and offered me a way out of the morass that still pulled me under way too often.

"So, tonight's a celebration of your fantastic new job for the best architectural firm in Providence."

He smiled. I returned it. Life continued onward and the best thing I could do was move with it.

I stepped forward and opened a cabinet next to him. I reached up on my tiptoes but couldn't quite manage the top shelf where my grandmother's art deco champagne glasses sat.

"That's why I'm there. Would you mind grabbing those?" I asked, looking over my shoulder. Was Knox staring at my ass?

He lifted his gaze with a faint shrug. Yes, he had been, and... was it hot in here? Definitely too hot. I stepped back as I pushed up the sleeves of my shirt. I wanted to fan myself but that would be too obvious. Instead, I crossed the room and cracked up the window over the sink. That had the added benefit of keeping me from returning the favor. I'd already checked out Knox's excellent butt more than once today.

I plugged the sink and turned on the water, adding some soap. "I'll just wash those," I said. "They may be dusty. I don't use them often."

I sucked in a breath when Knox set the glasses next to me, his body heat burning me through our clothes and the careful distance he kept between us.

"So, you know Mrs. Giovanni," Knox said, stepping back. I wanted to turn and curve into him, but that wouldn't do.

"Yep. My dad sat on her board for about four years. He was one of Joshua's doctors."

I rinsed off the glasses and pulled out a dish towel to dry them. "You talked like you know him, too."

"Of course. Josh is great."

I turned in time to see Knox's deep scowl. He cleared it when he caught me gazing at him and forced a smile.

"I get the sense that you're close," he said.

"I enjoy his company," I said, keeping my tone light.

Knox twisted the cork from the champagne bottle and it made a small pop. "Oh, wait! I have antipasto from Vincenti's to go with this."

Knox raised his eyebrows. "You sure do know how to party."

I pulled out a small tray of olives, cheese, thinly sliced ciabatta, and an array of salami. "I've learned to appreciate and celebrate all the good moments," I said. I took off the plastic covering and popped a green olive into my mouth. I chewed and swallowed, offering up a cheeky grin. "Plus, I love good food."

Knox filled the glasses each less than halfway. He raised his and clinked it to mine.

"To a great first day," he said. His eyes burned hotter than I'd seen them before, almost royal blue.

My breath hitched and he finally dropped his eyes to my mouth as I took a sip. "Let's sit in the living room," I said.

I grabbed the platter and my glass and headed that way, not waiting for him to agree. Knox dripped confidence the way most people breathed. I couldn't take being so close to him and not saying something stupid.

He followed and settled into one of the deep-stuffed armchairs my mother had loved but I'd always considered fussy and pretentious. Now, I loved them more because she had.

"So, you didn't decorate this place?" he asked. He tried to keep his tone neutral, but I understood his concerns.

I laughed as I set down the platter. "Oh, no. Not my style at all." I glanced around. "But it's home, and that's comforting."

"What is your style?"

I picked up a piece of bread and salami. I settled back on the couch and munched.

"I'm not sure I want to tell you," I said after a sip of my champagne. "This is good," I murmured, looking down into my glass.

When I raised my gaze, Knox was staring at me again.

"Of course you should," he said. "I want to know everything about you, Emmaline."

Time seemed to stop as his potent sexuality wrapped around me, tugging me, daring me closer.

He raised his glass, breaking the spell.

My heart continued to thrum with the what-ifs of the moment.

And I realized I was in way over my head with Knox Wright.

Chapter Seven
Knox

Emmaline Schooler was a sensual goddess who had no idea of her appeal. Typically, I scoffed at the idea that an unwitting woman could be more desirable, but that was before I met Emmaline. Her soft pink lips nuzzled her glass or opened wide enough to pop in the green fruit, and I struggled to maintain blood above my waist. Fuck if she didn't make me hard with that tiny noise of wanting or the soft flutter of her sooty lashes against her creamy cheeks.

She reminded me of the ephemeral perfection of Vermeer's painting "Girl with a Pearl Earring." When I'd seen the original, I'd wanted nothing more than to run my thumb down the smooth curvature of the girl's face, and I'd been desperate for the same connection with Emmaline.

Maybe I wanted Emmaline more because Nico put me on notice, and I didn't like being denied anything I wanted—especially women.

I'd go with that line of thought. That, and the fact she wasn't mine. She'd made a point to bring Joshua Giovanni into our conversation, which must mean she wanted me to know she was involved with him. While that could be good for us professionally, I felt...damn. I felt crushed.

I was deeply attracted to this woman, and that connection left me feeling jittery. Worse, I was tongue-tied, and I didn't care for the emotion at all.

"I prefer Spanish Colonial, which doesn't work here in the Northeast at all, so I tell everyone I'm a mid-century modern lover, which I am—who can go to architecture school and not appreciate the simplicity and beauty of those designs?"

"But it doesn't speak to you like Spanish Colonial. Huh. You and Nico have more in common than I thought."

She raised an eyebrow. "That's surprising."

"Agreed."

I didn't like the flash of jealousy that tugged in my belly. I wanted Emmaline's interest—her focus directed at me.

"Tell me about your impressions today," I said.

She sucked her lower lip into her mouth as she stared down into her glass. "Well, Nannette is bubbly."

I sat back. "She sure is."

"I've never met such an organized and ebullient person."

I finished munching my piece of salami. "What do you mean?"

She shrugged. "What I said. She cleared off all the folders from Aidy's desk when she was showing me around this morning."

I made a note to talk to my sister about the leeway she gave to the staff. Some of the projects we worked on required an NDA. All of our employees signed one for Wright and Associates, which should cover our asses in the case of leaked information, but Nannette wasn't the best at keeping her mouth zipped. That extroversion was what made her so good with the clients.

Like most people and situations, parts were winners and parts made working with them more of a challenge.

"Morris and Clint are nice," Emmaline said.

"I'm glad to hear they behaved themselves around you."

"Why wouldn't they?"

I leaned in, refilling her glass from the champagne bottle I'd brought out of the kitchen with me.

"Just that they're men, and you're beautiful."

She flushed and dropped the piece of bread she'd reached for a moment before. She rose, wiping her palms down the side of her pants. I'd noticed it before, thinking it was a nervous gesture. She fidgeted with her hair for a moment, then blurted, "I'm hungry, and the champagne is going to my head. Do you want any chicken marsala? I brought it home from Vincenti's, too."

I sat back with a small smile that I hid behind my glass. I was correct. I made Emmaline nervous—in the best possible way. I downed my drink. Not that I'd act on the attraction. But I liked knowing she was interested.

I *really* liked that.

"No, I should probably go."

She appeared both crestfallen and relieved. If I didn't understand those emotions, I'd be offended. But I did, and we were smart not to push this attraction further. Nico had gone out of his way to warn me away from her. That meant I must have telegraphed my fascination of her in the interview. Considering I'd never felt this strong a pull toward a woman before, I guess my lack of control wasn't surprising. But it did piss me off.

I slid back into the suit coat that I'd draped over my thighs. My mistake was turning to tell Emmaline goodbye, because I caught her unprepared for my scrutiny. Lust burned in her eyes, and her lips parted on a small exhalation as she took in my shoulders.

I put in years with weights—I understood my physical limitations and the mass of muscle I'd built. Emmaline's eyes skimmed down to my ass and a deep flush burned up her neck and into her cheeks.

She still didn't realize I had turned my head toward her. This reaction was unabashed and unfiltered.

Before my consciousness caught up to my reflexes, I turned and hauled her against my side. Her hands came up, fingers splayed wide on my chest. I dipped my head, desperate to taste and learn her. But I waited, unwilling to take if she didn't want it too.

"Knox," she whispered. Then, she tipped her head up, toward me. My lips molded over hers, drifting back and forth until settling into position.

She made a soft sound deep in her throat that turned off my brain and revved my passion. I sucked her lower lip into my mouth. She tasted of champagne and the spice from the salami with a hint of vinegar from the olive. Beneath that, though, was a wild, sweet flavor that was all Emmaline. That damn vanilla and citrus that drove me crazy. I pushed my tongue into her mouth, seeking it.

Her fingertips dug into my shoulders as she rose on tip-toe, conforming her curves to my hard lines. My free hand slid against her scalp, fingers tangling in her thick, silky hair. It smelled like sun-warmed orange blossoms. I needed more of Emmaline's flavor, of her scent, of her soft lips and warm curves. Fuck, I needed her.

I lifted her up with my arm around her waist, tugging her toward me so that she wound her legs around my waist. I palmed the back of her head, applying pressure with my fingers until she tilted her head, offering me deeper access into the recess of her mouth. I plunged my tongue in, wrapping it around hers, reveling in the slick, soft feel. She moaned, rocking her hips against mine. That felt amazing. I wanted her to do it again.

She did and I moaned, pressing my crotch into hers with more force. She gasped at my growing stiffy before she turned to wanton fire in my arms, her tongue tangling with mine as her body writhed and slid, pressing closer and closer still. I could feel the heat from her center.

I needed to touch her, feel her wetness coat my fingers. As I thought that, the kiss crossed the line into carnal. I'd never been this turned on by locking lips. This was...I had no words. Just that I didn't want it to end. Ever.

I stepped forward until my arm hit the wall. I removed my arm from her waist and supported her with the wall so that I could slip my fingers under her shirt to the soft, smooth skin of her belly. She turned her head, gasping.

"No." She choked, almost sobbing. "We can't. I can't do this with you."

I pulled back, trying to regain function in my brain. Her words finally connected in my mind. Fuck. Me. I'd literally lost myself in her.

I eased my hand out from under her shirt, my fingertips grazing her bare skin once again, thanks to the tightness of her top.

She sucked in a harsh breath. I met her eyes. They reflected the wild hunger on my face back at me.

"You're right. I apologize." My vocal cords felt as tight as my pants.

I let her slide down my rigid frame. She dropped her hands and stumbled away, her cheeks redder than they'd been before, and she turned her head aside, refusing to look at me.

"Thank you for bringing my purse over," she murmured.

Her voice was thick, but I didn't know if that was passion or tears sitting in her tone.

"You're welcome. But just so you know, I'm not sorry."

She raised her gaze to mine, and a deep, smug satisfaction lashed through me at the dazedness in her eyes. I leaned in, satisfaction pulsing deeper when her pupils dilated, and her breathing hitched. Emmaline wanted me just as much as I wanted her. I gave in to a brief slide of my nose along her cheek. I nuzzled softly into her neck as her lips parted and her breath spilled across them, warming my forehead.

"You're not?" she whispered.

The breathy quality of her voice made me jerk, almost as if it were a physical caress right across my dick. I took her biceps in my arms and managed to keep from sliding my hands upward in a caress—barely.

"No, but thanks to the contract you signed, we can't explore this attraction," I said with a deep sigh. "I can't ask you to dinner or touch your sweet, perfect lips. I can't explore your petal-soft skin."

I pulled back with effort. I wanted to push her farther, undress her, caress her, love every inch of her. That word caused me to pause. Love. I barely knew Emmaline. I wanted to fuck her, sure, but that's all this was—a passing attraction just like that's all it was with the women in my past.

Emmaline Schooler couldn't be that different from them.

Except that look in her eye... I wanted to see it in the morning from the pillow next to mine. I wanted to see her sleepy smile and hear her soft, raspy good morning before she opened her arms and I made her melt all over again.

No. *No.* Those thoughts were dangerous and would leave me open to a sexual harassment suit. I might already be well on my way, and Nico would literally have me by the balls.

"This cannot happen ever again." My tone was firm.

Emmaline blinked twice, and I watched her face shift from desire to worry to hurt. I wanted to raise my hand, to soothe her, to let her know I craved her and would keep desiring her.

I strode toward the door. Opening it, I stepped out onto the small porch. The cool night air hit my heated skin. I was doing the right thing—I'd put her needs before my own. But my stomach roiled at how I'd done it.

I pulled the door shut behind me but I turned to look through the window beside it. Emmaline crumbled back to the couch, her head in her hands, her shoulders shaking. Her misery settled in my gut.

I hesitated on the step, wanting to go back, wanting to pull her into my arms. I watched a tear slide down her cheek. No, this was best for her and for me. Having her at the firm but not having her was the only option.

That logic was *terrible*.

It wasn't logical at all. It might be insanity.

Could desire make me crazy?

I shoved my hands into my pockets and headed to my car, determined never to mention the hottest kiss of my life to anyone.

Chapter Eight
Emmaline

I'd kissed another man. That thought raced through my head like wildfire through dry grass. I'd kissed Knox Wright. And I'd *liked* it.

My lips still tingled, and my nerve endings danced with a need for more of Knox's kisses, and yes, please, his warm, slightly roughened fingertips against my skin. My belly quivered, and I collapsed deeper into the cushion, my face blanketed by my hands.

"I'm so sorry, Sebastian. So very, very sorry," I whispered.

I'd planned to live again, but kissing Knox... I'd pushed too far beyond my comfort zone.

Once the aftershocks eased, I managed to clean up the living area and washed the champagne glasses. My hands shook so much I nearly dropped them twice as I struggled to get them back into the cabinet. Dinner no longer held any appeal, so I trudged up to bed.

But that wasn't the worst of the situation. As soon as I closed my eyes, I saw Knox's face descending toward mine. I felt the soft brush of his lips settling over mine. I inhaled his intoxicating scent once more, willing him to continue to touch me—to make me feel again.

I rolled on my side and curled into a ball. Much as I hated my attraction to Knox, I also welcomed it. For years, I'd been locked in a purgatory, sure I'd never find the same love and passion I'd shared with Sebastian.

Not that I was ready to act on it—I still loved Sebastian. I always would. But, as Joshua and Ellie said, *my* Sebastian was gone. I'd never have a life with him, which meant I needed to start dating at some point—or at least to imagine a relationship with another man.

Now, I had. Except he was my boss.

My face burned with embarrassment at his final rejection: *this can't happen again.* It shouldn't have happened at all. Except, I kept returning to the softness of his touch, the way he nuzzled into me.

That made me ache for a return to the days when Sebastian was my best kiss, my future, my fantasy, all rolled up into a special, loving package.

Whoever claimed grief diminished with time hadn't grieved a living man changed by a simple decision. A decision that cost him the life he knew. And cost me everything.

I slammed my hand into my pillow, the growl building in my throat.

"You can't change the past, Emmaline."

I flopped onto my back and stared up at the ceiling. *Why* was I still here, in this house?

Because I was used to it.

Because it had been familiar and comforting when I came home, so alone. I hadn't been able to cope with moving into the wing of Ellie's mansion Sebastian and I had planned to share. So, I stumbled back into my parents' home, which held different ethereal memories that I couldn't escape.

Joshua's words from my last visit swirled through my head.

She could also do better. Knox is a notorious flirt and lady's man, Nana. That's not what we want for Emmaline.

Knox's tone tonight when he told me not to kiss him again had been arrogant, as if he expected to be obeyed. I'd lived on the same college campus he had, and I knew how revered the Cornell hockey team was. I'm sure he'd never been challenged to find a date—or a bed partner.

Still, his assumption that I would push for more than a kiss that he instigated irked me. The last man I was intimate with was Sebastian, and that was years before, leaving me at a severe disadvantage to Knox.

I didn't like the feeling.

How was I going to face him tomorrow? I blinked back a wave of tears. I'd let one fall earlier, but no more. I was stronger than sniffling into my pillow. I'd survived too much to let a man, *any* man, chip away at my self-worth. I'd go into the office tomorrow with my head high and do the work expected of me. Satisfied with my conclusion, though not my restless need for satisfaction, I rolled over and pulled out my seldom-used vibrator. I took it to my bathroom and cleaned it thoroughly, unwilling to meet my own eyes in the mirror.

And when I orgasmed later, the pulses of pleasure were courtesy of Knox Wright's slate eyes, soft lips, and warm hands.

A secret I never planned to share.

I rose early and arrived at the office five minutes before my scheduled time, settling in at my desk without bothering more than a smile at Nannette.

Luckily for me, Aidy was already in her office. She bopped out and smiled at me.

"Ready to get to work?" she asked.

"Absolutely," I said. I refused to glance over my shoulder, worried Knox was watching this interaction.

"Come on, then," she said. I followed her back into her office.

"I've been looking forward to working with you," she said with a smile.

"Not as much as I've looked forward to working with you," I said.

Some of my tension eased. I could handle Knox. I'd already dealt with much worse than forbidden attraction.

She settled in at her desk and frowned down at the cleared top.

"I swear, this whole pregnancy brain is such a truism. I thought I'd left two files on my desk."

"Nannette cleared it yesterday morning," I said.

Aidy seemed flustered by that statement. She picked up the phone on her desk and called Nannette.

"Hi, there," Aidy said. "Where are the Smithson and Carrington files?"

Aidy then swiveled in her chair and pulled two files out of her cabinet.

"Got them. Thanks, Nannette."

She hung up. "I'm going to have to start locking these two folders away." She smiled as she glanced over my shoulder.

"Hey, Knox. What's up?"

My shoulders stiffened, and I forced my face to remain neutral.

"Just wanted to see how your morning is going," he said.

His deep voice made my heart flutter. I placed my palms on my thighs and studied my manicure.

"It's going well, thanks. Emmaline and I are getting started."

"Morning, Emmaline," Knox said.

Dammit. Now I had to acknowledge him. I stared at his chest, refusing to meet his gaze. "Good morning, Mr. Wright."

"Knox," he said, his voice dropping, a little less stilted and more like the man in my living room last night.

"I prefer to keep the formality because familiarity can prove... problematic."

I flitted my gaze up in time to catch his frown.

"I'm going out to a site," he said. "If you need me, contact my cell."

I didn't have his number and didn't intend to use it.

He stepped out of the doorway, and I turned back to Aidy. She had her chin propped on her fists.

"That exchange was enlightening," she murmured.

The flush—from anger and mortification—that I'd been battling crested my cheeks. She sighed as she picked up a pen and tapped it on her desk.

"What did Knox do?"

"He brought me my purse last night."

"And he made a comment or a pass?" Aidy rolled her eyes and shook his head. "I think his arrogance with women is ingrained, thanks to all the fawning those girls did down at the rink."

I bit the inside of my cheek, debating whether or not to admit that he'd kissed me—and I'd been an active participant.

"I'll give him an earful later," Aidy said. "If you're

uncomfortable, you can tell me. I'll make sure you don't have to deal with him."

I swallowed. "Thanks," I said. "That would be helpful." Not for the reasons she thought, but I decided her conclusions were better than the reality.

I clearly wasn't prepared to jump back out into the dating world, and I wasn't ready to let go of the man I'd loved with all the passion of my youth. Plus, my interactions with Knox couldn't compare with my years together with Sebastian. Which meant I needed to keep my distance. He was, as Joshua and Aidy had pointed out, a man used to women fawning over him. I wouldn't be one of those women. Ever.

The man I fell for at some distant point in the future would romance me, show me I was special. Make me believe in love again.

Ridiculous and sappy? Maybe, but I needed that fantasy to get me through today.

"So...this project you wanted my help with?" I prompted.

She glanced down at the papers in front of her.

"You signed an NDA with your onboarding paperwork through HR, right?"

I nodded.

"Then, I can share some of this information. We're competing on these two projects, and I needed to add my specs to the Carrington file. I haven't had a chance to work on Smithson yet."

She unrolled her papers and showed me her digitized renderings based on the client interviews she had sat in on. Awe bubbled up causing my stomach to turn over. "These are amazing," I said, touching my fingers to the cantilevered second floor that spilled out over the water. "What do you plan to use for the decking material?"

"I don't know yet. Something that can withstand extreme temperatures, obviously. It will also need to bear a significant amount of weight since I want to try this cantilevered approach." She tapped her nail against the drawings. "This design only works well if the material withstands both New England winters and wave surge."

I blinked at her. "You think that's likely? I mean, that inlet is protected by the shoals and hills."

"True, but I don't want to do anything less than our best."

"May I help you find the best material?"

Aidy smiled. "I hoped you'd be interested."

"I am. Very." I hesitated but then blurted, "I own a small cottage on that inlet."

Aidy's eyebrows rose. "That's intriguing."

I'd started this conversation so I should finish it. "It was a gift from Sebastian for my twentieth birthday."

"Nice present," Aidy said.

I shook my head. "I'm not part of that world, but yes, it was. It is. We had so many plans for that place…" I closed my eyes. "It's why I ended up with an architecture degree. No other career or hobby made me happy."

Aidy blinked back moisture filling her eyes, her gaze filled with sympathy. "I'm sorry you had to go through that."

"Sebastian has it much worse than I do."

"Did you still want to marry him after the accident?" Aidy blushed. "I'm sorry, that's not really my business."

I smiled. "Yes, I did. But Ellie wouldn't let me. She holds the power of attorney and all the other requisite guardianships for Sebastian, and she refused to—in her words—destroy my life with a man who could never be one again."

Aide's mouth dropped open. "That's..."

I cleared my throat. "We were supposed to be discussing the Carringtons' residence."

"Right. It's just...wow. I cannot imagine how hard these past few years have been."

"It's why I don't like to talk about it. But Ellie was here yesterday, and now I'm concerned that I should have told your brothers and you about my relationship with the Giovannis before."

Aidy waved me off. "It's really none of their business. When you're ready, talk. Until then, just do your job."

"If you're sure."

"I am." She blinked rapidly and yanked a tissue from the box on the corner of her desk. "Your story is so tragic, and my hormones are vicious these days. Now, tell me about your cottage."

I pulled out my phone and clicked through to my album. Aidy's jaw dropped. "Yours is the property next to the Carringtons'."

"Really?" I asked, eyes wide.

"Yes. See?" She pointed at a distinctive red gazebo that sat at the water's edge in the middle of the Carrington's parcel of land. "That's not a structure you forget."

We laughed.

"I've noticed that cottage. It's small and charming."

"It's original, which is no longer an asset to the area. It really needs a total overhaul."

Aidy patted my hand. "You'll get there."

"I plan to move in once I make some of the more urgent updates. That wasn't a priority before, but now... It's time for me to jettison the parts of my life that aren't working, aren't bringing me pleasure, and start surrounding myself with the people and spaces I want in my life." I gripped my hands together. "I've lost years to grief. I needed that. But now, I need to find *me* again. And dive into making Emmaline Schooler the best version of herself." I winked, trying to lighten the mood. "To live my best life."

Aidy smiled but it was tinted with melancholy. "I know all about creating a better version of yourself. And I admire your convictions."

I laughed. "And I admire yours."

"Let's start with the material for the deck, shall we?"

I nodded, eager for the opportunity to learn from her. We spent the morning working through a variety of potential options. Each time we found a potential one, Aidy made a note on her phone. "We'll go check these out tomorrow to get a better sense of both flexibility and weight-bearing capacity." She wrinkled her nose. "The specs are always off."

I tucked that nugget of information into my ever-expanding file.

"When do you present these plans?" I asked.

"Next week." Aidy's green eyes lit with fire. "Sure, we could come in with vague ideas about what we think would work, but our reputation is on the line, and getting these details together now matters."

I thought about Aidy's comments the rest of the week, wondering what it was like to live with that much pressure to always push for new, fresh creativity while keeping true to deeply held design principles.

Thankfully, Knox remained out of the office, overseeing the various projects. That was just fine with me. I needed the time to catch my breath and reinforce all the reasons why I should steer clear of the man.

On Thursday morning, Aidy asked me to accompany her to various suppliers. We spent most of the day in Boston, with a nice lunch at a seafood bistro.

By the time we arrived back at the office, it was after hours, and Aidy had faded.

She let me into the office and sagged against the door frame, exhaustion turning her face pale.

Knox stuck his head out of his office door, and my breath caught at the sight of his blond hair and slate eyes peering at us. His gaze swept over me, heating, before turning to his sister. He stepped out of his office and headed toward us.

"I'll just grab my briefcase," I said as I scampered away from the oncoming sexy male.

Knox dipped his chin in my direction but kept walking. "You look done in, Aidy-pie."

"Growing a baby is tiring," she said on a sigh.

"Let me pack up a couple of files, and I'll take you home."

"That's okay," she said. Even her voice sounded done in.

"Well, I'd feel better if you let me drive you. I don't want anything to happen to you or my sweet niece."

I closed my eyes at those words, letting the sincerity and love in them wash over me for one long minute. Then I shook myself and slung my bag up onto my shoulder.

Knox had headed back into his office, and Aidy now sat in one of the club chairs, eyes closed.

"I'm heading out," I said.

Her soft snore answered me.

"She always was a good sleeper," Knox said from my shoulder, startling me.

"You're sweet with her," I said, glancing back at him.

He shrugged. "I'm her brother. She deserves my support."

It was more than that. I could see the love and sweetness in his eyes as he crouched down in front of her.

I should go. I knew it. Being alone with Knox was stupid. But I couldn't make my feet move as he touched Aidy's cheek with the same fingers he'd used to caress my bare skin.

"Aidy-pie," he murmured. "Let's get you home."

"Tired," she muttered.

He shook his head with a chuckle. He set his briefcase in the chair next to Aidy and bent down to scoop her up. I grabbed his bag and motioned for him to walk. He quirked a brow but did so.

I held his briefcase while he settled Aidy in his SUV. I thrust it out in front of me, like a barrier, when he turned.

"Here you go. Have a good night, Mr. Wright."

"Emmaline," he said on a sigh.

I trotted over toward my car, not willing to further engage him. He had other ideas and caught my wrist in his much larger hand.

"I'm sorry," he said, gaze fixed on mine. "For kissing you."

Of course I wanted him to apologize. I'd struggled with my own feelings even as I could still feel the tingle of awareness return. *Say something, Emmaline.* "Um..."

His gaze bore into mine. "You're beautiful, but you're so much more than a pretty face. You're smart, thoughtful, measured, and so talented. If you didn't work here, I'd ask you out in a heartbeat and do everything in my power to get you to agree to a second date—and a third."

My entire body started shaking. "I do work here," I whispered. "And I'd like for that to continue."

He stepped back, dropping my wrist after one more soft stroke of his thumb against my raging pulse.

"I do, too. Which is why I'm not going to ask you out. But I thought you should know that I dream about you, Emmaline. About what we could be."

He turned away, heading back up the steps to the building, no doubt to engage the alarm and lock the door.

I didn't move until he started to head back toward his car.

"Go home, darl...Emmaline. Go home so I can get Aidy to bed."

I scampered to my vehicle, my mind whirling.

He dreamed of me.

I chewed on the inside of my lip as heat washed over and through me. I wish he hadn't said that.

And I wished, more, that it didn't mean so much to me.

Chapter Nine
Knox

I woke with goosebumps covering my skin and flutters in my belly, thanks to yet another dream starring Emmaline. I rose from my bed and readied myself for the day. Maybe I'd been stupid to tell her I dreamed of her, but when I'd felt the thrum of her pulse against my thumb and saw the longing in her beautiful eyes, I couldn't help myself. Nico would say that showed my lack of control.

Maybe it did.

Or maybe I just had better instincts—and a higher level of game—than he did. I liked to believe it was the second option.

All week, I'd forced myself to stay out of the office as much as possible, trying to give Emmaline the space she needed—and my raging desire a chance to cool off. But I'd realized last night that my hunger for her wasn't going to diminish, let alone disappear.

When she'd collected my briefcase without me asking, and waited for me to get my sister situated, clearly concerned about Aidy's health and more than happy to lend a hand, something in my chest cracked open.

I wouldn't act on it. I wouldn't put Emmaline in the position to choose between her career and me. I'd been in that position when I'd had to decide between the draft and the firm, and it... well, it *sucked*. No matter what choice I made, I felt like I was letting myself down. Emmaline told me her parents were gone, and she'd been in a bad car accident. I didn't want to add more trauma to the woman's already grief-stricken life.

So, while I'd wanted nothing more than to share a meal with her Monday night, or better, to keep kissing her, a warning blared in my head. That and the fact I hated the idea of hurting her in any way. I couldn't be the reason for her tears. I simply couldn't. No matter how much I wanted to take those soft, pink lips again. And I did. Holy hell, I did.

Last night, I'd managed to force Emmaline's shocked gaze and slightly parted lips from my mind and spent a couple of hours on the Smithson presentation. Solidifying a relationship with that family would benefit our firm for years, thanks to their philanthropic efforts in the arts and well-known desire to build a new museum. The couple had also recently donated a few million toward the refurbishment of Providence's symphony hall, a project I really wanted to add to our list.

I'd been courting the power couple since I started with Wright and Associates, knowing they were the type of visionaries we needed to give us the leeway to create something lasting and worthwhile as well as creatively stimulating and beautiful. But something about Nico's initial designs felt clunky. I'd asked Aidy to look it over earlier and wanted to check her emailed response.

I toweled my hair dry as I sipped from a large mug of coffee just as the sun rose. I rarely woke before dawn, preferring to work late into the night—or work off any tension with a willing partner into the morning. Unfortunately, the latter became less appealing as the years passed—and completely unpalatable since

I'd met Emmaline, which left me with fewer late-night pursuits.

No doubt Nico would be thrilled to find out I was as celibate as he was. Hopefully, I didn't become as cranky.

I headed out of the kitchen, through my living room to my first-floor office. My house was a Shaker-style bungalow with three bedrooms and a killer view of the water. I'd purchased it last year and was in the process of upgrading the interior. I'd chosen to be relevant to the original design but not let the strictures of the genre keep me from some of my more flamboyant touches like the amazing den with its deep-seated couches and high-tech surround sound system. I didn't get to chill in the space often, but I loved it.

I grabbed my briefcase and laptop and returned to the kitchen. The room faced east, and I smiled, as I always did, at the warm glow of the wood casements as the sun sparkled off the glass. Once a small room, I'd knocked out walls to incorporate the dining room into the space, giving me a large, comfortable eat-in kitchen with a large island. That's where I did most of my work.

I poured myself another cup as I called Nico.

"Hey. I listed some ideas for the Smithson residence."

"I'm looking at them now," he muttered.

Of course he was. Nico channeled all his passion into Wright and Associates. I was proud of the work we did, but Nico kept the company his sole focus. Even when I played Division I hockey, I'd had other interests. Mainly architecture and sex, but those kept me from fixating on just one thing. My single business class had pointed out the importance of diversification, and I did like to practice the theories I'd learned at Cornell.

"And?"

"And I really like that initial sketch for the front. You were definitely onto something with that fall of wood and windows but where are the original notes?"

"They were in there when I handed it off to Aidy. Maybe they're still in her office."

"It's unlike her to misplace documentation," Nico said.

After nearly a decade of rocky years, Nico and Aidy were building a close relationship again—one I was happy to watch blossom. Nico protected her and championed her just as he had when we were kids. I hadn't realized how much I'd missed that dynamic.

Though, Ryder—my childhood friend—seemed to have taken a shine to my baby sis and might well determine to put himself in the role of Aidy's champion.

"Emmaline mentioned that Nannette cleared Aidy's desk Monday morning. I'd talk to Aidy first, though."

"Will do," Nico said. "But I'll wait until she gets in the office. I don't want to wake her up."

I'd texted Nico last night to let him know that Aidy fell asleep and I was taking her home. He'd written me back twenty minutes later stating that he'd just read that fatigue was a normal symptom of the third trimester and we better get Emmaline up to speed on some of the projects so that Aidy could reduce her hours back to a standard eight hours per day, preferably less.

I wondered, now that I'd seen my sister go through the process, if I'd ever have a child. I worried I wouldn't want to be with the woman who could give me kids.

"What are you thinking about Emmaline?" Nico asked.

No doubt that was related to his text last night, but my mind turned to the kiss we'd shared on Monday. She kissed better than anyone I'd ever met, and I'd made her cry. I shoved my thumb against my eye socket as I replayed our brief interaction yesterday.

She'd been so surprised by my words, her face softening nearly as much as her eyes. Those soft lips had parted, and it had taken all my willpower not to tug her against me and ravish her mouth.

She would have let me. I know she would have. But that made me doing so that much worse. I couldn't take advantage of my position as her employer. I wouldn't.

"Knox?"

I startled. Right. Nico asked about Emmaline. "You must have cut out."

"Well, tell me again," Nico said, tone impatient.

"I think she's a hard worker," I said my voice gruff.

Nico made an appraising noise. "Aidy seems to like her and the file she put together on materials for the Carringtons' deck are well-considered."

"You got a file on that?" I asked, surprised. She and Aidy hadn't returned until after six last night.

"Yeah, it came in about nine last night. I told her we didn't expect her to work so late. She said that she wanted to put together the schematics and notes while the information was still fresh."

"That's good," I said. But I didn't like the idea of her working so late. I didn't like the idea of her alone, rattling around that big house with its dated, bulky furniture and family photos that had to remind her of all she'd lost.

"What's good is the fact that she knows Eleanor Giovanni.

A few images popped up when I typed in her name, so it seems she's close with Mrs. Giovanni's grandson, Joshua."

"Like...they're together?"

My chest squeezed and I winced at the pain building there.

"Not sure. They attended the Giovanni Foundation Gala together last year. I'll look into it more later."

That sounded serious. And I'd kissed her. Then told her I dreamed of her. I dropped my chin to my chest, thankful Nico couldn't see my reaction. There was no reason for me to respond to Emmaline like this. None.

"Nah. It's her life, but it's good to know Mrs. Giovanni likes her."

"Fine. See you when you get in," Nico said.

I mumbled a goodbye, preoccupied with my thoughts.

And if Emmaline had a boyfriend, especially a rich, powerful one who was also a highly decorated war hero, I *really* needed to avoid her. Because I wasn't going to be able to ignore her.

The irony wasn't lost on me: Emmaline Schooler was the first woman I'd ever fantasized about. That's not to say I hadn't had fantasies because I had. But the woman had always been faceless.

Not anymore. Worse, I knew what Emmaline tasted like, and I wanted every single one of my kisses from now on to taste of her.

I was so screwed because I wanted a relationship like my parents. The way my father had looked at Mom—as if she were his sun, moon, and all the stars—that's what I wanted for me.

Even though they'd disappeared on their boat years before, they did it together, and that made their loss bearable. Since I'd never found a woman that created even a tingle of that devotion,

I'd decided to focus more of my energy on our firm, which was growing at an astronomical rate.

We were presenting with some of the biggest names in the field—and winning a decent portion of those contracts. Ninety-hour weeks were a regular occurrence. I thrived in the environment, but Nico seemed to be shutting down. Maybe a better way of putting it was he was shutting everyone out. His singular goal seemed to be creating the most celebrated firm in New England. While I liked the devotion, I'd begun to worry his drive might be fed by the demons of his past.

I finished my cup of coffee and put the mug in the dishwasher. I filled my travel mug to the brim, needing my next hit of caffeine.

No time to worry about my big brother now. I slung on my tie and made quick work of the Windsor knot. I grabbed my wallet, keys, phone, and my mug. Entering my garage, I settled into my crossover. While a sedan might have been more practical for work, I checked in on most of our projects during the construction phase, so I preferred a vehicle with all-wheel drive. Came in handy during the big nor'easters that ravaged the community throughout the winter.

I plucked my sunglasses from their space and backed out of my driveway, a smile lighting my lips. I might not be able to touch Emmaline, especially if she were dating Joshua Giovanni, but that didn't mean I couldn't enjoy looking.

Because I did plan to look—long and often. And if Emmaline became available, I'd find a work-around that Nico would live with.

Because there was no way I was losing the possibility of finding the same kind of spark my parents shared.

Chapter Ten
Emmaline

I rang the bell at the Giovanni estate that Friday evening. I let out a long breath, releasing some of the tension I'd held since Monday night. I'd completed my first week at Wright and Associates. Minus my ever-increasing obsession with Knox, work was better than I expected.

Eleanor opened the door. Her smile was wan. "Good evening, my dear girl," she said. "I'm happy to see you."

I kissed her cheek. "Here are your plans."

I pulled out the tube of papers and put them into her hands.

She smiled. "Thank you. I look forward to going over them."

She waved me in. I turned back toward her in time to see her shut the door. Her shoulders slumped, and she shuffled toward the room she called a parlor. She collapsed into one of her high-backed chairs—the kind that one would expect to see in a grand British drawing room with tufted chintz fabric I always felt as stiff and uncomfortable as the chair itself.

"Bad day?" I asked.

"Better now that you're here."

I smiled. "Those plans aren't just for veterans," I said, my stomach clenching with nerves. "I created them with both Sebastian and Joshua in mind."

"Now I'm even more intrigued."

She unrolled them onto the shiny teak coffee table between us as I settled on the edge of the chenille sofa. Her fingers traced the customizable counter height I'd considered for those who were wheelchair users part-time—as Sebastian had been when he woke. In this version, I'd included all his specialized equipment that TBI patients needed. Most patients with injuries like Sebastian tended to be former soldiers, which was why I'd taken the time to spec out options for those with prosthetic limbs as well.

"You thought of everything," she whispered.

I shook my head. "No. I'm sure I haven't. But I keep updating these each time Sebastian or Joshua have a challenge."

"We can do that here," she said, her eyes glowing. "The boys will *love* these modifications because it'll make their lives easier, fuller. Better. You really are a darling. I'm so thankful Sebastian brought you home all those years ago."

"I am, too."

"I tell you what. Once we get the beach house completed, we'll incorporate these changes into this place."

She clapped her hands together, a smile finally gracing her lips.

"That will be a wonderful present for Sebastian. Once we're sure he's happy, we can update Joshua's." She paused, a frown puckering her brow as she traced the lines for the ADA-compliant bath. "And perhaps for me as well."

"None of that, Ellie," I said, a catch in my voice. "You're healthy and you need to stay that way."

She blinked before refocusing on me. "Seventy-seven is looming, and I won't live forever."

I couldn't fathom a world without Ellie in it. More, I didn't want to. I leaned in and hugged the older woman.

"I know we don't have control, but try, for me, to stay well. Please."

She pulled back before patting my cheek. "For you. And for me, too."

—— Å ——

The next week passed smoothly because I spent most of my time with Aidy. Even better, Aidy informed me Wednesday that we'd be heading out to The Mac site where I would meet Chloe. We'd spent most of yesterday poring over plans and researching potential options for the new acreage and the large cinderblock and shingle structure that dominated the space. It had been a shipyard long ago but over the past two decades was transformed into a convention center-style space. Unfortunately, while large and able to accommodate bigger groups, there wasn't a hotel nor restaurants nearby, which caused it to fade into bankruptcy. That allowed the Macintosh Hotelier Group to purchase it at a huge discount but left the firm with the task of reconfiguring the space into something more useable.

I'd hit on a potential idea yesterday afternoon when I remembered the estate in Oxford I'd visited with Sebastian during our holiday there the summer after I graduated from high school. We'd met Joshua, who was on leave, in England. We'd visited one of Ellie's friends, a lord or something, and he'd served us tea in a large airy room facing south that led out to perfect English gardens, not unlike the ones I'd designed for The Mac. I mentioned it to Aidy, making a quick sketch on my pad to give her a better idea of what I was talking about.

"Oh! Yes, that's great, Emmaline. I can really see the potential, especially if we open up the south-facing windows. Let's run it by Chloe. I think she'll love this concept."

As Aidy anticipated, I hit it off with the older woman. Chloe was a vibrant contrast of flaming red hair, freckles, and a posh accent that I learned came from top finishing schools in Dublin.

"My parents are part of the aristocracy," she murmured. "They anticipated I should find a wealthy lord and settle down into a boring life in the country, managing the manor and weekend hunts. I pissed them off mightily when I took an interest in helping to run the Macintosh Hotelier Group, flouting marriage and hunts by moving to America," she said with a wink. "It's not as though they planned to deny their only child her birthright."

Aidy leaned in. "Don't you think Chloe would love Calliope?" she asked.

I nodded. "And Simon. They'd get along great," I said.

"Why's that?" Chloe asked.

"Because you're all so properly British and awesome," Aidy said with a laugh. "Now, I want you to tell Emmaline what your bosses expect. I've already gotten her up to speed on the timeline, and she'll be working closely with me to ensure we complete the gardens and renovations to the large pavilion in time for the grand opening you've planned for March."

Aidy patted her stomach. "Let's hope this little one decides to remain inside her handy carrying case so that I get to enjoy the ribbon cutting, too."

I admired Aidy's easy confidence and willingness to discuss her personal life, which made me feel even worse about having kept my close affiliation with the Giovannis from her. Chloe pulled my attention back to the present as she went over the list of possibilities for the five-thousand-square-foot building that came with the additional acreage.

I looked over the three-dimensional renderings Aidy and I had worked on to incorporate English-style gardens into the landscape.

"I have an idea that I ran past Aidy yesterday," I said, nerves causing my belly to flutter. "She suggested I mock up something, which she then improved upon. Since you're interested in a British experience for your patrons, with the formal gardens, I wondered if it would work to turn the large building into something like an orangery..."

"Like they have on large country estates," Chloe said, eyes wide and sparkling. "I'm liking this idea."

"Yes, that's where I got the idea. Well, Aidy created a breath-taking option that would be perfect for weddings or larger, formal gatherings as I understand these portions of estates are sometimes rented out for weddings," I said. "At least that's what Lord Higginbotham-Smythe told me."

"You know Herbert?" Chloe asked. "How delightful. Yes! His orangery is sublime, especially in January when England has been without sun for weeks."

"I wouldn't say know him, but my friends do. That's where I came up with the idea. We did some more research into others in the area, and Aidy believes we can knock out most of the ugly cinderblock wall and incorporate windows along here, which would give us prime beach views, adding to the romance of the location.

"We can cover the rest either in a New England shaker-style cedar shingle or skin the exterior in a veneer of stone to mimic the hotel, but the majority of the space will be windows to give it that conservatory feel, which means it'll be perfect for weddings either in mid-morning or evening, spring through autumn," I said, growing more hopeful as Chloe continued to review the drawings. "As an added bonus, you can create a destination-wedding package since the hotel is so close, allowing for out-of-town visitors to stay on-site."

"Which would no doubt increase the beverage billings. My bar staff and bottom line will love you for this," Chloe said. She smoothed her hand over the paper. "Let me send this back to HQ, but I have to say, I'm impressed. You don't think this would add too much time to the construction calendar?"

Aidy shook her head. "Because the building is in good shape, this is more of a revamp of the space. The kitchen is updated, so it's more an issue of adding those windows and knocking out all the non-load-bearing walls." She pointed to them on the drawing.

"You even have enough bathroom capacity. It's just a matter of changing out fixtures. And installing high-quality finishes to the main space to allow for a small chapel in this part next to what will become the banquet area. By adding French doors, guests will be able to enjoy the garden, and we can create a path that leads down to the gazebo for those who prefer an outdoor wedding."

"You've thought of everything." Chloe breathed. "I want to get married here." She chuckled. "First I'd need to find the right man."

"Don't we all," Aidy said, her mouth twisting in disappointment.

I dropped my gaze, my heart fluttering. I'd thought I'd marry Sebastian one day, and I'd poured every bit of my imagination into the orangery/chapel design. I'd never get my wedding, but that didn't mean other women wouldn't be able to fulfill their dreams.

I'd have to find enough pleasure in my career because I wasn't going to get more.

Knox's face flitted through my mind, but I shoved it away, just as I had each of the previous times I thought of him. He was wrong for me and I wasn't interested in pursuing a relationship with anyone anyway. End of story.

— Å —

I attended yoga and brunch with my girls, enjoying their camaraderie. After years of imposed isolation, the joy of companionship washed over me. Aidy had an activity with Ryder, so she bailed before brunch, which left Calliope and me to help Bridget waddle down the street to our favorite café.

"How ya doing there, Bridget?" Calliope asked as Bridget struggled to wrestle her belly close enough to the table to enjoy her minestrone. She gave up and settled the bowl on her bump, causing us all to laugh, but I saw the longing in her eyes as she stared at Bridget's large bump.

Bridget must have noticed, too, because she leaned over and captured Calliope's hand. "Your time is coming."

Calliope shrugged. Clearly, there was history behind that exchange. I sighed as I contemplated my half-eaten lunch. Sebastian used to talk about our family all the time. He wanted three children and a Newfie. He wanted to live on the coast, but he'd been willing to wait for me to finish my education. At the time, I'd planned to be a doctor, and he'd been so proud of my choice.

I sucked in a long breath, trying not to fall into the dark tunnel that led back to Sebastian's crumpled SUV.

"Right, Emmaline?" Bridget leaned in my direction, concern written across her face.

I shuddered, much as a wet cat does in an attempt to fling water from its paws.

"What?"

Bridget placed her hand on my forearm and the warmth helped push back the memories. "Are you okay?"

"I was just remembering," I said.

Bridget's soft gaze filled with understanding. She'd been in the ER the night the EMTs brought in Sebastian and me. I'd been sick with worry and loopy from my own injuries. Bridget was assigned as my nurse, and she managed to keep me updated on Sebastian's progress. She, more than anyone, understood what I'd lost that night.

I touched the edge of my plate. "He wanted kids." I lifted my head to look at her. "Three." I gestured to her. "Like you."

"Oh, honey."

Calliope rose from her seat across the table to hug me. We'd all known loss, the four of us. Maybe that's why we made such a strong bond, as unlikely as it might seem.

"I'm okay," I murmured. "It just hits me sometimes."

Calliope cupped my cheeks. "Understandable."

I closed my eyes briefly, wishing for a different outcome that would never happen. I sucked in a deep breath. "We were discussing Bridget's beautiful babies and Simon's overprotective impulses," I said, managing a smile.

The look on the other two faces told me I failed but they let my history fade back into the past where I wanted it to stay. Sebastian was no longer mine, not to care for nor to hold. He and his family made that choice for us, but part of me couldn't let the Sebastian Before go.

He'd been my dream man. Tall, athletic, confident and caring. He cherished me, put my needs first. Until he glanced at his phone that night and we ended up with a very different future.

I smiled at my friends' comments, no longer fully engaged in the conversation. At least not until Bridget laid her hand on her belly and grimaced.

"Well, Calliope, I think your class sent me into labor," Bridget said, as calm and collected as she normally was. ER nurses amazed me.

"Oh, no. Not here," Calliope gasped.

Bridget chuckled though it ended with a grimace. "Emmaline, will you grab my phone? I'll call Simon. My guess is he's already parked outside, waiting for me."

"On it," I said. I pulled her phone from her purse and handed it to her. She dialed the number while the rest of us stared at her, clearly out of our element.

She spoke quietly. The waiter came by and I told him he could take our plates and to bring the check. Calliope shoved her credit card at the guy as he turned to walk away. "Just put it on there."

Simon appeared in the doorway, blond hair tousled and eyes a bit wild. They landed on Bridget and he stalked toward her. As soon as he reached her side, he dropped his phone into his pocket, and pulled her up, into his arms.

"Brendan?" she asked.

"With Ben's mum. I'll help you to the car." He turned and focused on Calliope for a moment. She nodded. "Ladies," Simon murmured.

He slid his arm around Bridget's middle and helped her toward the door. She settled her body against his and he realigned to her, taking her weight.

"Her purse," I began.

"We'll take it to the hospital. Simon's going to worry, so let's let him get Bridget sorted," Calliope said.

She closed the bill's folder with a flourish and a smile that bloomed over her face. "Well, I'm going to be an auntie. I can't wait to hold my nieces."

—— Å ——

Aidy called me into her office Monday morning. She pulled out her file for The Mac. "Chloe said the designs are approved. The gardens need to be romantic for a magical wedding experience."

She looked a bit dreamy, but she shook her head just a little, seeming to pull herself out of whatever fantasy had been building there.

"The good news is that I already have a crew on-site. Since we're into the finish work on the main hotel, I can move the main construction crew over to demo the space and get the walls prepped for the windows. That should start this morning."

"Whoa. You work fast."

Aidy's expression was grim. "We meet our deadlines," she said.

I sucked my lower lip into my mouth, unsure how I'd handle the pressure of the project. Its scope grew exponentially with the additional parcel-and-building purchase, but Aidy and her brothers rolled with the changes, coming up with a spectacular plan that would be beautiful and add additional revenue to the hotel.

"I'd like you to come with me to the site while I talk to the contractor and their subs. We'll go after lunch. Then, I thought we could stop by Bridget's to drop off our gifts."

I frowned. "I don't have mine with me."

Aidy waved a hand. "We'll pick it up."

"You're sure? I don't want Nico or Knox to think I'm not working—"

"We know you are," Knox said from the doorway. "And if you're with Aidy, then it's fine."

My back straightened, and my heart thrummed against my ribs. I hadn't heard him enter the space and wasn't prepared yet to see him. I breathed out through my nose, trying to find my resolve, but it crumbled as I turned to look at Knox. He was potent, and he moved like a predator. Something big and lithe, well aware of his dominance. I knew I had a type: All-American and very fit, but Knox Wright put even Sebastian's lean muscle to shame. The man was built for power, agility, speed, and, yes, dominance.

It was the last that made me shift in my chair as heat bloomed through my belly. My attraction to Knox started with our first meeting, but that low-level awareness had grown the more we interacted. I might have wanted to kiss him and touch him before—as I had on that first Monday—but the more I watched him interact with his employees and clients, the further I fell under his spell.

My body continued to warm for him, and I hated that reaction. This attraction needed to stop. I kept my face lowered, hoping that Aidy couldn't see my flushed face.

"Thank you," I said.

"I have to meet with Lance Jericho to deal with an issue in the support wall."

"Oh? Did he put in the middle post?" Aidy asked.

"Yes, and it's not going to work with the glass wall system we purchased for the space. I really wish the contractors would follow the plans."

Aidy sat back in her chair with a sigh. "Good luck with that."

Knox's palm hit the door jamb, causing me to jump. "I'm going to need it. Hey, make sure Emmaline has time to go over the specs for the Giovanni's residence, will you? I'm going to head out there once I finish with Lance."

Aidy nodded. "We'll do those next. I wanted her input on the kitchen and back deck." She beamed at me. "After that brilliant save for The Mac's new building, I'm pretty sure coming up with an integrated solution for the limited outdoor transition from kitchen to beach won't be any kind of challenge at all."

I flushed again, this time from pride.

"Great," Knox said. "I'll look forward to your ideas. Put the folder on my desk when you finish, will you?"

His gaze flashed to mine and the warmth in my stomach expanded. His gaze heated up and my lips parted. I dropped my gaze to my lap.

"See ya later, Aidy-pie," Knox said, his tone gruff. "Emmaline."

"What did I tell you about calling me that here?" Aidy's voice held both exasperation and affection.

"That I'm the only one allowed?" he asked, humor lacing his tone.

I turned in time to catch his unrepentant grin. His slate eyes lit up, appearing warmer than usual. My heart squeezed. I wanted him to look at me with that level of affection.

Wait. No, I didn't. I was steering clear of Knox. I was focused on my career.

She shook her head even as she laughed. "See ya later, Hat Trick."

His gaze slid from Aidy's to mine, a deep scowl furrowing his brow as he mumbled his goodbyes.

I frowned at Knox's reaction. Once I was sure Knox was gone, I asked, "Isn't that a hockey reference?"

She raised an eyebrow. "It was. You don't know hockey?"

I shook my head. I knew about hockey only through college. Sebastian rowed, so I'd been to many crew competitions.

"How do you live in New England and not know all about hockey?"

I swallowed with difficulty. Bringing up Sebastian typically caused Aidy to get teary-eyed. "My mom was from Brazil, and my dad was rarely home to watch sports."

"Gotcha. Yes, a hat trick is when a player scores three goals in one game. But that's not why Knox got that nickname." She wiggled her eyebrows. "He hates it when I call him that, so of course I do it every chance I get," Aidy said with a self-satisfied smile.

I nodded but I must have looked uncomfortable. "Don't worry, Emmaline, he won't try anything with you."

For some reason, that reassurance left me bereft.

Chapter Eleven
Knox

I stopped at the sight of Emmaline's dark head bent over her desk. Even after weeks of her consistent presence, I still thrilled at the sight of her.

We'd managed to work around each other, only talking when others were within earshot. And after each of our chats, I was rock hard, which led to more time at the rink and in the weight room. I was in the best shape of my life—all because I was sexually frustrated.

But it was more than about my desire to kiss her plush lips and taste her soft skin. Emmaline drew me in a way I could barely understand and never explain.

She held a pencil in her hand and seemed deep in concentration, so I took a moment to study her in greater detail. Her hair lay smooth against her skull in a thick black cap that ended at the base of her neck with the hair bundled neatly into some kind of twist. Her dark lashes fluttered down toward her cheekbones and her soft pink mouth firmed into a line of concentration as she moved the pencil over the paper in economic, determined strokes.

The long column of her neck slid into her emerald-colored blouse that had a frilly collar but left her arms and part of her shoulders bare. As she worked, her shoulder blade shifted under the smooth pale skin.

I managed to bite back the groan but even I knew I had it bad if I were salivating over a shoulder blade. Still I wanted to kiss and lick every inch of it, which made Nico's suggestion this morning an even worse idea.

But because I didn't want him to know just how much I craved Emmaline, I forced myself to go along with his plan. I made my way to her desk. She looked up, surprise lighting her eyes as I settled across from her.

"Did you get to see your friend yesterday?"

Em nodded, her cautious expression opened as she smiled. I smiled in return, unable to stop her happy glow from improving my mood.

"Bridget's doing well, and so are the babies. They're adorable. So tiny and perfect."

Seeming to realize she was gushing, her cheeks flushed. She twirled her pencil with anxious energy. The idea of her being tense or upset around me caused something deep in my chest to ache. I cleared my throat.

"That's what Aidy said when I talked to her this morning. She's going to be out a while longer than she expected. Her OB had to go to the hospital for a birth, but she still wants Aidy to keep her appointment today."

Emmaline's eyes widened but then she reached forward and laid a soothing hand over mine. "I'm sure she'll be okay. She's had a wonderful pregnancy up to this point."

Her small hand was warm on mine. Comforting and perfect. Maybe that's why I voiced my concern. "I just worry about her, both of them. I want... I want the world for Aidy and her baby."

Emmaline's eyes softened and her lips parted. She looked too much like the soft, sweet woman I'd gotten to know that night I delivered her purse or even the evening I took Aidy home. I craved more of *this* side of her. I pulled my hand away from hers before I managed to do something stupid like tug on it and pull her into my lap right there in the middle of my office for Clint and Morris to see.

I stepped back, putting her desk between us. I settled into the chair and crossed my legs, needing another minute to calm myself.

"Chloe called."

"Oh?" Her delicate black brows rose. They reminded me of a segmented arch—with the same perfect curve to support her forehead. This was a bad idea. I was waxing poetic about her fucking eyebrows.

"She's thrilled with the orangery, which is what they're going to call it, and the landscape crew is finishing the plantings. She called it a paradise."

Her eyes widened, and she managed to stop twiddling the pencil, her focus all on me. "That's lovely."

"We aim to overshoot our clients' expectations."

She tilted her head, studying me as one would a fascinating piece of art. My chest puffed out a little.

"That can't be easy to do."

I leaned forward, desperate to smell her subtle perfume. The fragrance didn't waft like some; whatever she wore clung to her skin as if it, too, didn't want to let go.

I pinched my thigh, in a desperate need to realign my thoughts *again*. She couldn't know she'd starred in my dreams every night since that kiss. The mere idea of touching another woman was laughable—Emmaline took up all my extra thoughts. So much so I'd almost broken down and talked to Aidy about my feelings.

Thankfully, I'd come to my senses. Aidy had enough to deal with at the moment. I'd handle my issues. I hoped.

I refocused on Em as I'd begun to think of her. Emmy, the nickname I'd heard once from Mrs. Giovanni didn't suit her. She was elegant, poised, no-nonsense, not a child as the name suggested.

"It's not. But it's necessary. A vision on paper," I flicked the edge of her paper to make my point, "is simply a possibility until it's fully executed."

She waited, gaze fixed on me. That prim top swelled over her breasts, outlining their shape before cinching in at her waist, which was wrapped by a thick black leather belt. I wanted to undo that belt and shove my hand under her top.

I clenched my hands into fists.

"We're going to tour the grounds this afternoon."

"Who's we?"

"The entire team. I want you, Clint, and Morris to see the translation of your work. We've also been invited to the grand opening there next month."

She smiled. "Sounds fun."

I chuckled. "That's the best part of the job. The unveiling." I sobered. "But that's not what I wanted to talk to you about."

I hesitated, partly out of self-preservation. If I invited her, I was going to have to find the willpower to keep my desire in check—and something about this woman made such a feat impossible. Except I couldn't fail. Aidy had been correct when she said Emmaline fit into our aesthetic. She worked hard and absorbed information quickly. Seeming to sense my tension, she picked up the pencil and began to tap it on the paper.

"Nico wants me to take you with me to the Giovanni's site now that all the demo is completed and the kitchen is installed."

Her pencil stilled. "On Martha's Vineyard?"

"We leave tomorrow morning."

"Who is we?" she asked, avoiding my gaze.

"You and me."

She made a soft sound. She didn't want to go. Not with me. Since that kiss at her house, she'd remained coolly professional, managing to never be alone with me. That caused my belly to clench because I was the only person in the firm she chose not to speak to in semi-private areas. Even Nico had warmed to her, and she'd spent a good twenty minutes in his office yesterday, going over a bid to convert an old warehouse store into a loft/work space. Her ideas were fresh and intriguing.

Like her.

"Of course, Mr. Wright."

That caused my fists to clench tighter. I both loved and hated her insistent use of my last name.

Only years of compartmentalization, honed by sporting events at the highest level, allowed me to pull myself out of the memory. Now wasn't the time. Thanks to my big brother, there wouldn't *be* a time as long as Emmaline worked here, and her talent was much too bright to let go and have one of our competitors snap her up. Such a damn conundrum. I'd pondered that problem almost as much as her sweet lips and the soft rasp of her tongue against mine.

"Great. I'll pick you up at seven."

She shook her head before I finished the sentence. "I'll meet you here."

"That'll add an extra twenty minutes to our drive, Em."

Her fingers tightened around the pencil at the nickname, but her gaze remained cool. "I'll be here at 6:30."

I sighed. "Fine."

At the stubborn thrust of her jaw, I rose, not willing to push her further. Still, I looked forward to a day in her company—that was more than I'd had since the night I stopped by her house and kissed her.

And... I was back to thinking about her taste, the way she moved against me, restless, as if she couldn't get close enough. That damn kiss. She'd ruined me for other women. None of them had those Marilyn Monroe—Emmaline—curves. Or those full, rose-colored lips that tasted better than heaven.

"See you later, Em." I rose, needing to escape the chair and her soft vanilla-and-citrus scent.

"My name is Emmaline," she said.

"Mrs. Giovanni calls you Emmy sometimes," I pointed out.

She slammed her pencil onto her desk and her cheeks suffused with color. "I don't want you to call me that."

I smirked. "Which is why I call you Em."

I strode back to my office quickly before she decided to throw the pencil at me or worse. Not that I didn't deserve retaliation for needling her. I did. And I knew if Aidy had been in the office and seen that, she would have given me a piece of her mind with the sharp side of her tongue.

I chose to keep my distance at the walk-through at The Mac later that afternoon. No reason to push my luck—or Em's temper. The shortened name really did suit her, and I felt pleased to have come up with it.

I walked behind the rest of the group, struggling to keep my eyes off Em's pin-up-worthy ass. Nico slid back to walk with me, and I forced my gaze upward and out over the grounds.

"These turned out well."

"They did," he said.

I struggled to keep my gaze away from Emmaline's shapely back. She was my employee, and she was becoming a treasured companion.

Treasured companion? What the fuck was my mind reeling off? I sounded like one of those nineteenth-century British romance novels. I shook my head. No way I'd dress up in those ridiculous clothes they forced onto Colin Firth—it was Aidy's favorite movie, and I'd watched it with her earlier this week. That's the only reason I knew about it.

Fine. I'd watched it again at home, wondering if Em liked it, which was part of the reason I'd picked up my phone to call my sister and unload my emotionality. That was, until I realized how obsessed I sounded. No way anyone could know I'd completely lost my shit.

I refused to become the fool who didn't learn from past mistakes. But Em wasn't Melinda. Nor was she the scheming seductress of Nico's ex, Amanda. Em was a thoughtful woman. My employee. My *responsibility*.

The rest of the team stopped, forcing Nico and me to as well.

"I think you taking her tomorrow is a mistake."

My shoulder muscles tensed. "You're the one who suggested it."

"I've changed my mind."

"Too bad."

He studied me. "Because you're doing it anyway?"

I met his gaze. "You and I both know the best learning experiences are hands-on."

"I brought this firm back from failure of mismanagement. I brought it back again when our cash flow problems nearly destroyed us. Not even you know how long I went without a paycheck."

"The fuck, Nico?" I asked, frustration welling in my chest. "I made the mistake with Melinda, not you. I told you to let me bear the financial burden."

He tipped his head. "You wouldn't have been able to keep your house."

My stomach knotted tighter. I jutted my jaw. "All the more reason I deserved the financial punishment."

He shrugged. "Aidy didn't need any help through school, and I'd set aside money for that. I was okay." His eyes narrowed with menace. "Because you thought with your dick first, I almost lost this company. There won't be a third time. I'll make sure of it."

He stepped up into the cluster of our employees and asked if they had any questions. Clint pointed to the additional structure on the inlet and Nico led the group back toward the large open-air pavilion.

I stayed still. I'd played hockey for most of my life, starting when I was barely old enough to walk. I trusted my gut and what I could see. Those, together, hadn't steered me wrong—even with Melinda. I'd never trusted her, and I'd never *liked* her.

Now, finally, I understood why. Melinda's gaze never met mine and clung, like Em's did. She never once focused on me like I was the only person she *could* focus on.

And, dammit, I needed to know if I could trust Em. Not just as an employee but with my heart.

Because I feared she'd already managed to snag much more of it than I'd ever planned to give.

Chapter Twelve
Emmaline

Even though Joshua and Ellie suggested at our last dinner together that I start spending more time on my own pursuits, I drove from The Mac's impressive grounds to the Giovannis' grand home. I rang the bell, as always. Neither Joshua nor Ellie were at home, so Gina, a tireless woman in her late fifties who'd managed the house for years, answered the door.

I smiled but it felt a little off. I'd been unnerved since my conversation earlier that afternoon with Knox. The idea of traveling with him left me unsettled. I was too aware of his presence—even during the tour today. I spent more time attempting to ignore him than I did on the beauty our team had managed to create.

No man had affected me like Knox. Not even Sebastian, whom I fell for hard, fast, and fully. Loving Sebastian had been easy, like sliding into a warm pool as snow sprinkled my hair, lashes, and body. Sebastian radiated affection and reassurance. Being around him caused my whole body to unwind, to let go.

Not Knox. A man used to giving orders; he expected them followed. He might use charm in the conference room—until it didn't get him what he wanted. Then he turned cold and ruthless. He became a man I didn't recognize and didn't want to know *even* as my attraction to him skyrocketed.

My body's reaction upset me. I'd known eventually I'd be attracted to another man. Now, nearly four years later, I once again saw a future—just as I'd planned. I'd given up on a family of my own because I couldn't have it with Sebastian but holding Bridget's infant daughters earlier this week caused a deep pang to flutter through my belly. And I could picture myself holding my own child with Knox's arm wrapped around us both.

Stupid.

Knox might want me physically, but he'd said that first day of my employ that he had no intention of settling down. So my dreams would remain silly fantasies.

I walked up the stairs and down the long hall, trying to reorient my see-sawing emotions. Still, my ability to picture a family proved Ellie's harsh pronouncement that Sebastian and I never marry smart. I'd fallen in love so many years ago. No one expected us to last once Sebastian began attending Yale. But our love had been true, solid and deep.

I would never regret our time together, but I could finally see I would have resented tying myself to Sebastian in a fit of loyalty. What had once seemed romantic now showed itself as martyrdom.

I swallowed back my emotions and knocked on the door. No one answered.

I knocked again and then pushed the door open.

Sebastian wasn't in his sitting room. I hurried into his bedroom and found him asleep, snuggled deep into his pillow. I sighed, brushing the hair back from his forehead. I bent down and pressed a kiss there, a well of tenderness bursting forth.

He opened his eyes and smiled. The sleepy pull of his lids and the warmth in his eyes reminded me strongly of the time before—when he'd been my Sebastian.

"I miss you," I rasped.

"I miss you, too," he said.

I settled my hip on the edge of his plush mattress as he struggled to sit up. I leaned forward to fluff his pillow and his arm slid around my waist, pulling me closer—just like the Sebastian of old. For a moment, I closed my eyes and luxuriated in his warmth.

But, he no longer felt right against me, and he hadn't smelled like *my* Sebastian in years. I wasn't sure what had changed until I read about how our brains processed pheromones and chose the healthiest specimen to be a potential partner. It was an unconscious choice but one that had kept the species alive for millennia. I hated that my body rejected Sebastian as an ideal partner now. All because of a momentary lapse in his judgment.

He buried his face in my neck and made a smaller choked sound. "You smell good."

"Thank you."

He pressed a kiss to my neck. It was wet, sloppy.

"What are you doing?" I asked, my stomach seizing.

"I'm kissing you," he said in a sweet voice, not unlike that of a young boy.

A chill slid down my spine. Sebastian was still a large man at five-eleven, and even in his thin state, he outweighed me by at least forty pounds, but these kisses weren't from my Sebastian. He wouldn't kiss my neck.

"Why?"

"It's what adults do. I saw it on…"

He pulled back as he trailed off, his arm loosening enough for me to inch backward. I needed space between us. Coming here hadn't eased my confusion; this interaction compounded it.

"Did we do that, Emmy?"

I pressed my lips into a firm line as I gathered my emotions. I reached forward and cupped his cheek. The bristles there lightly abraded my palm. *My* Sebastian had always been clean-shaven. Just another change I documented in my mind.

"Yes," I said. I shut my eyes as pain radiated through me. I startled when his lips settled over mine. Like the kiss to the neck, this was too wet and without the dynamic we used to share. I shuddered.

He pulled back, hurt written all over this face. "I did that wrong?"

"Not one thing."

I pressed my hand to his chest, unsurprised to feel the pounding of his heart. Mine raced, too, but for a different reason. I'd hoped… I'd hoped if he kissed me again, it would be *my* Sebastian. But as I looked up into his face, the last of my dream crumbled. My Sebastian was gone. He'd bled out in the car, next to me, all those years ago.

This man wasn't mine. He was a beautiful soul but damaged in ways I didn't fully understand and might not ever be able to. Tears formed in my eyes as I realized I didn't want to be responsible for him. Ellie had been right. A sob rose in my chest but I forced it back.

Sebastian winced.

"Headache?" I asked.

"It always hurts."

I cleared my throat. "What does Nana say about that?"

"That we'll keep trying to find a different medication. But they're getting worse. It's hard to keep my eyes open or to eat."

I bit my cheek in time to stifle my gasp. "I didn't... I didn't know that."

"Nana said I asked to you marry me that night. Did I?"

I clenched my hands into fists so tight, my nail broke the skin on my palms. But I met his gaze. "You did."

He leaned forward, expression avid. "What did you say?"

"I said I'd be so proud to be your wife," I whispered.

He wrapped his big hand around mine, engulfing my hand in his. "I'm also glad that this happened then."

I blinked back the tears that threatened to fall. "Why?"

"It was better to happen before you were stuck with me."

Shit. Just what I'd been thinking. Did that...guilt ate at me. I was a bad person. If I loved Sebastian, really loved him, I should want to be with him, even now.

But I felt...relief. I closed my eyes, hating the truth.

"Will you visit me again?" he asked, snapping me out of the nightmare that came after his most perfect proposal.

In the years since the accident, I'd never seen Sebastian like this—both introspective and clearly unhappy.

"Of course."

"Maybe you shouldn't."

His words caused the ache in my chest to deepen, but I managed to ask, "Why not?"

His gaze drifted before it returned to mine, and that conviction I loved glinted in their depths.

"I'm not good for you, Emmy. Not now."

"Sebastian…"

"Nana said I was the one driving that night."

I nodded, my breath caught in my throat. Please don't make me relive that...*please*.

"She said I looked down at my phone to check a text."

Tears slid over my lashes and down my cheeks. "You did."

"So I didn't see the car coming at us."

"No, Sebastian. You didn't. It was—"

"My fault. I won't ever drive again, you know. Or...or do more like we did. Because I made a mistake."

My lower lip quivered. "She...the other driver was drunk and skipped the median."

I swallowed the bile that rose in my throat. My chest burned with the need to release the fear and pain that came next.

Chapter Thirteen
Knox

Getting up at five was worth my fatigue because I was able to hand Em a large cup of coffee. While she appeared tidy with her hair pulled back in a simple low ponytail that fell more than halfway down her slender back, her eyes were slightly bloodshot and puffy. She'd either spent the night crying or partying.

I didn't like either option.

She took the cup from me with a murmured thanks.

"Got everything you need?"

"I hope so," she said. She took off the plastic lid and inhaled before she took a tiny sip. "How did you know I liked cinnamon and cream in my coffee?"

"Aidy."

She reattached the lid and set it into the empty cupholder, then buckled her seatbelt. "Ready when you are, Mr. Wright."

Something seemed off. She was clearly miserable. Because she was hungover?

"We can stop for breakfast—"

"I'm fine. Let's just get to the site."

I pulled out of the lot, wishing I understood what had caused Em to go from cautious with me to closed off.

"Look, if you don't want to go with me today, just say so. I won't be mad."

Her gaze flew up to mine. "I really want to see the house."

"Okay, then. But it comes with being in the car with me."

Her normally sensual lips compressed into a thin line. "I'm aware."

She picked up her coffee and took another healthy sip, wincing slightly when the heat slid down her throat.

"So, do you want to talk about why you look like you spent the night crying?"

She shook her head. "I visited an old friend," she murmured. "The conversation steered toward the accident."

Ah. Well, at least I could understand that.

"If you want to talk about it—"

"I don't." She dropped her gaze to her lap and remained silent. Well, her lack of interaction might make the day spent together easier to handle.

I turned on my radio, needing something to ease the tension building in the vehicle. I steered onto 1-95 heading east. The glimpses of water helped me relax, but we soon picked up traffic and our commute slowed to a crawl. I tapped my fingers against the side of the wheel, trying to catch a glimpse of Em from the corner of my eye. She sipped her coffee but otherwise sat still.

My mind spun out a variety of scenarios that would lead to such sadness. All I knew from Em was that the accident had been bad. Did that mean she'd been in the car with someone else? With each new possibility, my own mood took a further nosedive.

Another sip of her coffee.

This wasn't the woman I was used to seeing in the office. I hated that I didn't know more about her—or how to help.

My phone rang and I leaned over, intending to press my screen to check out who was calling. Emmaline smacked my hand, shocking me enough to sit back with a yelp.

"Keep your eyes on the road," she said.

Her voice shook and tears pooled in her eyes. We were near an exit, so I flicked on my blinker—it wasn't as though we were making much progress anyway. I ignored my phone, which rang again. This time the screen showed that Nico was calling.

I pressed my handsfree button as I looked for somewhere to pull over.

"What's up?" I asked.

"You already on the road?" Nico asked.

"Yeah, we're in Fall River. Why?"

"The contractor had a snafu. Something about a bad lumber shipment. She wanted to know if you could push back your meeting by an hour or two."

Emmaline didn't turn toward me, but tears continued to trickle from her eyes.

"Sure. If that's best. We'll do a bit of sightseeing along the way."

"Research," Nico said. "You should at least try to sound like you're working."

"Definitely research," I said, cracking a smile. It faded quickly. Emmaline worried me.

"I'll call and reschedule with Sarah," I said. "And I'll let you know what we plan once we've planned it."

"Good. Talk soon."

Nico hung up.

Abrupt and growly were kind of his thing. Too bad those traits weren't attractive to many women. Or maybe it was good that women rarely approached him. I didn't see my brother changing.

I turned onto Wilson Road, pleased to see a packed diner up ahead. Emmaline might say she wasn't hungry, but no matter her ailment, a good meal should help. I pulled into the lot.

She twisted her fingers together. I wanted to smooth my hand over hers but wasn't sure she'd accept the comfort.

"I owe you an explanation," she muttered.

Her expression cleared. "That accident. My..." She hesitated. "My fiancé happened to glance down at a text message. It only took a moment, but in that time, a car crossed the median and slammed into us. We flipped, many times."

I swore softly. No wonder she had such hang-ups about phones and cars.

"He was injured, badly. The car was too mangled for me to help him. I was stuck, also bleeding, but my injuries weren't as severe. I broke my collar bone, my arm in multiple places, my leg. I had a concussion, lots of scrapes, some glass. I was lucky."

Shit. If she considered that lucky, I couldn't imagine what happened to her fiancé. Considering she no longer wore a ring, I could guess. But I needed to know for sure.

"And your fiancé?"

"He hit his head in the initial impact. Probably more times as we rolled. I'm not sure how long it took the firefighters to cut us out."

I laid my hand over hers, needing to offer what comfort I could. Her fingers were cold and trembled. I turned her hand over and interlaced our fingers.

"I'm sorry that happened to you."

She glanced over. Her tears had stopped, though tracks still gleamed on her cheeks. "It's why I was so weird about you looking at the phone when you're driving. I apologize for my behavior."

"Ah, Em. There's nothing to apologize for."

She withdrew her hand, and I missed her touch. I smoothed my hand through my hair. "Let's eat, then we have another hour or two of research to do before we head out to the build site."

She exited the car, leaned in, and grabbed her purse, then patted her hair.

To look at Emmaline now, you'd never know she'd been through so much trauma. What was the saying? You were never given more than you could handle...something like that. Well, that saying was a stinking load of fish carcasses. I'd been at my lowest point, grieving for my parents when Nico came to me, stating he needed my help to keep our father's legacy alive.

That had meant the end of the life I'd planned for myself.

I didn't regret it. At least not often. I had a good life—one built on hard work, talent, and skill. I also lived a much lower profile life than I would have otherwise and was able to spend quality time with my siblings.

We'd turned the firm around, and I was sure our father was proud of our accomplishments. So, I guess I hadn't been given more than I could handle. Just more than I wanted to bear.

Emmaline, however, lost the man she'd planned to marry and, from what I'd gotten out of Aidy, her parents died around the same time. Sometimes the burden of life was too heavy. We just didn't have any choice but to go on.

— A —

Emmaline excused herself to the restroom, so I settled into the booth. I eased back, more comfortable in my dark jeans and an untucked button-down dress shirt than I would be in a full suit—one of the perks of making most of the site contacts. The waitress brought over two coffees, and I asked for two glasses of water and a small dish of cinnamon, not caring at her strange look. Emmaline came back and settled into the opposite seat.

"You got me cinnamon. Thank you."

"Sure. It was no problem."

Her eyes softened further, and her mouth lost its tautness. "Still, it was sweet, and I appreciate the gesture." She dipped her spoon into the dish of cinnamon and liberally sprinkled her coffee before adding a generous splash of cream. She stirred the liquid three times and then tapped the side of the mug.

"I've never been here before," she said, her large eyes taking in the clientele and plates of steaming food. "Do you know what's good?"

I smiled, pleased by her enthusiasm. "No idea. It's a foodie adventure. But you like food experiences, so I'm sure we can find you something interesting."

She picked up her menu, riveted to her choices. After a short time—before I'd made up my mind—she hummed and laid down her menu. "Stuffed French toast."

"That's what you're going to have?" I asked, surprised.

"I've never tried anything like it, and it sounds delicious."

All true, but most of the women I dated would never order something so decadent.

"You're not into omelets?" I asked, trying to remember what any of the women I'd shared breakfast with preferred.

"Oh, I love them. Especially with sun-dried tomatoes, olives, and feta, but this isn't the place to order something so Mediterranean. We're at..." She glanced down at her menu, and said, "Gina's Restaurant, and this place makes pineapple cream-cheese stuffed French toast topped with fresh berries."

I glanced down. She'd recited the menu verbatim. "You do like food."

She smiled and this time it reached her eyes. "Love it."

My breath caught a little as my skin flushed. I kept staring at her, watching the way her mouth moved as she spoke to the waitress. Endorphins flooded my system, reminding me of how I'd felt after my team won the Frozen Four, the college hockey term for the playoffs.

"Me, too," I said after Em ordered, handing over my menu to the waiter.

She sipped her coffee, a soft smile on her face. She tilted her head. "Why are you looking at me like that?"

"Like what?"

"I'm not sure—but..." Her face suffused with the same heat that burned through me. "Like you want to undress me," she said, her voice dropping.

"Well, I do. But it's not happening. So, why don't you tell me something else about you? You said you'd started school at Cornell."

Her eyes widened. "You don't forget anything."

"Not about people I'm interested in."

"So, a new woman each week?" She lifted her mug and took another sip.

"I haven't been seeing anyone for a while." I shrugged. "It's been..." I tapped my chin. "Since before you came in to interview."

She made a noncommittal noise.

"Regardless of Aidy's attempts to irritate me, I've never been with three women in one night," I said, annoyed enough by Em's previous comment to need to defend myself. "And I don't go out with a different woman each night or even each week. I'm running a successful company that deserves my focus."

She met my gaze, surprising me when she said, "I apologize for my comment. It was insensitive and really none of my business."

I settled my elbows on the table and leaned in closer. "I want my life to be your business. And, yes, I know you're my employee, but that doesn't change the fact that I care for and about you."

We sat in awkward silence. She re-situated her napkin and her silverware.

"What about you?" I asked.

She pulled the napkin at both edges. "Dating? Not interested."

"I thought you had a thing for Joshua Giovanni."

She threw her head back and laughed. My lips curved at the jovial sound emanating from her. She wiped her eyes with the heels of her hands. "Oh, that's funny."

"Why?" I asked.

"Because Josh is—"

"A friend," I said, remembering her words from that first

night. "Who gave you a bottle of champagne to celebrate your gainful employment."

She smiled, her gaze locking on mine. The moment spun out, and I saw a promise of a future in her eyes. At least I thought I did until she broke the connection and re-straightened her silverware. Something about being here, with me, made her nervous.

"He is. And he has been, for years. Almost a brother."

"*That's* why you're so familiar with his cooking habits," I said, thinking about the kitchen she'd helped us design.

She nodded. "And entertaining preferences."

"But you're not dating?" I hesitated but the question erupted past my lips. "Because of your fiancé?"

She inhaled sharply through her nose. "Yes. Well that, and because Josh is already in a relationship."

My stomach rolled, and I shifted.

"You must have been young when you got engaged."

She sighed. "Young, yes, but not *that* young. We'd known each other for six years."

"Oh?" Any way I could find out more.

She lifted her head, and I noted her eyes were soft, far away, and filled with happier memories.

"We started dating when I was sixteen. He chose to go to Yale so he'd be relatively close. I saw him every weekend."

"You must have had to give up your social life here to do so."

She shrugged. "He was my future, not the kids from my high school."

I frowned, not really understanding her thought process.

My high school friends, my hockey team, were my entire social sphere. But now that I thought about it, I couldn't remember the last time I'd seen any of them in person. I didn't care much for social media, finding it tedious rather than useful, so it wasn't as if I sought out my former closest friends there, either. My friends who'd gone on to the pros kept much more public lives—ones I didn't think I'd enjoy, not even for the fame or the money.

"Seb...he proposed to me the night of the accident."

I leaned back, feeling like I'd taken a hit from a two-hundred-pound defenseman without any pads.

"*That* night?"

She fiddled with the creamers, stacking the little bottles. "Let's talk about you, Knox. Tell me about your dating history. You know, the one that doesn't include three women in one night."

She was rattled enough to call me by my first name. Much as I didn't like the reason, I loved hearing my name in her voice. It wasn't especially husky or sensual. A mid-range voice...Em's. And that's why I liked it. Her eyes beseeched me.

I forced a chuckle. "Never happened, though I appreciate Aidy's beliefs in my prowess."

Em wrinkled her nose.

I leaned in closer again. "Agreed," I said.

Her startled gaze flew up to mine.

"I didn't mean to—"

"It's fine. But my point was you don't get to judge me. At least not for that. Have I been with my share of the ladies? Yes.

Normally, I wouldn't answer because I don't like to brag."

Her lips flipped up and she shook her head, but her eyes were somber and filled with pain.

"I pushed you," I muttered. "My questions were a bit invasive."

She raised her hand and spread her thumb and forefinger a quarter of an inch apart.

"Sorry. So, what did you study at Cornell?"

She toppled her stack of creamer cups. "I thought I wanted to be a surgeon, like my father."

I raised an eyebrow. Em in scrubs. Now, *that* would be a sight worth seeing.

"What changed your mind?"

She raised her eyebrow as she met my gaze.

"The accident," I said with a sigh. "I keep sticking my foot in my mouth here."

"That's a pretty big foot." She giggled.

I smiled. "And an even bigger mouth."

She laughed again.

"I'm even more impressed by you than I was before, and that's saying something, Em. You've overcome a lot of misfortune."

She shrugged. "Not like I had a choice."

"There's always a choice." I hesitated but then added, "I didn't feel like I had any reason to keep getting out of bed, to keep trying, once I refused the draft."

"You could have been a professional hockey player?" she asked, eyes wide.

"I didn't accept the spot," I said, my stomach tumbling. Would Em see me differently, act differently, now that she knew about my brush with fame? That reminded me of Melinda and a sour taste built in my mouth.

She canted her head. "I can't see that," she murmured. "Oh, I'm sure you were good. But you at a drafting table is pure poetry. Plus, you look damn good in a suit, Knox Wright. I can't imagine the pads and weird jerseys could be a better look for you."

Her eyes widened and she blushed from the roots of her hair straight down her neck. She clapped a hand over her mouth.

I chuckled. "Good to know Tom Ford is more your speed." I inhaled, my gaze locked on the waitress as she hefted two loaded plates that had to be ours. No way I'd be able to pack all that food away. We should have shared.

The waitress set them down and we both thanked her. I caught her mortification from the corner of my eye and continued my story.

"I fucked up my life pretty hard and good before Nico figured out I was in a total funk and managed to pull my head out of my ass."

Her brows pinched. "Why is it so hard to admit you guys have feelings?" she asked.

"Because feelings mean we have to feel. And that shit hurts."

Or it caused us to watch stupid period movies that talked about love in high-brow terms, trying to understand what was so appealing about small gestures of affection—why romance seemed to bring a softness and acquiescence that merely expressing our intentions never did.

"Or expressing feelings allows you to soar." She smiled a little, her tone so wistful that I felt emotion clog my throat.

"Did you soar with your fiancé?" I asked.

"I did," she said.

We looked up at the same time. Her eyes were clear and fathomless. I felt a pang before she spoke again.

"But when I crashed, it was a really bad landing."

Chapter Fourteen
Emmaline

We ate in relative quiet, and I relaxed, hopeful he'd no longer pursue the topic of how the accident changed my life. Part of me felt as though I should tell him my ex-fiancé was Sebastian Giovanni, but I'd overheard enough of Nico's comments to know how important the Giovanni Foundation's commitment to Wright and Associates would be.

Much as I loved working for the company and even appreciated the brothers' ambition, I wanted to be respected for my work, not for an informal tie to a wealthy family.

I looked down at my half-eaten meal, emotions slugging at my gut and causing my appetite to vanish. Sebastian's words last night caused pain to ripple from my chest, outward.

"Finished?" Knox asked.

"Yes, thanks."

He studied me for a few minutes as we waited near the register for him to pay. "Let's walk."

He placed his hand on my lower back, leading me out the door and into the bright sunshine. I pulled my sunglasses out of their case and settled them on my nose. Knox turned left, away from the car, and I followed.

I didn't know how to live without Sebastian in my life. I'd lost both my parents—my entire family. I couldn't lose Sebastian, too.

Except, I already had. I just couldn't accept that.

"I opened a painful wound," Knox said as we walked. I appreciated him not stopping, not trying to look into my eyes.

"Yes."

"I'm sorry, Em."

I blinked hard to keep the tears from spilling over my lashes. I'd cried enough last night. Nothing would change because of my tears. "Me, too."

He turned down another street, stopping in front of a large, weathered building. I stopped too, standing by his side.

"My parents disappeared in the fall of my last year at Cornell. It was devastating. Aidy was so heartbroken and Nico shell-shocked by more than just their loss, though he didn't talk much about it then. Still doesn't."

Knox paused. "I was unable to help with the firm or Aidy. Nico didn't want me to come home. Coach wouldn't release me from our season. I was so pissed at everyone. Luckily for my team, that translated well on the ice. I became more aggressive. We won more games."

His smile was more of a grimace.

"Winning the Frozen Four was supposed to be the pinnacle of my hockey career, and it was, but it felt so damn hollow without my parents there to share it." Knox's lips pressed flat. "I worried my going into the draft would cause Nico to lose the firm. I worried about Aidy's partying, which Nico seemed to ignore. If I traveled with a team, I wouldn't be able to help with that."

We moved on to another building, looked up at it as the silence built. I remained quiet, unsure why he was telling me this.

"It came to a head when Aidy was hospitalized. She'd had too much to drink, and they had to pump her stomach. I came home and found Nico so overwhelmed with the firm that he literally couldn't handle Aidy, who, in turn, needed her brother's attention and affection. It was an absolute cluster fuck."

He shook his head.

"I couldn't leave them. Not as they were. But even though I gave up my hockey career, Aidy and Nico still fell apart. I can't tell you how many weeks I was sure were the last for Wright and Associates."

I couldn't help it. I reached over and slid my palm against his, squeezing.

"But you fixed it. All of it. Aidy and Nico seem close. And the firm's reputation is one of the best in New England. You have so much to be proud of."

He made a noise, deep in his chest. "I almost broke it again when I started dating our intern the next year."

I swallowed. "Melinda Schoals, soon to be Miner."

"I figured you did your research on us." But the slight lift of his lips flattened immediately. "She stole my designs. I'd brought her into my home, and she stole from me."

His hands fisted, the muscles in his arm so tensed, it was like rock.

"That's terrible. I'm sorry you had to go through that, Knox."

"Not as sorry as I am. Which is why I can't get involved with you." He turned to face me. Gently, he lifted my sunglasses to the top of my head. His gaze swept over my face like a heated caress.

"As long as you're at the firm, I'll leave you alone. I think..."

He searched my eyes. "I think you need that space, anyway. That you're still healing."

I blinked back the ache in my chest. "I am. You see, my fiancé is—"

He pressed a finger to my lips. "Not now. We've had enough sharing. I feel...I don't know. I need to process." Those big shoulders shifted as if he were restless. "Emotions aren't really my thing. I'm a fixer. On the ice, I could simply slam into a man who pissed me off. With you, your past, I can't take away your hurt, and that's fucking with me."

My heart melted. "Maybe we're supposed to help each other shoulder the pain." I bumped into his side and then almost bounced back. He slid his arm around my waist to steady me.

The connection between us was warm, perfect.

But I wasn't ready for Knox, and he wouldn't break his promise to Nico. I finally understood the employee handbook policy—it was in place to protect Knox. From *me*.

I frowned, not liking the realization.

He squeezed my waist before dropping his arm. I mourned the loss of both his warmth and our connection. He turned, this time pulling me across the street and back toward the car.

"Let's get to Martha's Vineyard. We can continue our research there."

I slid my sunglasses back into place. We settled in the car and Knox drove us back to the highway while I mulled over his story.

"Do you regret it?"

"What?" he asked.

"Not going into the draft?"

He chuckled a little. "At the time? Hell, yes." His face turned somber. "It took years for me to stop regretting that I missed out on the opportunity to play pro hockey, but that it was the right decision, at the time, and it turned out well in the end."

He drove forward, keeping more than enough distance from the car in front of us and causing me to relax. From the slight shift in his gaze, I assumed he'd noticed. Knox didn't miss much. Maybe that was the former hockey player in him.

"I promise you this, Em, I'll always put my full attention to driving."

"Thank you."

We drove to the ferry at Quonset Point and pulled into one of the lines that would allow us to board.

"Let's go up to the deck," he said. "I don't want to spend an hour and a half down here in the dark."

Oh, good. I loved ferry rides. Plus, I hoped being out, in public, around others would keep me from doing something stupid—like leaning over the console of his vehicle and kissing Knox again.

That wouldn't be prudent or professional. I opened my car door and hopped out, following him up the stairs to the top-most deck. He settled on a bench well away from the few tourists. I sat a few spots from him—far enough away that his fingertips didn't quite reach my shoulder when he rested his arm on the back of the bench.

But the thought of his fingers on me caused my belly to clench.

I looked out across the water, wishing I knew what to say to Knox, how to feel about our talk this morning.

"There is one more thing I wanted to mention."

I turned my head, thankful for my sunglasses. He jutted his jaw, which made him look more masculine, more in control. My belly quivered.

"I readily admit I was a willing and attentive participant during my early college days. Hot, willing chicks and hormones." He shrugged. "But once I was no longer the big college star, going on to bigger NHL stardom, I found out real fast who my friends were, and I realized I didn't have that many."

Once again, I felt compelled to offer him sympathy. I clasped my hand over his wrist and inched in a bit closer. A cool breeze skimmed our cheeks and lifted some of my hair as the ferry's horn sounded.

"I'm sorry you had to go through that."

The ferry hummed as we moved out into the water, which looked blue and peaceful from here. A sharp tang of salt air hit my nose. I wondered how Knox felt about being on the water, out in the same bay where his parents disappeared. He stared out, lost in thought. A few seagulls wheeled overhead, diving and darting back toward the shoreline.

"It's okay. I made my choice." He turned to smile but it was just a hint—too sardonic to be actual good humor. I wished I could see his eyes, but it was probably best they remained behind his aviator-style frames.

"And I learned really quickly that women—at least the women I'd hung out with before—loved the allure of a professional athlete but had little interest in an almost-college graduate or even as an up-and-coming architect. The change opened my

eyes to how few people I could trust. How few people
were genuine."

—— A ——

We arrived at the residence at eleven, still before Sarah Martin,
the contractor, expected us. Knox grabbed a couple of hardhats
from his SUV's trunk space and offered me one. I settled the
hat on my head and trailed behind Knox for a few steps, sighing
in relief. We'd both shared our deepest hurts. Like he'd said, I
needed to process—especially since I hadn't shared some of those
emotions with anyone else, not even Bridget.

He stopped and waited for me to catch up.

"Sorry. I forget not everyone has as long of legs."

"It's fine," I said. "You go ahead."

"I brought you here to go over the project together."

His jaw was set in a stubborn line. No way to foster
much-needed space. I stifled a sigh and walked beside him,
catching Knox's occasional glance to ensure he had matched his
stride to mine.

Sebastian used to grab my hand and pull me forward, sometimes making me trot to keep up. I shook my head, trying to
knock out the comparisons forming in my mind. They were
ridiculous and unnecessary.

We walked into the main entry through a gaping space that
should house a stylish, hammered wood front door with leaded
glass panels to both sides. Knox grunted, his eyes narrowing as he
took in the heaps of broken wood and bent nails.

"This needs to get cleaned out, stat. It's a hazard."

"Which is why I'm getting it taken care of," a lithe woman

with long dark hair pulled up into a high ponytail and sloe-eyes said. She walked nearer, her stride loose-limbed and her hips swiveling as if she were on a runway, not in steel-toed workbooks and grimy jeans. Her long-sleeved T-shirt hugged her figure.

"Abe," she called over her shoulder.

"On it," Abe said. His bushy ginger beard hid his lips, but his hazel eyes twinkled behind safety glasses.

"Good to see you, Knox," Abe said.

"You, too."

Knox shook Abe's hand, then introduced me. I held out my hand and Abe's engulfed it, making me feel puny.

The woman offered me her hand, and Abe turned toward the mess, easily loading up a large wheelbarrow he'd brought with him.

"I'm Sarah, the builder." The woman held out a hand to me, and I shook it.

"Emmaline works with us at the firm," Knox said, stepping in closer. "She's the one who came up with the patio extension off the kitchen."

Sarah's eyebrows rose and a small smile quirked her lips. She dropped my hand. "So you're the one we've been cursing all week."

I tried not to take offense, but between Knox's proximity to the beautiful brunette and her comments, my response came out stilted. "Joshua likes to entertain large groups, which requires extensive space."

Sarah's eyes cooled. "Must be nice to have those opportunities," she murmured. She slid in closer to Knox and the ease of her frame as she pressed it against his spoke of intimacy.

"I'd hoped you'd stay for...dinner," she said.

I couldn't see her eyes but the sultry note in her voice left no doubt Knox had slept with her at some point in the past—and that she'd like it to happen again.

I spun on my heel, mentally working through the schematics of the house until I ended up in the kitchen with the builder-accursed patio. I laid my hand on the cool granite countertop, trying to realign my emotions, but jealousy continued to fizz like acid in my veins.

"Like it?"

I spun around to find Abe leaning against the archway that led back toward the great room. I could see Knox and Sarah beyond. She still had her hand on his chest. I turned back to the kitchen and the large patio that flowed to the stairs that led to the beach beyond.

"It's beautiful."

"Yeah, it is. I heard Knox say you came up with the idea."

I glanced up to find him watching me. "What?"

"You look familiar." He snapped his fingers. "You're the girl—the one who was engaged to the younger Giovanni."

I tensed and my stomach fluttered. "I was, yes, but that was before a car accident."

Abe's gaze softened. "That's gotta suck."

I leaned against the counter edge, sadness tugging at my shoulders. "You have no idea."

"So, does Knox know about your connection to the Giovannis?" Abe asked.

A niggling of a realization burst into my mind. "You know Knox well, don't you?"

Abe chortled. "We played hockey together all through peewees, straight through high school. You didn't answer my question."

"No, he doesn't know about Sebastian. But, yes, he knows that I'm close with the family."

Abe tugged at his beard. It was long, falling to the middle of his chest. I'd never seen such lush facial hair, and I wondered how difficult it was to keep well-groomed.

"And you don't want him to," Abe said.

"I'd prefer he not."

"Prefer who not what?" Knox asked, coming up beside us.

He glared at Abe, who remained unperturbed, maybe even smiled. It was hard to tell with his riotous beard.

I stiffened, irritated that Knox now smelled of Sarah's perfume. The idea of him kissing her in the middle of the job site, especially after what we'd shared earlier, caused those ants to feast in my blood again. I clenched my fists.

As he'd told Sarah, I was an employee, and so I'd remain because I wasn't quitting my position. So what if he'd told me I was beautiful and all he thought about? Clearly, Knox used lines on all the women.

"Emmaline here was telling me about the Giovannis," Abe rumbled.

I shot him a hot glare and this time I was sure he suppressed a grin. Asshole.

"Not quite," I said. "But I did say that the sight lines to the beach were beautiful."

Knox turned, eyes narrowing, as he studied the newly installed glass wall. He dipped his head in a brief nod.

"It is. Let's tour the rest of the place."

Knox rested his hand on the small of my back and led me through the butler's pantry toward the dining room. I didn't miss Abe's raised, bushy brows or the hot scowl forming on Sarah's face.

And I couldn't deny my fierce and jubilant reaction to Knox's touch.

Chapter Fifteen
Knox

After what I'd thought was a breakthrough, with Em and I connecting during breakfast and our walk, Emmaline withdrew as we worked through our checklist that included the new copper dome on the atrium's cupola and the large windows in each of the eight bedrooms.

"The renovations are coming together. I think Joshua and Mrs. Giovanni will be happy to see the transformation," I said.

"Yes."

Emmaline held the paperwork in her hands but kept her head bent to avoid making eye contact. We moved through the next room, the last of the bedrooms—this one closest to the stairs and the large, airy main room. I checked the bathroom while Em hovered in the doorway. I looked back at her while I was in the farthest corner, partially shrouded in the shadows made by the window on the wall nearer the door. Em sucked in a long, slow breath, her shoulders folding further inward. She glanced up at me from her lashes, and the longing in her gaze caused my stomach to dip. I slid back and touched the wall, as if inspecting the space.

"That's the last of the items. I'll email these to Sarah tomorrow," I said.

"If you'd like to discuss the issues with her now, I'll go wait in the car," Emmaline said.

"I'm not going to have you wait in the car," I scoffed.

She fingered the edge of her documents.

"Want to grab a bite?" I asked, hopeful. "It can be an early dinner since we won't get back to Providence much before five anyway."

"I'm not hungry."

I frowned. I wanted to spend more time with her, and she shot down my best chance. I led her down the rear stairs and onto the large patio that now snuggled into the sandy dune a few hundred feet from the ocean. The faint tang of saltwater tickled my nose. I paused to enjoy the view.

"The use of the same slate inside the kitchen outward onto the deck was inspired. A great call, Em."

"Thank you." She walked a step behind me as we headed toward my car. She removed her hard hat and set it into the trunk. Sarah called my name from the patio, her hands fisted on her hips. Emmaline tensed and her lips compressed into a slash of displeasure.

Ah. Something warm and heady stirred in me as I noted Emmaline's strong reaction to the other woman. Not unlike my response when I caught Em talking to Abe in the kitchen. I wanted to scream at my long-time friend that she was *mine*, dammit.

But the truth was, Em wasn't mine. Though, how I'd watch her date another man proved mind-boggling. My hands fisted at the mere idea of some douche walking into my building and laying lips on hers.

Sarah called my name again, pulling me out of the pleasant

fantasy that had me smashing my fist into the potential boy-friend's asshole face. I held up my hand, not wanting the other woman to interrupt the moment. She stalked toward us anyway.

"You can drop me at the ferry so that you can have...dinner with Sarah."

I managed to keep my smile from forming. "I haven't shared anything with Sarah in years. And I don't intend to do so again."

Em's gaze darted to mine before skittering off. "Oh? Why not? She's beautiful and obviously more than willing to pursue your attraction."

Abe appeared from the front door, and great wingman that he was, he swooped in, heading off Sarah.

"I want to talk to Knox," Sarah said, her voice higher and thinner as jealousy bled through.

I sighed.

Dammit.

I considered my options briefly before I turned to find Sarah marching toward us once again, Abe's face transformed into dismayed anger.

"Abe can handle the problem," I called out.

Sarah stumbled to a stop, no doubt shocked I'd basically told her not to come closer.

"And if he can't, you can call and speak to Nico. Now, I need to finish my discussion with Emmaline."

I turned my back on Sarah and edged in closer to Em's warm, soft body, my hand cupping her chin. Satisfaction flowed through me when her pupils contracted then dilated. She might want to ignore the desire coiling around us, but her body reacted to mine just as fiercely. We might not be ready for more, but the possibility shimmered.

For now, that would have to be enough.

"You didn't need to do that," she murmured.

"Yes, I did. Let's get a few things cleared up," I said. "One, I told Sarah to keep her hands to herself. She didn't listen the first time, and she may not listen now even though I've made it clear to you, Abe, and her that I'm not interested."

Em dropped her lids to cover her gaze but I'd seen the flash in her eyes.

"Two, I told her I won't have dinner with her or anything else, which she didn't like. Three, the reason we haven't worked with her in this time span was because she made it known she wanted more than I did. Yes, I had sex with her, but that was many years ago, back in college one summer I was home."

I inched in closer, bowing so that my nose rubbed against hers. I pulled back, needing her to see the truth in my eyes when I said, "But she isn't my future. I've told her that gently, but now I'll tell her that in blunt terms, with you at my side, Em. She's not for me."

The tip of Em's tongue darted out, wetting her plump lower lip. I inhaled as desire slammed through me, tightening my groin. She inched closer, her lips a mere whisper against mine, her gaze still locked on mine.

"I…I don't know what to say," she murmured.

"For now, you don't need to say anything. You're the only woman I think about. I'm sorry if Sarah made you uncomfortable. I'll let Nico know about the unsolicited touching. Professionalism is why we've made it as far as we have, and I won't work with people who don't match that same level."

Em gulped as she brought her gaze up. "You don't need to chastise her for me. Like you said earlier, we couldn't go anywhere. And…" She closed her eyes, breathed deep, and met my gaze. "I'm still heartbroken, Knox. I lost my whole life that night. *Everything* changed."

"Your parents?" I asked, my voice soft.

Her face paled so much I worried she'd faint. She swallowed with clear difficulty. "I'll never understand it. My mother's blood-alcohol level was right at the limit of legal. So, she had a glass, maybe two of champagne over the course of the evening. None of that explains why she skipped the median." Her voice trailed off.

"Oh, Em." Realization dawned. So much clicked into place. Her mother drove the car—the car that slammed into Sebastian's.

"I can't even imagine."

"I've only just started to wrap my head around a world that doesn't have them in it. I love working for you. This job—it's better than I hoped it would be. Aidy and Nannette are my *friends*." Her lower lip trembled, and I realized I could never jeopardize her happiness by crossing the line Nico drew in the sand.

"And, I better understand the employment policies. I don't want to get you in trouble, Knox."

"You won't. Nico wouldn't actually fire me."

She searched my eyes. "Are you sure?"

I hesitated.

She nodded. "That's what I thought. And, anyway, I still love him," she murmured. "That's why I don't date."

She turned her head and tugged her chin from my grasp and pivoted around both me and the vehicle. She opened the door and settled herself into the seat. She never said a word.

I shoved my fingers through my hair and grunted. I caught sight of Abe from the corner of my eye. He shook his head as he turned away.

I gave her space on the ferry ride, but the drive to Providence was long, seemingly longer because the conversation was stilted—when we conversed. Emmaline spent most of the time with her knees pressed tightly together and her hands wrapped around her legs—almost as if she were holding herself together.

I hated watching her suffer.

Not wanting Em to know how much her pain hurt me, I turned on the radio and hummed along, tapping my fingers absently against the steering wheel. My mind kept trying to spin out from her revelations, but I managed to keep my attention on the road, as I'd promised.

The moment I pulled into my assigned parking spot, she nearly tumbled out of the vehicle before grabbing her purse, slamming the car door, and heading into the office. I gritted my teeth. She wanted to go there, fine.

I needed a break. I pulled out of my spot and drove toward the arena. A couple of hours on the ice might just clear my mind.

Chapter Sixteen
Emmaline

I returned to the Giovannis' mansion the next night, unsure of my reception by Sebastian but unable to stay away. Sebastian's last words continued to flit through my head. I paused on the flagstone walk, staring up at the large house.

Instead of ringing the bell, I turned on my heel and headed back to my car. I pulled out my phone and dialed Aidy's number.

"Would you like some company tonight?" I asked. "I'll bring dinner. And ice cream."

"Can we watch a rom-com?" she asked, her voice a little fuzzy.

"I'm sorry. Did I wake you?"

"No, though I am sleepy." She hesitated. "My ex showed up."

"I'm on my way. It'll take me thirty so that I can get the ice cream."

"Can we trade that in for chocolate white chocolate chip cookies? My mom used to make them, and I have a craving." Her voice was wistful. My heart squeezed with sympathy.

"On it."

"You're the best."

"See you soon," I said.

I arrived with a bakery box stuffed full of cookies and an-other bag of chicken noodle soup and sourdough. Nothing else sounded as comforting as the soup, and both Aidy and I needed food support tonight.

I balanced the box with the bag of food and raised my hand to knock on her door. A moment later, it opened, and I stared into Knox's hard chest. My knees trembled as I forced myself to follow the strong muscles up over the tanned throat with its dipping Adam's apple and to that chiseled jaw I daydreamed about. He hadn't shaved and tiny blond hairs poked through his cheeks. How some men managed to pull off the vaguely scruffy look was beyond me, but Knox did. My belly quivered, and the box in my arms tipped.

"Whoa there," he murmured.

He snatched the box as it teetered, the back of his hand sliding across my breast. We both caught our breath, gazes locked as heat burst along all my nerves.

"Emmaline?" Aidy said, padding closer. "Good, it's you."

She looked haggard, her eyes puffy and red.

I shook myself out of my fog and brushed past Knox. I mostly managed to ignore my body's further heating as I set the bag on her dining room table and wrapped her in a hug. The baby in her belly rolled and tumbled, oblivious to her mother's plight...or my own.

"Why didn't you tell me you were this upset?" I asked.

"Because I didn't want anyone to know." Her lip quivered. "I shouldn't be. It's not like Ryder and I are anything other than friends."

Knox stepped into our space and I stiffened, which caused Aidy to narrow her eyes. He set down the pink bakery box and gently extracted Aidy from my arms. He took her by the biceps and turned her to face him.

"Listen to me, Aidalyn: Ryder is dealing with his own shit right now, but he would be torn up if he knew you were this upset—"

"Which is why you won't tell him," Aidy said, her voice edged in steel.

Knox sighed. "I'll handle this however you want because I trust you to make the best choices for you and my niece. But if you need me, for anything, any time, I want you to promise to call me."

He held her gaze for a long moment, his face solemn, his hands gentle as he offered her the comforting glide of his palms up and down her arms.

Aidy's lip quivered but then she straightened and raised her chin. "I promise."

He leaned in and pressed a kiss to her forehead. "Good gir...er woman." He sent a smirk at Aidy, and she managed a wan smile.

His gaze shifted to me, where I stood, aching at this display of affection. I wanted that. No, I *craved* their closeness.

Joshua and Ellie cared for me, deeply, but I wasn't a Giovanni and never would be. Up until recently, I hadn't realized the lack of intimacy in my life—not just with a man, but with any close relationship. Bridget had stuck with me these years when I'd needed her, but I'd been hell-bent on managing my own grief. That pushed those who'd wanted to help away, which was the main reason Bridget and I hadn't been closer.

Now, with Aidy, who had more than her share of heartache, I'd found a kindred spirit. But it wasn't Aidy who held my focus at the moment. Knox, the powerful, successful, even arrogant professional showed a soft, tender side to his sister—much as he had with me during our time out at the Vineyard. These different facets of his personality fascinated me.

I turned away and began unpacking the food.

"I wasn't sure what you wanted, but I thought chicken noodle soup seemed about right," I said with a false cheer.

"And the cookies?" Aidy asked, moving closer.

"That's the box."

She smiled, a real one, when she opened the lid. "There have to be more than two dozen in here."

"Thirty-eight," I said. "I bought them out. The owner was there, and she was over the moon."

"I bet."

Aidy grabbed one and popped it into her mouth. She hummed as the sugary goodness dissolved in her mouth.

She grabbed two more and thrust them at Knox.

"Like Mom's," she mumbled around another bite. "Not as good, but..."

"They never are," Knox said. He, too, bit into the treat. His strong, white teeth carved off a large piece. He nodded. "It *is* good."

"Take some," I offered.

His gaze met mine and his lips quirked up. "Thanks. I'd like that."

I headed into the kitchen and searched through drawers while Aidy and Knox spoke quietly. Finally, I found the plastic baggies and pulled one out of the box. I busied myself with transferring a dozen cookies to the bag.

"I'll leave you ladies to your night," Knox said. "We're doing dinner soon, though, Aidy-pie. I want to celebrate your thesis."

He hugged Aidy tight to his chest even as he snagged another cookie from the box. His mischievous look told me he expected a chastising, but I simply shook my head.

"Em, would you walk me out?" Knox asked. "There's something I'd like to discuss."

Nerves fluttered through my belly. "Oh, um. Sure."

My voice squeaked.

I closed my eyes and took in a long breath. Then, I grabbed his bag of cookies and headed toward the door.

"Be back in a sec," I said over my shoulder to Aidy.

She appraised first me then her brother. "Take your time."

No, I wanted to say. *It's not like that.*

But I feared it was *exactly* like that, especially when Knox placed his hand at the small of my back and my entire body warmed to his touch.

He ushered me from Aidy's condo and down the hall toward the elevator. "What you did for her—it means a lot to me."

I tilted my head back and met his gaze. "She's my friend."

He raised his hand and cupped my cheek. "I know. Thank you."

My brows tugged together. "I love Aidy. She's great…"

"Thank you for worrying over her and caring for her when she doesn't think she deserves it. Thank you for being a kind-hearted soul who looks after her friends."

My face flushed and those nerves skittered. "You're welcome," I stammered.

"How are you?"

"Wh-what?"

"You were raw yesterday, and I worried..." He ran his hand through his hair. "I brought up a bunch of emotions." He met my gaze. "Are you okay?"

My heart fluttered. Knox was out of his depth, unsure how to talk about feelings—and trying so hard.

"I'm okay," I said, my voice soft. I cleared my throat. "I *will* be okay."

He cupped my cheeks and his thumb pressed to my lower lip.

"I want you happy, Em. That matters to me. I love seeing you smile."

Before I even thought about it, I'd touched the tip of my tongue to his finger. He leaned closer, his warm breath puffing against my cheek.

"You are so beautiful. Inside and out." He groaned as he stepped back. "You should go back to Aidy."

I frowned. I didn't want that—I wanted him to kiss me again. He ran the pad of his fingers over my swollen lips and up my cheek. I loved how large his hand was against my nape. He tugged me closer again and dropped a peck on my nose.

"You need to go in. And I need to leave."

I stepped back, stumbling over something. Knox grabbed my biceps, ensuring I was stable before letting go.

"Thanks for the cookies," he said with a wink.

I stood still, trying to recover my breath and my wits as Knox opened a door on the left side of the hall and sauntered down the stairs. I took in another breath, counted to fifteen and released it slowly.

I pushed open Aidy's door and stepped inside, unsurprised to find Aidy setting out bowls of soup and the cutting board with slices of the sourdough boule I'd bought.

"Want to tell me how long you and Knox have been fighting that attraction?" she asked, the same mischievous smile gracing her face that had been on Knox's moments before.

"I..." I collapsed into the nearest chair and buried my face in my hands. "Nothing happened, but I want to—"

Aidy held up her hand.

"I don't really want to know. First, gross, because he's my brother. Second, as your boss, don't say that to me again."

I snapped my jaw shut, flushing. My muscles tensed and I prepared to rise. Aidy pressed her hand over my fisted one. "Let me have plausible deniability."

"Third," her voice and gaze softened, "as your friend, I don't have the answers to love and relationships. I've managed to mess up two in mere months. But Bridget keeps telling me things have a way of working out. Never how I plan or want, but somehow for the better." She patted my hand.

"How is she?" I asked.

"Good. You should visit her. Holding those babies is magical."

I would do that. Soon.

Aidy slid her arm around my shoulders and squeezed. Pulling away, she slid a steaming bowl toward me.

"Eat," she said. "You'll feel better. Then, we'll gorge on cookies and some Hemsworth men."

I fiddled with my spoon. "Maybe I should quit," I said.

She dropped her spoon into her soup, ignoring the splash of

broth on her blouse and back of her hand. "Why would you do that?"

"Because I'm causing problems for you and Knox."

She leaned closer. "You're not quitting."

"But—"

"*No*. You're fabulous to work with. You're more capable than most more-experienced designers. Nico can pull his head out of his ass and deal."

I continued to fidget. "But I never told Knox about Sebastian."

She tilted her head. "Are you ready to do that?"

I sucked on my lower lip. "It hurts," I said. "Not just that night, but since. I was so mad at Sebastian at first. If he hadn't looked at his phone..." I sighed. "Then I was angry with my mother for driving when she shouldn't have." I laid down the spoon and pressed my hands to my chest. "They both made mistakes, but my parents shouldn't have had to die. Sebastian shouldn't have a traumatic brain injury that destroyed his life. So, it hurts, and it always will."

She squeezed my hand. "Do I sense a *but*?"

I nodded. "But I'm learning to live with that pain. You and Knox, Bridget, and Calliope have helped."

"I'm glad," Aidy said with a smile. "But I don't think you should tell Knox that you were engaged to Sebastian Giovanni."

"Why not? I mean, *you* know."

"I'm your friend, not your possible lover. And, Knox, bless him, doesn't seek out confrontation, but he also doesn't shy from it. Probably because he played hockey. So, if he thinks there's an issue with the Giovannis because you were almost one, he'll voice his concerns. Mrs. Giovanni is very protective of you, and the resulting fallout could be bad for our firm."

"I don't want to cause problems," I said.

"Then, I recommend you keep that relationship to yourself."

I nodded, stunned by how much of a mess I'd made of my life.

"I think," I said slowly, picking up my spoon and dipping it into the golden broth. "That love and relationships are much harder than I ever expected."

"Preach, sister," Aidy muttered.

Chapter Seventeen
Knox

For the second time in two nights, I headed to the ice rink, my refuge when the world around me grew too tumultuous. After an hour on skates that led to burning thighs and lungs, I managed to work off enough of the adrenaline from my interaction with Em to think rationally.

Nico would find out soon about my continued interest. There was no way I could keep that from him. Nor did I want to. I'd never longed for a woman before. It sucked. As did the knowledge we had a strong connection that my brother and her past threatened.

When I thought of my future, I saw Emmaline. That meant *something*. We could manage the roadblocks—we just needed to be savvy about our choices. After another hour of meandering on my skates, Skip announced the facility would be closing in thirty minutes. I took a quick shower and changed into sweats and a T-shirt before shouldering my bag and heading home.

Seeing Nico's car in my driveway caused my mood to tank further. I gritted my teeth as I walked in the door. Nico unfolded himself from my couch. He stood and stretched as if he had all the time in the world.

"A bit late to be getting in, wouldn't you say?"

I walked to my fridge and opened it, pulling out a beer. I

popped the cap and considered drinking it straight from the can. Nico, who had meandered over, opened my cabinet and handed me a glass. He also made a big production of sniffing me.

"I figured you'd smell like her."

"Well, you're wrong," I said through gritted teeth. "I was at the rink—after I went to check in on our sister, who's feeling sad about the jerk-off trying to worm his dick back into her life."

Nico stepped back, anger hardening his eyes and flattening his lips. "I'll deal with him."

"You don't need to. Aidy did a magnificent job." Pride in my sister swelled my chest.

"So you didn't run into your dark-haired Marilyn Monroe?"

"Would you stop calling her that? It's rude."

"Why?"

"Because…it's like me calling you a wannabe Frank Lloyd Wright. She has a name, a personality, and it's *hers*. Not something you can superimpose with your own biases."

He tilted his head and studied me. "She's under your skin."

"As you said, she's our employee. When are you going to get off my case about her?"

"When you quit eyeing her like she's a steak and you're a half-starved lion."

I slammed my beer on the counter, ignoring the slosh of cold liquid onto my hand and wrist. The foam dripped onto my counter below it.

"That's *it*, Nico. You need to go. I won't have you here, baiting me in my own home, and I won't have you questioning my integrity again."

I glared at him, continuing, "Emmaline is not a criminal. And she's a detail-oriented draftsman—better than Clint or Morris. Probably better than you or me. That's number one. Number two, I find her attractive—I already told you that, but I am not having sex with her currently, and three, this is about you being unable to put your shit with Amanda behind you. Why is that Nico? What really happened?"

His muscles bunched and his hands fisted, and for the first time in nearly ten years, I wondered if my brother would hit me. We used to whale on each other all through childhood and our teen years, but Nico outgrew the need when he started college, leaving me no choice but to comply. That and the fact I had thirty pounds of muscle on him.

"I told you, she stole my designs and took them to our boss. She got a promotion. I got shown the door."

I shook my head. "That's not enough for you to obsess over my love life. And to act like a complete ass to both Aidy and me." I looked straight into his eyes. There was a deep-seated pain there, but he masked it quickly with that icy overlay that I hated so much. This man was *not* my brother.

"You're pushing us away, again, still. I had your back; we stayed close, even when Aidy cut ties. She's back and working hard to build a relationship with you, so now you're lashing out at me. Which makes me think this was never about either of us—or Emmaline. This is your hang-up with Amanda, and you're letting it fuck up the most important relationships in your life."

Nico turned away. He walked into the living room and

collected his suit jacket. He slid his arms into it and shrugged it up until it fit over his shoulders.

"You don't get to question me," Nico said, his tone stilted as he continued to face away from me.

"I should have done so sooner. And I shouldn't have to follow a stupid, arbitrary rule in your human resources handbook. Would you *really* keep me from falling in love?"

He paused, mid-tug on his jacket and shot me a look. "You think you're in love with her?"

"I think I have feelings that are much stronger than lust."

He cursed, long, low, and vicious. "A woman who has that much power over a man's passion, over his dick, will use it."

I raised my eyebrows. "Because Amanda did?"

"Because your precious liar was Sebastian Giovanni's fiancée."

My heart pounded. Her fiancé who'd hit this head in the crash. That was Sebastian Giovanni, heir to one of the largest fortunes in New England? And Em hadn't told us? I shook my head.

"She dropped him faster than a hot potato when he needed her most." He narrowed his eyes. "Still think she's the sweet little angel sent to warm your bed? She's ambitious and willing to work her way up through the wealthy elite to solidify that position. She chose our firm because of our reputation. She was truthful about that. But I bet she likes rubbing elbows and other body parts with all those rich assholes."

"No," I muttered.

He raised an eyebrow, triumph stamped in his features. This is what my brother had become. He'd rather see me hurt than see me happy. And Em...the way she'd talked about her fiancé...Sebastian.

Dammit. No. She hadn't used him to get close to Ellie. She'd loved Sebastian. She told me she still loved him, and I'd seen the haunted look in her eyes then; Nico hadn't.

I didn't have the whole story.

"You're not firing a woman for being too close to a client."

"Whenever I asked Emmaline about it, she was evasive." He pinned me with his glare. "I cannot tolerate half answers."

I washed my hands, unable to stand the stickiness of the beer. After wiping up the mess on the counter, I picked up the glass and downed it in three long gulps. It hit my stomach like an avalanche.

Em had been engaged to Sebastian Giovanni. There would be pictures of the two of them together online. He was two years older, she'd said. They'd started dating in high school, she'd said, and she'd visited him at Yale most weekends. That meant he'd brought her into his dorm or apartment—he'd loved her body there.

Before this, I'd managed to keep the idea of another man's hands on Emmaline strictly hypothetical. But if I saw the photos, it would be real. That's why I hadn't looked her up. I didn't want those images in my head.

And I knew Sebastian Giovanni wasn't dead. Joshua spoke of him last time he'd been in the office—mentioned him to Emmaline and she'd hung on Joshua's every word.

Fuck. What if she had played us?

But I couldn't figure out why. How was keeping that relationship secret an advantage? Why wouldn't she just tell us...at least me?

"She and Aidy are close. I bet Aidy knows."

"Doesn't matter. I didn't. And I run the company. If she's lied about her past, what's to keep her from stealing our designs and our clients?"

"That's a big stretch and you know it. Your attitude is a liability. We're not firing a woman for being attractive or for knowing wealthy clients. That's the epitome of idiocy, and you're not stupid Nico."

He huffed out a breath, and for the first time in months, maybe years, I caught the Nico I'd known and looked up to staring back at me, unguarded and clearly unhappy. "She reminds me of Amanda. More with each passing day."

I blinked. "In looks?"

"No, they look nothing alike. I wouldn't have been able to stand...no."

He clenched his teeth and balled his hands into fists. I waited, unwilling to encroach on this honest moment—it's what I'd been waiting for with him, and I could be patient while he worked on releasing his poison.

"In ambition. In her intelligence. The way she asks questions and listens intently. Her smooth, simple line strokes."

As Nico continued to tick off reasons, I gaped. Nico had paid more attention to Emmaline than I had, which was saying something.

"You're still in love with her," I muttered.

His head snapped back as if I'd punched him. "Don't be ridiculous."

"It's eating you up inside that she picked your boss over you."

This time, when Nico's muscles bunched, I knew he was going to follow through. I managed to block both his arms, grabbing his wrists. Instead of fighting me, he yanked me forward.

"I don't love Amanda Krantz. I'll *never* make that mistake again."

I straightened. "Fine. But that doesn't mean Em is like her."

Nico studied me, and I forced myself to stay relaxed.

"Then, we test her," he said.

I narrowed my eyes. "What the hell does that mean?"

Chapter Eighteen
Emmaline

Knox seemed preoccupied most of the week, sending me strange glances. I spent my time with Aidy, as I typically did, preparing for yet another client presentation. I'd found I didn't like those much. Nico seemed tense, calling me into his office a few times.

But it was Knox's constant time out of the office that worried me most. Each time I did see him, he busied himself with a task. I was beginning to think he didn't want to be around me, which hurt because I was more drawn to him with each passing day.

That night, I visited Bridget. Aidy was right. Holding a small baby close to my chest was an instant stress-reliever. Bridget's smile was indulgent as I cooed at the baby.

"You have to see the space Aidy helped us with," she said.

She walked through her kitchen and flicked on a light. I smiled. The small apartment had been transformed into a nursery/playroom.

"They don't use the cribs yet, of course, but I think this is going to work out well."

I touched the soft fleece covering one of the mattresses. "It's beautiful."

Bridget beamed. "The girls will have to share a bathroom, but this way, they also have their own space."

We chatted until Simon arrived home with their son, Brendan.

"I won't keep you from your dinner plans," I said, rising from the couch and reluctantly handing back the baby to Simon. He whispered something into the baby's ear, and my heart melted.

"Oh, I meant to ask—do you know a good realtor?"

"Your parents' house?" Bridget asked.

"It's time."

She hugged me, rocking me gently. "You are so brave," she murmured into my hair.

I called the realtor from my car, unwilling to postpone my decision. I scheduled an initial walk-through for the next evening, and because I was antsy with the Knox situation, I made a big dent in cleaning out some of their closets.

—— Å ——

I worked at my desk, squinting against the bright late afternoon light filtering through the transom windows when Knox dropped into the chair across from me. I raised my head slowly, unsure of how to approach him. We'd left our situation unsettled, and I felt as though I owed him a more detailed explanation about my life regardless of what Aidy said. But to do so left me exposed to the very man I feared could do me the most damage.

Confusion continued to swirl through me as it had all weekend. That's why I'd finally headed out to my beach house and begun the unenviable task of demolition. The hard work proved satisfying and I'd made a good dent removing the decayed drywall and rotted sub-flooring.

"Aidy had her baby," Knox said, a wide smile gracing his lips. Just as they did with Chris Evans' eyelashes, most women moaned over Knox Wright's lips...and eyelashes...and behind...and...

I cleared my throat.

"That's great. Are they both well?"

"Yes," he said his deep voice deeper than usual. "They're resting. Aidy popped the baby out at the supermarket last night." He shook his head and chuckled.

I bent down and rummage through my purse until I found my phone.

"I'll text her and give her my congratulations and love. See when I can stop by. Thank you for the heads up."

Knox leaned forward, his brows pinched in an utterly sexy display of confusion. Was there anything this man did that wasn't sexy?

I dropped my gaze back to my computer screen.

"I'd like to drive you over to visit her later," he said. "And before you ask, that was Aidy's request."

I snapped my jaw shut and nodded because I wanted that, too.

— ✦ —

Aidy lay sleeping when we entered her room. Her long lashes lay on her cheeks, her breath rising and falling in long, slow pulls. I was glad to see her so well. The idea of birthing a baby freaked me out—but having a child in a public place? No, thank you.

We tiptoed toward the bassinet, trying not to wake Aidy. I smiled down at the tiny bundle snuggled in a fuzzy white cap and swaddled tightly in a bright pink blanket.

"Courtesy of Whole Grocer's. I guess people have been coming into the store all day, wanting to donate items to Lilia and me." Aidy struggled to push up into a seated position. My chest warmed when Knox helped her, then fluffed her pillows. She smiled at him, her gaze sharpening as she realized I was with him.

"Maybe it's been positive publicity."

"Mm. Must be," Aidy agreed.

"How you feeling, Aidy-pie?" Knox asked, his tone solicitous. He leaned down and pressed a kiss to her forehead. "What can I do for you?"

"I'm good." Aidy yawned. "Tired but good."

"We brought you some dinner," Knox said.

"I'm hungry," she said, smiling. "I bet Ryder is, too."

A broad-shouldered man around Knox's age with hair nearly as dark as mine but gray-gray eyes. This must be Ryder. While I'd heard about her neighbor, I hadn't yet met him.

Aidy's face lit up with a smile, which told me everything I needed to know. She was smitten. And who could blame her? The guy rocked his dress pants and button-down. His hair was a bit longer on the top and flopped toward his kind eyes—that hadn't left Aidy even while he answered Knox.

The infatuation ran deep between these two.

"We brought you gifts," I said, my tone chipper. The baby stirred in her tiny plastic bed. Knox strode to the side and looked down, his face softening. My earlier frustration with him dissipated. This was a man who cared, deeply, for his family.

"Nico's on his way. May I hold her?" Knox asked, his voice quiet.

"Of course," Aidy said. She slid her feet toward the side of the bed, but Ryder clamped his hand over her calf.

"You stay there. Either Knox can pick her up or I will and hand her to him *after* we wash our hands."

Knox, who reached out to run his finger along the infant's cheek, checked himself. He went into the bathroom and washed his hands then came back.

"Would you pick her up for me, Ryder?" Knox asked. "Show me how it's done. I don't want to hurt her."

Ryder nodded, serious, as he squirted hand sanitizer on his hands before he walked Knox through supporting the baby's neck. He transferred the infant to Knox, whose face slackened into awe.

"She's so little. Smaller than you ever were, Aidy-pie."

"She was only five and a half pounds, which was plenty big."

Aidy winced, and I couldn't help but cringe in sympathy.

"If she'd been much bigger, I'm not sure I could have managed," Aidy said.

"You were a rock star," Ryder said with a grin.

After I washed my hands, I stepped closer to Knox, drawn by the invisible strands of sweet baby. I wanted to hold her but didn't want to ask Knox to stop bonding with his niece. His sublime expression told me how much he loved this experience.

I bit my cheek, once again thinking of the life I'd planned with Sebastian. Sure, the moment hurt, but the pang wasn't as soul-crushing as it used to be. I stared down at the tiny sleeping face and felt much of my own body soften. I might hate hospitals, but this was a place of happiness, not death, pain, and misfortune like the ward where my father worked.

"Here," Knox said, his voice low, soft. "I know you want to hold her."

"You two look happy together. I'll hold her another time."

Because his head was bowed over the baby's our eyes were level. "I know you don't have good memories of hospitals, Em. Let's make you a new, positive one."

I sucked my lower lip into my mouth as he carefully transferred the baby to my eager arms. "Oh," I said.

"Yeah, she's kind of addicting," Knox muttered. He touched his long, index finger to her cheek and I marveled at their size difference. The likelihood of Lilia ending up six-three and two-hundred-plus pounds of muscles seemed highly improbable, but Knox couldn't have started out too much bigger than Lilia. His tenderness touched something in me—a fiery need I didn't want to acknowledge. The baby gripped his finger and he inched closer.

The warmth from his body and her tiny weight nestled to my chest flooded me with endorphins.

"I hated being an only child, and Sebastian wanted three as close together as possible. He and his brother are nearly ten years apart, which he said was too big of a gap to really share a childhood."

I blanched, realizing what I'd said.

"Sebastian, huh? That was your fiancé?"

I nodded. *Please don't ask. Please don't make this perfect memory weird.*

Without another word, he settled on the edge of Aidy's bed and went through a list of questions—all designed to ensure she was well and cared for. To hide my confusion, I bent in close to the baby and began to sing her a lullaby my mother used to sing to me.

When I finished, Knox said, "That was beautiful."

Knox moved off to talk to his brother, who had shown up looking harried. I heard Jeff's name and winced, knowing someone would have to tell Aidy her ex was calling and checking up on her.

That person ended up being me. Thankfully, the baby squawked soon thereafter, her small face crumpling in consternation. Ryder lifted her from my arms.

"She's wet and no doubt wants to nurse."

Knox leaned down and pressed a kiss to Aidy's forehead. I hugged her with the promise I'd stop by again this weekend.

I trailed Knox back to his vehicle, my mind flitting with partial thoughts. But one kept coming back: Knox knew how much I wanted to see Aidy, and he'd realized why I struggled to set foot in a hospital. He'd done what he could to protect me from my frightening memories.

As we pulled into the parking lot at Wright and Associates next to my car, I unbuckled my seat belt and opened the car door.

"Thank you for tonight," I said. "I really enjoyed seeing Aidy and meeting Lilia."

"I'm glad," Knox said.

I sat there for another moment, not sure I wanted to head home. Knox's phone jangled, and he picked it up.

"Oh, hey—I need to respond to this. Would you take my keys and run into the office? There are a couple of files on my desk that I need to look over tonight."

"Sure," I said, scooping up his keys. "Which key is it?"

He showed me the ones for the door and the one for his filing cabinet. "It's the Carrington file and another labeled Top Secret."

I raised my eyebrows but nodded again. "Do you mind if

I grab a couple of things from my desk? I need to go over the museum's renovations again before the presentation tomorrow."

"Sure," Knox said, bent over his phone. "Get what you need."

I stepped out of the car and headed into the building, careful to pocket Knox's keys on the way. I stopped in his office first and pulled the files he asked for, once again intrigued by the one titled "Top Secret." I clasped the folders to my chest and made sure to lock his cabinet. After I exited his office and shut the door, I headed to my desk.

I quickly found the Modern Art Museum file, which was in the center of my desk. Next to it was another folder that I didn't remember. Keough was printed on the top. I hadn't been helping with that project, so I frowned, wondering why it would be on my desk. I grabbed my landline and pressed the speed dial option for Knox's cell.

"Yeah? Did you have any trouble? I finished my call. I'll come inside and grab them."

"No, no trouble with your folders, but I'm concerned about the fact that the Keough file is on my desk. I'm not part of that team."

I heard the front door open and turned to find Knox striding toward me, his brows tugged low.

Once he neared, I pointed to the folder. He grunted, his lips compressed. He picked it up and I held out his other files and the keys.

His eyes softened as he took them. "Thanks for helping me out, Em."

"Sure," I said. "Any time." I hesitated, wondering why he was looking at me like that.

We turned in unison and headed toward the door. He locked up behind him while I waited on the sidewalk below. I needed to grab my briefcase and purse from his vehicle before I could head home. I sighed, unhappy with the idea of another solitary meal in my kitchen. Sure, I could read my Kindle but the lack of company most nights was getting old. Bridget had invited me over, so I guessed I'd see if she wouldn't mind if I dropped in.

"I'm looking forward to The Mac's opening next weekend," I said.

"Me, too," Knox replied, but he seemed preoccupied. He opened his car and set the files on his center console. He fired off a text, ignoring me.

I grabbed my items and stood awkwardly for a moment, half hoping he'd ask me to dinner.

He scowled at the phone and typed something else.

"Well, goodnight," I murmured, my hope dwindling.

"Night, Em. I'll see you tomorrow."

"Yeah. Sure."

I dropped my stuff into the car and turned back toward him. He was staring at the building, phone to his ear.

"You don't need more proof."

I wondered what that was about.

Chapter Nineteen
Emmaline

I slid my arm through Joshua's, laying my palm on the forearm of his dress uniform. I smiled at the cameras as they flashed all around us.

"Seems that The Mac Hotel is creating quite the splash," Joshua murmured as he, too, smiled. "I haven't seen this many reporters in one place for any of the events in town, including our annual gala."

"Mr. Giovanni, Mr. Giovanni." Reporters continued to shout his name, but he waved as he continued to walk us up the red carpet and into The Mac's lobby. The area was modern and sleek without feeling cold or too precise. How Aidy'd managed to pull that off using stainless steel and a cool white marble boggled my mind.

"I know that look," Knox said from my left. His deep voice sent a shiver down my spine, causing Joshua to glance first at me before turning toward Knox.

"Oh?" I managed to keep my tone neutral.

"You look just like Aidy does when she wants to soak up everything about an existing design," he said with a chuckle. "What part caught your eye first? Start there and work your way out."

"You obviously know Emmaline well," Josh said, his gaze drifting around the space.

Knox took the moment to let his gaze sweep over me in a leisurely caress. When he returned his gaze to mine, his eyes burned his approval. I'd worn an emerald green ankle-length satin sheath similar to the one Audrey Hepburn wore in Breakfast at Tiffany's, my all-time favorite movie. My hair was clasped in a complicated twist the hairdresser said complimented my long neck and high cheekbones. Much as I liked the end result, my head already ached from the heavy weight of too much hair and the smell of hairspray.

Knox's smile grew as Joshua brought his attention back to Knox. "It's good to see you again," Knox said. "I had no idea you were attending with Em tonight. I would have thought, as one of her bosses, she'd give us the honor of escorting her to this affair."

The men shook hands, and I noted how Joshua sized Knox up. His face remained inscrutable and I didn't know what he was thinking. The slight bite to his words caused my back to stiffen. He never asked me to join him, so how dare he act as if I'd disappointed him?

The longer I tried to tease out Knox's actions last night, the more tense I became. And because I didn't understand the situation, I'd felt it best to distance myself from Knox, so I'd fallen back into old patterns—turning to Joshua and Ellie for support.

"I'm sure if you'd asked her, Emmaline would have happily accepted," Joshua said, his tone smooth and easy—as it always was even in these stressful situations.

Josh had told me once that he'd lived through life and death—even longed for the black slide to end his pain, so a little cattiness or pettiness remained where it should: in the ridiculous corner. I pressed my lips together before I remembered my cranberry lip stain. No reason to destroy my beautiful makeup simply because I couldn't manage to contain my attraction to Knox.

Knox's gaze clicked to mine, and I felt the heat burning up my neck and over my throat. After a couple of long, intense breaths, I looked away, unwilling to be caught mooning over my boss. The fact that Joshua knew of my crush mortified me. If it hadn't been for the accident, Sebastian and I would have been married by now, and I would have attended this event on his arm, beaming with pride that he'd chosen to spend his time and lavish his love on me.

I snatched up a glass of champagne from a passing tray. I blinked back the melancholy that was my life with difficulty to find Joshua and now Will, Joshua's boyfriend, discussing hockey with Knox. The men agreed that Boston had a decent chance this year but worried about Toronto and Chicago. Before I zoned out again, Nico sauntered up. Nannette popped up next to Nico, looking sleek and beautiful in a silky lavender dress that stopped just above her knees.

"So, this is how rich people party," she murmured. "I can see the appeal."

"You'll like it better once you taste the champagne," I said.

"I like everything better when it's served with champagne." Nannette practically bounced in her heels. "I'm going to work on securing myself a man from that line over there."

She fluttered her hand toward a group of good-looking men in their early thirties. She flitted off before I could mention that group was known for how quickly they changed partners—in bed, not in their financial and business circles. I shook my head, trying not to be overly concerned. Nannette was an adult and she'd learn quickly that playing with this wealthy crowd came with a different set of rules.

"Ah, hell, she's going to land herself in trouble," Nico muttered. "I knew I shouldn't have brought her."

Before I could ask him what he meant by that, he high-tailed after Nannette, steering her away from the group of men now blatantly checking her out. Nannette pouted but seemed happy to have Nico's attention.

Joshua pressed a kiss to my cheek and moved off with Will, their heads bent close together, leaving me alone with Knox. My stomach fluttered.

"You look nice," I said.

He looked spectacular in his tux, which is why I turned outward, facing the crowd. Ogling my boss's ass was not professional.

He leaned in so that his warm breath slithered over my neck. "So do you, Em."

I turned my head quickly, unsurprised to find his pupils dilated. I'd heard the passion in his voice.

"My name is Emmaline," I said, though my argument was half-hearted.

My entire life, I'd insisted on being called by my full name because there were so many other Emmas in my age bracket. My mom would sigh and say it was like the Traceys and Jennifers of her generation. "That's why we named you Emmaline, honey; we wanted something as unique and beautiful as you are."

"Then please make sure you don't abbreviate my name because then I'm as interchangeable as any of the other girls with the same name."

She'd cupped my cheeks and pressed a kiss to my forehead. "You'll always be special to me," she'd whispered.

I scowled, hating how I kept falling into my past tonight.

"But I like to call you Em." Knox smiled. "It's special, just between us." His brow drew down. "What's wrong, really? You seem unhappy."

I shook my head, not wanting to admit seeing Bridget's and Aidy's babies each week opened wounds for me, reminding me again of what Sebastian and I had lost. A waiter drifted past and Knox lifted two glasses of champagne from his tray with a brief nod. That's when I realized I'd set my first glass down, untouched.

"Is that why you didn't want to come alone? Bad memories?"

I nodded.

"And you asked Joshua to escort you?"

Again, I nodded. "He understands."

"Understands what?"

I hesitated, not wanting to bring up the car accident again. It kept getting between Knox and me, and I needed to move past it. Not that I could act on my attraction as long as I worked at Wright and Associates. I caught my lip between my teeth and tugged.

"What's been going on through that pretty head of yours?"

"Just thinking."

"About your past?"

"Yes. I don't really enjoy these types of engagements anymore. They remind me of what I lost."

Knox's mouth dropped open at my comments. I drained my glass of champagne to cover my embarrassment and thrust it into his hand.

"Excuse me. I need to speak with Nannette."

I strode by Knox. He managed to turn and set my empty glass and his full one on another waiter's tray and snag my elbow before I made it three steps. He leaned in, nuzzling the spot behind my ear. "I can't stand to see you sad."

I shifted away from him but kept my face forward. "Please don't," I whispered. "Not here. First, Nico's been watching me like a bug under a microscope. And second—"

"Kissing you was the highlight of my life," he said.

He anticipated his comment causing me to turn toward him because he wrapped an arm around my waist and leaned in closer so that once again, his breath whispered over my skin when he spoke. I shivered in response.

"I want to be there for you, to help you find your happiness again."

I leaned back so that I could stare into his eyes. His were earnest.

"All right," I said. I forced myself to step back from him.

His hand reflexively tightened on my wrist before he let go. "What does that mean?" he said.

I felt a smile tug at the corners of my mouth. "It means I heard what you said." I stepped back further, turning from him. I needed a chance to regroup away from Knox, to focus my thoughts and clarify what I wanted.

"I'm going to find Bridget and Simon. They should be here."

Living was hard. Adding dating to the mix...my guts clenched.

"If I can talk Nico out of the no fraternizing clause, will you let me take you on a real date?" he asked, his voice tinged with desperation.

I glanced back over my shoulder. "Do you think that's wise?"

"Could be the smartest decision I've ever made." His smile was wolfish.

"What if we both get burned?"

He leaned in even closer, his lips grazing my cheek and ear. Heat coiled through me like a spring, waiting to be released.

"I can't think of anything hotter than playing with fire and you, Em."

Chapter Twenty
Knox

The light fragrance drifted away as Emmaline did. I wanted to follow her but now wasn't the time.

Instead, I sipped my champagne, attempting to find my brother in the growing crush. Before I could, a pale hand with a gaudy diamond engagement ring landed on my arm. I tensed, the scowl already building.

"What do you want, Melinda?" I asked.

I braced myself before turning to face my former girlfriend. She looked stunning with her red highlights glinting in the soft chandelier light, dangling softly around her heart-shaped face.

"I want to know why you were talking to Joshua Giovanni."

"Not really any of your business."

"I'm making it my business, especially since you seemed close with the crippled brother's ex."

I blinked at her rapidly, trying to process what her words meant. "Crippled brother?"

"The hot younger one," Melinda said, her tone short. "Sean or Simon or something."

"You must mean Sebastian," Ellie Giovanni said. She appeared on my other side, her bearing regal in her understated black gown. "My *grandson*." Her gaze flicked up to mine but returned to Melinda, her lip curling in distaste. "And while he does have a traumatic brain injury, he most certainly isn't crippled."

Ellie wrinkled her nose, allowing the full weight of her displeasure to spill over onto the younger woman.

"Mrs. Giovanni," Melinda said, her eyes widening. "I wasn't aware you were here."

"I assumed that from your crass terminology applied to my family," Eleanor said. "And, yet, here I am, not dead yet, and still filled with these amazing opinions like one shouldn't speak ill of the unwell or that your fiancé clearly felt the need to mark you as his with that grotesque rock weighing down your finger."

The first twenty years of my life consisted of hockey fights. Both friends and opponents yelled insults and pummeled each other with their fists, but Eleanor Giovanni dismantled Melinda in a few sentences in the most vicious takedown I'd ever witnessed.

"Ah, here he is now. John, be a good man and rein in your fiancée's nasty tongue-wagging. Please explain the detriment of irritating me further with talking of my family—of which Emmaline Schooler is still an important part," Eleanor Giovanni said, her voice turning even frostier than an ice rink at opening.

Melinda's face paled further under Eleanor's light tone. John, face a mask of displeasure, whisked Melinda away before she had a chance to open her mouth. I heard him hiss, "What did you do? You know we need her—"

They disappeared into the crowd. I turned toward Eleanor, who inclined her head toward a passing server. I plucked her a glass of champagne from the silver tray and handed it to her.

Eleanor Giovanni drained the glass in a single long pull, not unlike Emmaline had moments before.

"Humph. Champagne is inferior to scotch when I'm in a mood." She laid her hand on my arm, which tensed further under her touch. She turned her shrewd gaze toward me.

"I see that you were already aware of my connection to Emmaline through Sebastian."

"Nico mentioned it last week."

"Nico, hmm, not Emmaline? Is that why you're upset with her?"

"I'm not..."

But I was. She should have told me the truth when we were eating breakfast together. Or last night when she mentioned Sebastian. The hurt welled up once again. I didn't enjoy being the last to know and I was unsure how to get Em to open up to me.

"Is that why he wants her fired?" Eleanor said.

"I don't know what you're talking—"

"Don't play coy, dear," Eleanor said. "I make a point of keeping an eye on Emmaline. She deserves my unfailing support. Did you know that she fought with me about—I feared we'd come to blows—about Sebastian's care?"

To blows? This night had taken a surreal turn.

Ellie grabbed another glass of champagne and downed it with the same speed as the first. She grimaced.

"Emmy wanted to be involved more, but she was so young and so broken. She wanted to marry him anyway. I've never seen her angrier or more devastated than when I told her I forbade such a decision. If Sebastian hadn't been in my house,

I fear she would never have spoken to me again. Only recently have I begun to see any glow in her cheeks or a spark in her eye."

I took a long, slow sip of my champagne. "You're correct. Nico's unhappy. He said if she'd lie by omission nothing's stopping Em from lying for her own personal gain. Or stealing our secrets."

Eleanor snorted. "Your brother has had a giant tree branch up his ass since he was fired from Gerard, Bernstein, and Mathers."

A tingle of shock rippled over my skin. "You know about that?"

"Of course. Due diligence is how I've kept most of my money all these years."

I shook my head, a little dazed by the older woman's continued truth bombs.

"And what about me?" I asked.

She raised a brow. "*You're* the one I chose for my Emmaline, Knox. Nico's too much of an automaton. But you—you have fire. Emmaline will burn bright for the right man—brighter even than she did for my grandson."

For a moment, her face morphed into one of unspeakable grief. She inhaled sharply and closed her eyes.

"I expect the first girl to be named after me, naturally."

"Naturally," I said, tone dry. I liked this woman more and more with each passing moment. She was witty, charming, and entirely too aware. I hoped to be half as plugged in and sharp at her age.

Her lips thinned. "And you might want to inform Nico that Emmaline choosing not to share a detail about her past was because she knew it would impact your willingness to hire her. She and I discussed it. Emmaline deserves a chance to be seen for her genius—not the sad sob story of a girl who lost her life at twenty."

For the first time since I met her, Eleanor Giovanni looked tired. Her eyes appeared misted, and I realized she mourned for her grandson just as one would an actual death. Whatever his current state, Melinda struck a painful chord for Eleanor when she called Sebastian crippled.

Mrs. Giovanni turned on her heel and was soon swallowed up in the crowd. If it hadn't been for the car crash, Emmaline would be Eleanor's granddaughter-in-law. Quite possibly, she would be the one accompanying Eleanor to our firm to discuss the beach home's renovations.

Without conscious thought, my gaze landed on Em. She sparkled in her dark gown, her cheeks lightly flushed, and her dark hair gleaming in the lights. Everything about her tugged at me.

I wanted nothing more than to bury my nose into the soft curve of her shoulder as I held her tight against me.

If life had aligned differently, Emmaline Schooler would be just as forbidden to me. In fact, she might be more so—married to another man.

I didn't like that realization, just as I didn't like the pang that ran through me at the thought of what Sebastian and his family lost in order to let Emmaline have *this* life.

I noted Em disengaging from the group and walking toward the gardens...just as Melinda peeled away from John's tight grip and headed the same direction.

Chapter Twenty-One
Emmaline

I made a loop but hadn't seen Bridget yet. I waved at Calliope, who sparkled next to her financier-husband.

I excused myself from Nannette and Nico, feeling a bit overwhelmed by Nico's narrow-lidded gaze. What had I done this week to deserve his clear standoffishness? I wasn't sure what to make of his current behavior, but he seemed to be sizing me up in an entirely new way than he had when I first interviewed with him.

"I'll go with you," Nannette said with a throaty giggle.

Nico rolled his eyes. "Can you get a glass of water in her before she embarrasses herself?" he asked, his voice low enough not to carry to the still chortling secretary. Nico had never shown such solicitude toward Nannette before and I wondered if he were interested in her, but then I noticed that his gaze was caught on a willowy brunette across the space. She was tall and lithe with a compact build. I felt like I'd seen her somewhere before.

"Sure," I said, but I wasn't sure if Nico heard me.

"Knox hasn't taken his eyes off you all night." Nannette giggled.

I shook my head at Nannette as I moved toward the peonies that rioted blues, pinks, and purples in the next flowerbed. "I don't know what you're talking about. Do you see a curvy blonde with a tall blond-haired guy? I wanted to say hello to them."

I craned my neck, searching the growing crowd. I spotted

Bridget, her smile wide, a moment before Nannette squeaked. Something wet and sticky splashed the side of my neck and down my arm.

Nannette's eyes widened as she took in the splatters. I couldn't look. I'd loved this dress and now...I swallowed hard.

I glanced down, shocked to see a thick red substance dripping toward my fingers. I slammed into a statue across the path, my vision blurring. A whimper rose in my chest. *Blood*. My whimpers increased.

I had a deep-seated fear of blood. I started to black out, my legs trying to fold under me. I forced myself to stay on my feet. If I didn't, I'd get more blood on me—there was a pool under my shoe.

I opened my mouth but nothing came out.

"Emmaline?" Nannette's voice.

"Help," I said, my voice faint. I was going to be sick all over my beautiful dress. My dress that was saturated with the fluid. I could feel it against my ribs, dripping down my fingertips, just as it had when we'd rolled and rolled, and I couldn't get to Sebastian. He was dying but I couldn't reach him.

My fingers fumbled and my vision blurred. I was losing consciousness. *Breathe, Em.*

"I'm going to be sick." Churning returned to my belly.

"I'll get some paper towels."

"No, don't leave me. I don't...I can't...not alone. Not again."

"Okay, I won't go." Nannette frowned at me.

Bridget arrived on my other side, already taking my pulse. "Are you okay?" she asked. Her mouth was set in a thin, angry slash.

"No." I shuddered, unable to stop my teeth from chattering.

Her lips pressed together even tighter. "Let's get you to the bench."

I gripped her wrist tight. "What if...what if she comes back?" My voice cracked. I didn't care. The panic hadn't subsided, and the mere idea of more liquid splashed on me caused my stomach to heave and crash.

"Simon's here," Bridget said. "He won't let anyone hurt you."

Nannette leaned in toward Bridget, who was checking my pupils now. "We need to get her out of here. She's really not in good shape."

"We will. As soon as I'm sure she isn't going into shock."

I might be. I flashed back to the moment when I'd managed to reach Sebastian's hand, our fingers slicked in blood. The thick substance dripped and pooled onto me, under me. I gagged and whimpered.

Sebastian's voice, all scratchy and filled with pain sifted into my mind. "Love...you...Emma...line...Never...forget...love...you."

I'd talked, sung, anything to keep his mind from spiraling too far into the pain. He'd quit talking. I wrapped my arms around my head, no longer caring about spreading the substance that coated my arms, a strange, keening ripped from my throat. I need the images to stop.

"Em, look at me." Knox's deep voice coaxed. He knelt in front of me, his gaze filled with concern.

"Why are you here?" I gasped.

His gaze darted to Bridget who still sat next to me, her hand cradling my bare, sticky arm. "Bridget had Nannette call me."

"Oh."

"I'm going to take you home."

He reached for me, but I put out my hands. "Someone dumped...it...I'm covered." My eyes filled with tears and my chin quivered.

"Is it...is it blood?" I managed to push past my numb lips.

"No, darling. It's red wine, which doesn't make it much better. But it's not blood. It's not like Sebastian, Em. You're safe."

I searched his gaze, needing something. His eyes were filled with compassion, waiting. At least he wasn't angry with me for my dismissal earlier. I couldn't handle that now, too. I sniffled. He swept me into his arms.

"I can walk."

His smile was soft and sweet. "I'm glad to hear that. But I'm still carrying you. I need this moment, Em. I need to feel that you're safe."

I rested my head on his shoulder, my arms creeping around his neck. He was warm and bulky and alive. I closed my eyes, trying to will down my panic. Mostly, though, I didn't want to look at the crowd that would be staring at me.

"I'm sorry, Knox."

He stopped at the valet booth and handed the attendant his ticket. "What could you possibly be sorry for, darling?"

That was the second time he'd called me that. I would never have taken Knox Wright for a terms-of-endearment kind of guy. I'd never been a woman who liked them before. But from him, I thrilled each time he said it.

"For freaking out."

I lifted my head in time to see the muscle in his jaw tick.

"You held up pretty well, I'd say, for getting attacked like that." His jaw clenched. "And yes, it was an attack."

"I don't understand," I mumbled.

"Neither do I. Yet. But I will."

Chapter Twenty-Two
Knox

I continued to cuddle Emmaline to my chest, thankful her gaze was more alert. Seeing her cowering and shivering on that bench, soaked in a deep crimson fluid, caused my heart to lodge in my throat. For a moment, the floor shifted under me, and I wasn't sure I'd be able to step forward.

Her slender hand settled on my nape, her skin warming. She'd been so pale and cold when I touched her—like a porcelain doll. But Emmaline was already reviving. Not that she could return to the gala in a stained dress.

Anger flared hot and hard in my chest. Someone sought her out. Someone frightened her, bullied her. I planned to find out who and why.

Though, I had a pretty good guess. And if I were correct, Melinda definitely wouldn't like the consequences.

Until then, I planned to keep Emmaline close…and safe. My crossover slid to a stop. The valet hopped out and hustled around to open the door for Emmaline. I thanked him and slipped him a fifty.

"Don't mention this to the press, please," I murmured, hoping Em couldn't hear me. "She's pretty shaken up and it would make it worse to find out someone blabbed about the incident."

The teen met my gaze, his firm. "I got a sister. She's been

bullied since elementary school. No one'll hear a word from me."

I hoped he kept his word. I patted his shoulder and walked around the hood of my car. I slid into my seat, glad to see Emmaline sitting upright, her seatbelt buckled. She twisted her fingers in her lap, her gaze out her window, throwing her profile into stark relief. Her forehead was high and smooth, her nose precisely sculpted. Her mouth was a lush pink bow—the best kind you'd find on a present, and her chin softly rounded.

She stole my breath.

Her long lashes settled on her cheeks and a single tear slid down her cheek. And, in that moment, a large piece of my heart.

"Let's get you home."

—— Å ——

I pulled into the driveway of her house, and she stared up at the two-story Colonial with a bone-deep exhaustion.

"I miss my parents. Coming home each night makes my chest ache."

"Ah, darling. I know that feeling."

"Yes, I imagine you do." She continued to stare.

"Let me walk you in," I said.

She shook her head. "I'm fine."

"You had some kind of flashback. You are not fine."

She rolled her eyes. "It's *my* body, *my* mind, and I said I was *fine*."

I huffed, frustrated that she wouldn't let me shoulder part of her burden. "I'm trying to help you."

"I don't need help."

"Yeah, you do, and that doesn't make you weak. It makes you

human." I gripped her chin, and she shivered as warmth transferred from my palm to her skin. My heart thudded a painful rhythm.

"You think Aidy, Nico, and I were all okay after our parents' disappearance? We weren't and in some ways we're still not. Aidy attached herself to a man, knowing he didn't love her, simply so she wouldn't be alone. Nico refuses to date and insists he's happy working hundred-hour weeks."

"And you? What is your vice, Knox?"

I looked into her eyes, wishing they weren't shadowed. "It's evolved," I said, my tone husky. "Before, it was work, blowing off steam with hockey...an occasional, no-strings hookup."

One of her dark brows rose. It was a sardonic gesture, one meant to flail me. Instead, it inflamed me.

"And now?" she asked.

"I'm still learning to live with the hole my parents left. But that doesn't mean I don't crave affection. That I don't value close relationships."

With each word I spoke, I inched closer to her mouth. I would kiss her again. Tonight had been a fascinating peek into Emmaline's life. Dressed as elegantly as a movie star, she fit in with the rich and powerful at the gala as if she'd been born to it—or at least planned to marry into it. Tear-stained cheeks and a quivering mouth, she snuggled in tight and let me comfort her. But that was overlaid with images of her dressed in her professional attire, pencil poised over paper, or her pale, composed face as we entered the hospital and then the soft affection as she held my niece.

Emmaline was real—a multi-dimensional woman whose passions ran deep. I wanted to be her passion. Without thought, I whispered those words as my lips brushed over hers. She shivered and opened for me.

I loved how she responded. Her taste flitted along my tongue, saturating my senses. I cupped her cheek and tugged her closer. The kiss burned past hot and into ravenous. From the moment I'd seen her tonight in that sexy dress, I'd wanted to strip it off her and feast on her body. Now, I would.

I kissed her and nibbled, licked, and sipped from her lips and mouth. I couldn't get close enough; I couldn't taste her enough. Her flavor seeped into my pores and I felt drunk with lust.

I broke the kiss, pulling back enough to meet her shadowed gaze.

"I'm going to tell you goodnight," I rumbled.

"You are? But…"

"I am," I said, my voice firm. "Because you've been through enough, and I refuse to take advantage of your emotions."

She sucked her lower lip into her mouth, which made me groan.

"I don't want to be alone," she whispered.

I studied her for a long moment. I couldn't leave her. But I also couldn't continue to kiss her—I wanted her too badly.

"I'll walk you in."

I pecked her lips before I opened my door and strode around to open hers. She slid out, all elegance, and moved past me toward the house. She glanced over her shoulder. "Come in? I need a shower."

I sighed even as I nodded. I follow her into her home, once again my eyes were harassed by the overwhelming array of doilies and overstuffed furniture.

"I know," Em said, voice soft. "It's too much. She was a cluttered person. She never threw things away. My dad and I would sneak the worst items out when she was gone." She touched a ragged piece of lace. "But, when they died, I found the memories buried in the items, and I began to understand why she kept them."

Em surrounded herself with ghosts. She pushed so hard to return to her life, to carve something out for herself, but each time she did, she was backhanded with her history. Instead of clenching my fists, I wrapped her in my arms.

She sighed, resting her cheek against my chest. I wanted nothing more than for her to be happy. I wanted to be the one to make her smile, make her eyes light up. I tilted her head back and resisted the urge to kiss her.

"Why don't you take a shower?"

Fear crept into her eyes, but she dropped her gaze, lashes hiding her reaction.

"I won't leave you. Not until you're ready."

Her gaze flew back to meet mine. Relief and something fierce—something that felt very much like the soft, melting that was currently occurring in my chest, eased through her eyes and then into every part of her body.

"I—" She shook her head. Rising on tiptoe, she pressed a soft kiss to my lips. "Thank you."

Before I managed to react, she'd slipped from my arms and up the stairs.

Chapter Twenty-Three
Emmaline

I hugged my arms around me, but it was a cold substitute for Knox. I turned on my bathroom light and began to pull the pins from my hair. Dried red wine saturated my gown, ruining it. I frowned at the waste, wondering who could possibly hate me so much as to throw drinks on me.

My shower was long, and I relaxed into the water. Since the accident, I'd fought hard to keep the memories at bay. Tonight, in a place I felt safe, they'd been forced on me.

I inhaled, the steam worming into my sinuses, as I stopped fighting with my memories. Sebastian's proposal flitted through my mind, the certainty of my answer, of our future, the shock as I looked into my mother's wide eyes the moment before Sebastian's SUV slammed into their car. The pain, the scream of metal, the slash of glass fragments into my skin. And Sebastian...knowing he was hurt, his blood dripping onto my cheek, sliding down my neck...me unable to help him, pinned.

I slammed my fists against the tiles. I gnashed my teeth. I cried, big, harsh sobs. My knees wanted to give out, but I pushed back into my feet, rooting to rise as Calliope would say. Finding my foundation, finding my strength, I used my legs and stood up.

I turned my face into the cooling spray and heaved a breath. I was alive. Sebastian was, too. He was finding his place in this new world, as was I. Aidy, Bridget, Calliope—all helped me find the joy of friendship, of being present and laughing, again. Knox helped me feel smart, capable, attractive.

I was alive. I deserved a life. Slowly, the tension eased from my muscles.

I heaved a final breath as I turned off the faucets. I left some of the weight of the grief in that shower. I was alive. I was…

I'd let go of the past. I would live. And I wouldn't take these moments, my friendships, these connections to others for granted.

I wrapped myself in my robe, feeling lighter than I had in years.

—— Å ——

Knox rose from my couch, where he'd been sitting, his gaze roving over my face before dropping to take in my fleece pajama set.

"You look better," he said even as he reached out and touched the corner of my eye. The skin was puffy and red from my crying jag in the shower.

"I feel better," I said. "Do you want a drink?"

He shook his head, stepping back and resettling on the sofa. He tucked his phone into his pocket. "I let Ellie know you're okay. I figured she'd be worried."

I settled next to him and it seemed right to slide into his side, which quickly became an embrace. "Yeah. Thank you for thinking of her. And, Knox?" I tilted my face up so that I could see his expression. "Thank you for tonight. I'm sorry you had to see me like that."

He pressed his lips to my temple—a soft brush to let me know that he was there both with me and for me.

"Your friend Bridget saw Melinda throw the wine on you," he

said, pulling back enough to meet my gaze again. This time he searched my face. I sucked in a breath and blew it out.

"That was really mean of her, but you know what? Maybe I needed the push to finally let myself remember."

His features hardened. "No, Em. She needs to be held responsible. That was cruel."

I clasped his much larger hand, reveling in the warmth of his fingers as they slid between mine. "Those memories held me captive for a long time," I murmured. "They were the reason I gave up med school, the reason I quit volunteering at the hospital. I let that night take those dreams from me. But now..." I wasn't sure how to explain myself.

"Remember when I asked you if you missed hockey?"

He nodded. "And I told you I'd made a life for myself. A good one. That's what I'm doing, finally. I'm making a life. Part of that meant facing those memories." I sucked my lower lip between my teeth, worrying it. "Would you stay here tonight?"

He cupped my cheek and met my gaze. His solemn. "I'm glad you asked because I really didn't want to fight with you about that. I'm not sure I could leave you alone."

I smiled at him. There was more we should talk about, and we would, but for now, I rose and pulled him upstairs. And into my bedroom.

He hesitated at the threshold. "You want me to sleep in here? With you?"

Shyness slammed into me, but I nodded. "If you're okay with that?"

He swallowed, his focus on my bed. He lifted his gaze, eyes

blazing. Light played over the strong angles of his face. Goodness, he was gorgeous. Thoughtful. What I needed.

"I'd like nothing more than to slip into that bed with you and hold you all night."

That warm, gooey feeling grew. I wasn't sure how I'd gotten so lucky with Knox. He was thoughtful and caring while also protective and fierce.

"I'll get you a toothbrush," I said.

When he stripped down to his undershirt and boxer briefs and climbed into bed behind me a few minutes later, my body relaxed. Knox was here with me. I felt safer and more cared for than I had in years. And I reveled in that feeling.

Chapter Twenty-Four
Knox

I woke early, as I often did still even after all these years of a more typical workday. Hockey hours were ingrained. But unlike most other mornings, I didn't try to fall back asleep. Instead I drew Em closer, content to hold her.

She snuggled in even tighter, her nose rubbing against my shoulder, her breath puffing against my neck. I wanted this, I realized. Not just this morning, but every morning. I wanted to wake to Em in my arms. This was what my father had been trying to explain. *This* was love.

I was sure of it.

I considered how Nico would react and decided I'd talk to Aidy first. She and Em were tight, and Aidy would want Em to stay at the firm even after Aidy returned in another few weeks from her leave. And we'd need Em because Aidy wasn't coming back full time immediately.

I'd figure it out—I had to because now that I knew how right Em was for me, I refused to let her go.

"You're thinking about something awfully hard," she murmured.

Her voice was still raspy with sleep. I cherished this piece of Em, and I tried to memorize every detail.

"What are you doing today?" I asked.

She blinked up at me, her eyes focusing on my face. "My plans? Isn't it Saturday?"

I nodded. "Let me take you to breakfast. Spend the day with me."

She searched my face for a long moment—so long I caught my breath.

"I'd like that."

I smiled. "Me, too." I rolled over so she was atop my chest. "I like this, too." I ran my hands along her ribs and over her hips.

Her breath caught and her eyes clouded. "I'm not ready for sex yet, Knox."

I levered up and pressed a soft kiss to the corner of her mouth. "Who was asking for sex?"

She pulled back, frowning. I didn't want her to remember Aidy's comments about my sexual habits, so I smacked her softly on the bottom. "Time to get up. Day's a-wasting."

She squeaked and rolled off me, nearly tumbling out of bed. I caught her and she laughed, eyes bright, cheeks flushed. I brushed her hair back from her temple, loving this moment—loving *her*.

I wished I could tell my father I'd found her—my woman. A pang hit me but it was muted by the joy of Em's smile.

I sat up and smacked another kiss to her lips. "I have a change of clothes in my car. Mind if I grab a shower?"

She shook her head. "Make yourself at home. I'll fix some coffee."

She rose and stretched, and I struggled with the need to grab her and pull her back into the bed. She needed time.

And I needed to make sure Em understood just what I was committing to her.

Over breakfast at a small neighborhood café, she admitted she'd never been ice skating before, and my jaw dropped right before I was about to take the first bite of my omelet. I pointed my fork at her.

"This must be rectified. Today. *Now.*"

Flustered, she grabbed her napkin, wadding it into a ball. "I don't know, Knox. I mean, skating's dangerous."

"Not with me, it's not." At her continued consternation. I leaned over the table, grabbed her hand and kissed her knuckles. "I'm a pro. Well, basically. I won't let you fall."

Her wide eyes captured mine. "Promise?"

"Promise," I replied, heart pounding. She thought this was about skating, but I meant in life. I'd tell her that—soon. As soon as I figured out how to make Nico see reason and that my happiness was tied up in Em's.

She held my hand as I chose a pair of skates for her and even as I dropped to my heels. I extricated my fingers from hers to pull off her pink Converse. But once I had her laces tied and she tried to stand, wobbling more than a newborn colt, she wavered.

"You go. I'll watch," she said.

I placed my thumb on her lower lip before she could sink her teeth into it. "I've got you, Em."

She met my gaze, hers filled with anxiety, and, dammit, I wanted to believe that was hope. She'd been through so much.

The fact that she was giving me a chance, especially when my ex was the person that hurt her last night, caused butterflies to explode in my belly. I'd never felt like this about a woman before.

I cupped her cheek, my thumb cradling her jaw instead of sliding my hand into her hair like I wanted to. She'd pulled it up into a ponytail and I liked the thick, long cascade down her back. I brought my lips so close to hers I could feel the warmth of her skin. "Trust me, Emmaline."

I held my breath until she whispered, "Okay."

As if it were the most natural thing in the world, I let my lips drift over hers in a light caress before I pulled back and settled on the metal bench, tugging off my hiking boots and sliding on my skates.

I did up the laces with practiced ease and grabbed Em's wrist. I tugged her lightweight sweater from her fist and clasped her hand. She'd dressed in jeans, like me, and topped it with the silver sweater over a hot pink camisole. She was casual but still sexy as fuck.

She squeaked, falling against me as soon as her skates touched the ice. I chuckled, enjoying her chest rubbing against mine. Instead of kissing her again as I wanted, I lifted her and turned her so her back was to my front. I wrapped my left arm around her waist and grabbed her right hand.

"Let's go."

Her skates clawed at the ice, but I continued to glide. Eventually she relaxed. With a soft laugh, she dropped her head against my shoulder. "You're better than training wheels."

I smirked as I wove between the sparse crowd. A couple of teen boys turned toward me, eyes widening as we skated past.

"Dude," one of them whispered. "He's practically holding her up. Think I could do that with Chelsea?"

Em and I shared a laugh.

"Dude, you are really strong," Em said, imitating the boy's deep voice. Her eyes softened, and her eyes dipped to my lips. She brought her gaze back up to mine, her breath a little choppy.

"Thank you for this. I like skating with you."

I slowed as we neared the furthest corner. I turned her, easing her against the boards and pressed my body to hers. "I like skating with you, too," I murmured.

I lowered my head, giving her time to pull away. Instead she raised her chin and pressed our lips together. Instead of the light soft brush I'd planned on, Em opened her mouth and ran her tongue along my bottom lip. I slid my skates forward until they bumped against the boards and took her mouth.

"Dude, he's getting some. I definitely need to bring Chelsea."

I broke away from Em as we both cracked up.

"I guess making out at the rink isn't my best move," I said.

She glanced at me through her lashes. "I enjoyed it."

I pressed into her tighter so that she felt my hardening cock against her belly. "So did I."

Her eyes widened and fear crept in, darkening her beautiful eyes. I sighed as I pulled back. "That's enough for today," I said.

She nodded, but we both knew I wasn't just talking about skating.

Once we were back on the bench, sliding our feet into our shoes, I glanced over at her. Her brows were tugged low and she stared at her laces as if they held all the world's answers.

"So…"

She glanced up at me.

"I'd like to date you. I mean, more than just today. I enjoy spending time with you, Em."

The frown returned. "What about Nico and the employee policy? I don't want to cause any trouble."

I clasped her hand in mine and tugged her to her feet.

"You haven't, and you won't. There's no reason for Nico to be upset with you."

Not now that Em had proven herself trustworthy. My muscles tightened as I remembered those tense seconds before Em had called me to tell me about the strange file on her desk. But she'd passed Nico's stupid test, and now I was going to make him see reason.

"Let me worry about Nico," I said.

Trust shone from her eyes as she nodded. "Okay."

Chapter Twenty-Five
Emmaline

Instead of taking me home, as I'd expected, Knox asked if he could take me on a drive. I swallowed as I considered my options. I wanted to spend more time with him—I enjoyed his full attention and those large, warm hands cradling me with such gentleness. My other option was to rattle around in my parents' house or rip out the flooring in my beach cottage. There was no contest: I wanted to spend time with Knox.

We walked out of the rink into the bright sunshine, both of us sliding on our sunglasses, laughing at our simultaneous reaction. He looked really good in his Aviators. Once in his vehicle, he drove toward Newport.

"Why are we here?" I asked.

"I wanted to show you one of my favorite places," he said with a grin.

He turned off the main street onto Ferry Road. I could make out the sound of waves nearby through our open windows as he turned again at a sign for Blithewold Mansion. Once parked in the large lot, he walked around and opened my car door.

"Have you been to the Gateway to Spring?" he asked.

I shook my head, and Knox grinned.

"You're in for a treat."

He bought tickets and then walked me around the side of the building.

"You want to give me a lesson?" I asked, looking up at the large residence.

"This place isn't as popular as The Breakers, but it's another summer estate built around the turn of the last century."

I eyed the pale yellow brick-and-stone façade. "This is an amazingly well-maintained example of the Country Place Era," I said, awed by the deep portico with its white columns.

"I do love the arts and crafts era," Knox said, giving the large home a look of approval. "There was a fire in 1906 and it was rebuilt. Now, it has forty-five rooms. But that's not why I brought you here."

We rounded the corner, heading into the warm afternoon sun. I raised my eyebrows as he led me to the gardens. My jaw dropped at the rows and rows and happy yellow daffodils swaying in the cool ocean breeze, a carpet of sunshine that ended at the beach. A few people wandered through the paths while others settled at benches, watching the waves crashing against the brown sand.

"This is amazing," I whispered. "There are thousands of them."

"Over fifty," Knox said.

I glanced up at him. "You've been here before?" A pang hit me as I considered Knox bringing another woman here.

"With my parents, Nico, and Aidy. My mom liked Daffy Days," he said. "Spring in Rhode Island can be short, so she made the best of it."

I nodded, my gaze darting back to the happy yellow flowers. He tucked a few strands of my hair back behind my ear as the wind kicked up. I shivered and he wrapped his arm around my shoulder, pulling me against his chest.

I looked up at him. His mouth was soft as he leaned down, his motion slow, measured, giving me plenty of time to deny him. I didn't want to; I rose up on my tiptoes and covered his mouth with mine.

The kiss was languid, slow, soft.

He pulled back, continuing to cradle my shoulder in his large palm. I wished I could see his eyes, grasp what he was thinking.

"Thank you for bringing me here. Thank you for wanting to spend the day with me."

"Ah, Em. It's truly my pleasure."

I tilted my head back and tried to peer through the mirrored lenses of his sunglasses—to no avail. "Nico won't let me stay at Wright and Associates, will he?"

Knox squeezed my shoulder. "I don't want you to leave, and neither does Aidy. We'll figure this out, I promise you."

I returned my gaze to the ocean, but the moment of giddiness had passed. Being with Knox like this would cost me my job. The problem was, in that moment, I wanted Knox more than I wanted to return to the office.

And that realization scared me.

Chapter Twenty-Six
Knox

I took Em home after dinner at a small seafood restaurant on the water. She seemed lost in thought, her brows pinched, and I didn't want to push her about her former fiancé—or the fact that I wanted to be more than her current kissing buddy. But hockey had taught me patience, and this wasn't the moment to skate forward and steal the puck.

So, I kissed her goodnight and settled back in my vehicle with a heavy sigh. Longing poured from me as I started the engine. Soon. Soon I'd get Em to realize how much she wanted a relationship with me.

—— A ——

Thankfully, Nico stayed too busy with travel and catching up in meetings to focus on the office. I needed to talk to him, but I dragged my feet. Em and I were professional in the office, so it wasn't as if Nico had any cause for concern.

That next weekend, I took her back to Newport and we toured Marble House. As we entered the dining room, Em caught me up on her thoughts about Richard Morris Hunt's depiction of the Petit Trianon at Versailles in Newport. We chuckled at the opulence of the red drawing room and stood wide-eyed at the painted dining room ceiling.

"The amount of gold filigree…" Em murmured.

"It would probably solve world hunger for a year or two."

Em shot me a glance and I raised an eyebrow in return.

"You don't say what I expect you to," she said.

"You don't either." I linked our fingers together and pressed a kiss to her knuckles. "That's part of why I enjoy spending time with you."

"Aidy will be back in six more weeks," she murmured.

"So she will, but that doesn't mean we won't keep you, too."

Em turned away, but I saw her catch her lower lip. So that's what worried her—her continued employment. I guess I should have realized.

I'd have to find time to talk to Nico. The mere thought of his response caused my mood to sour. Nico and flexibility were never in the same sentence—or the same universe.

We both were quiet the rest of the afternoon, lost in our thoughts. Nico was called out of the office on a last-minute trip to the West Coast for a possible museum build in Seattle, which he followed up with a trip to Des Moines about an arts center. Both opportunities were fantastic, and I hoped we'd land one of the contracts. But more importantly, I was able to spend the week with Em, unburdened by my concerns about Nico.

The next Saturday, I took her on the Cliff Walk, a scenic three-and-a-half-mile walkway bordering the back lawns of many Newport mansions. I set out a thick wool blanket on the beach, and we watched the sunset while enjoying a bottle of local cider. When she rested her cheek on my shoulder, my heart beat with pleasure.

This feeling was what I'd been missing, and I wanted more.

Nico strode into the office that Monday and my heart seemed to drop like a speeding puck right into my guts. Em and I needed more time. I needed to convince her everything would be okay with Nico. More, I needed to come up with some contingency plans if Nico refused to budge on his stupid policy. I'd tried to talk to Aidy about it yesterday, but her ex had shown up, and she was so far past stressed; I plucked my niece from her arms and shooed her into her bathroom for a long soak.

"Aidy's ex is in town," I said, deciding to pre-empt any questions about Em and me with Aidy's current issues. "She's going to need you to run interference there tonight so she can shower."

Nico turned to glower at me over his shoulder. He seemed even angrier than he'd been all those weeks ago when he accused Em of lying.

"I can go tonight, maybe tomorrow, but then I have to head out to New York." He undid his suit coat and settled into his chair. "I've been called in as a potential witness for a trial."

"Trial? One of your projects?"

His lips thinned further. "No. I almost wish. This is a civil case between Amanda," he sneered her name, "and another man she manipulated and cheated after me."

I shook my head. That woman had really gotten around. "So she has a pattern?"

"Definitely."

"Any more details on that one?" I asked.

Nico buried his fingers in his hair. "None. But I wish to fuck that woman would quit haunting me. It's been ten years."

I bit the inside of my cheek to keep from offering any advice—Nico wouldn't want to hear it anyway.

"Let me catch up on some stuff and we can meet in a few hours," he said, clearly worn out. I nodded as I rose. I wondered if there were a way to help him, but I could only do so much, especially if Nico didn't want my help.

Fifteen minutes later, Emmaline walked in, her gaze drifting toward Nico's shut door. She said hello to Morris and Clint. I completed my task as Emmaline worked on hers. She was developing sketches for a special needs dance studio, and her ideas so far had been refreshing. I'd grinned as I clicked through the schematics, surprised by how much I liked the idea.

I finished up the sketches for a presentation to an up-and-coming restaurateur later in the week and fielded a few inquiries.

"What's on the schedule?" Nico asked.

"Well, you had the two presentations. We've started the demolition on the Carrington reno, the Smithson and Giovanni projects are ahead of schedule, and I took a meeting about a new restaurant and another for a dance studio."

Nico curled his lip. "Dance studio?"

"It's a cool project," I said. "It's for special needs kids. Already backed by the Carringtons—they gave her our name—and the woman running the place is a famous dancer."

"Like a ballerina?"

I nodded. "She's big time. The lead in Swan Lake and all that. I don't know why she's opening a space here, but we'll need to come up with some ingenious engineering for the wheel-chair users.

"Point is, we're on top of everything, and I can hold down things here if you want to get ready for that project," I said.

He raised his head, eyes glassy, darkness swirling in their depths. "I'd...you know what? Yeah. I'd like that. I just need a break."

He wasn't speaking of time off from the firm. Whatever Amanda did to him, he wasn't over. I cleared my throat.

"Get out of here, Nico. Go see Lilia. Dick-hole Jeff will hate that you're there as an added bonus to niece snuggles."

The corner of Nico's mouth lifted briefly. "Sounds like a solid plan."

I grinned back, pleased to have bought myself more time. I refused to let panic override my joy. I'd figure it out—Em was it for me.

Nico left early, and the next few days were dreamlike in their perfection. I spent every evening with Em, taking her to dinner or even just a stroll along the waterfront. That Friday night I took her to dinner at a Chilean-fusion restaurant. She'd released her long, dark hair from its daily updo and it cascaded over her shoulders and down her back in shiny tresses that begged for my touch.

She eyed the menu with enthusiasm I found contagious. "My grandmother used to make a *cazuela*," she murmured. A soft smile drifted across her mouth. "I think I'll get that."

I wanted to ask if she were sure, but her eyes were clear as she launched into a story about her mother's attempts to make feijoada, a black bean and pork stew.

"She managed to burn the meat so badly, my father took the whole mess out to the trash bin, pot and all."

She pressed her hands to her stomach, her giggles making it harder for her to talk.

"It was terrible. Sebastian was the only one who even tried to eat it."

I jolted at her ex's name, but she continued to laugh, her eyes bright with happiness. I reached over and clasped her hand in mine, telling her a story of the time Ryder and I tried to recreate my mom's cookies.

"I thought we'd managed to burn down the house when I saw the black smoke pouring out of the oven."

The waiter dropped off our plates, and Em pressed her napkin to her lips as my laughter joined hers.

When I drove her home, our mood was mellow, content. But as we approached her driveway, I hoped this time—tonight—she'd invite me in again. Since the night of the gala, I'd stopped at her doorway, not wanting to push for more than she was ready to give—that and because my failed relationship with Melinda weighed on my mind. I didn't want Nico to have another reason to attack Em, and that meant I couldn't invite her to my place. Not that she'd asked to come over.

But after spending every free moment with her lately, I wanted nothing more than to lose myself in her body. I wanted her to know just how much she meant to me.

She sucked on her lower lip as we sat in her driveway. She turned toward me. Shadows drifted over her skin, but her eyes were steady as she faced me in the car. "Would you like to come inside tonight?"

Chapter Twenty-Seven
Knox

I hesitated. "What do you mean?"

She blew out a breath. "I want you, Knox."

She exited the car, not waiting for me to open her door, as I usually did. I hustled out my side and met her on the porch. She slid the key into the lock and opened the door. Soft light spilled out from the hallway as we stepped inside.

I hesitated for a moment.

"Em, you have to know I want you."

The soft curve of her lips was nearly as erotic as her slow, deliberate release of the buttons that held together the bodice of her black dress. While not overly revealing, the skirt showed off a few inches of her toned thigh, and I'd been salivating with the need to touch her soft skin since I picked her up.

"Good. I want you too."

She dropped her hands away, so I got faint hints of lavender lace, and wound her arms around my neck. My hands fell to her hips.

"I want this, Knox."

"Tell me if you want to stop."

She nodded, her gaze trained on mine. I bent my head and kissed her. First, a gentle rub of lips that soon became a soft dance of tongue. She tasted like the cinnamon and chocolate of her dessert, that faint vanilla and citrus scent wafting from her hair and skin, driving me wild. I tilted my head and plundered her mouth. She whimpered, crushing her chest against mine.

Finally, we broke apart.

"I'm desperate for you."

She shuddered. "Take me upstairs, to bed."

"Are you sure?" I searched her face. This moment—it mattered.

"Yes. I feel…"

Before she could say any more, I rained kisses on her chin, her cheeks, her neck.

"Feel with me, darling. Let me help you fly."

"Don't make promises you can't keep," she said with a breathy chuckle.

"I *always* keep my promises."

She sobered as she studied me. I waited. She needed to make this choice. I held my breath, waiting, desperate. Her gaze still on mine, she leaned back in. When our lips touched this time, magic tingled through my veins.

As my lips molded over hers, taking her higher, my hands slid down her jaw, over her neck. I hesitated. I licked across her lower lip.

"Are you okay with me touching you?" I asked against her mouth.

"Yes. Please."

I loved the sultriness of her voice. I cupped her breasts and we both moaned. She was soft and her flesh fit well in my hands. I slid my palms over her, contouring her curves to my hands.

She brought her hands up to my hair, her fingers sliding through the unruly mess and took my mouth in a searing kiss. Her tongue rubbed against mine, and she arched her back so that her breasts overflowed my hands. Her hard nipples pressed into my palms.

"Upstairs," she gasped against my mouth.

I gathered her in my arms and bolted up the stairs to her room. It was as neat as the last time I'd stayed there. And it smelled of Em. I set her on the bed and leaned in as I claimed her mouth for another kiss, ecstatic to be in her space, giddy with need.

I managed to tug my lips from hers and slid them along her jaw, her neck, taking the same path as my palms. My tongue darted out to taste the sweet flesh of her collar bones before I dipped it into the lush valley between the globes of her breasts. I smoothed my hands over her rib cage as I slid my lips back up to her jaw. I nipped and nibbled over to her ear, and Em shuddered. I wrapped my arms around her as I settled against her multitude of pillows. With a quick lift of my arms, Em settled over my lap. I rested back against the pillows as I tugged her closer, enjoying the feel of her breasts rubbing against my chest.

"Just where you belong," I murmured against her neck.

Her fingers bit into my biceps as she stared down at me, her lids heavy. She licked her lower lip—I watched the slow drag of her tongue across the lush cranberry stain. This time, I cupped the back of her head and pressed our lips together. I was a starved man, and she was my perfect meal. We kissed and kissed. I lost time and self in her, and I never wanted the moment to end.

I worked my hands under her skirt and slid my hands up her outer thighs. She ground against my aching dick, and my hips bucked into hers, seeking the right friction. "Em. I want you.

So bad."

"Yes," she moaned. "Yes."

Never had I felt such a ferocious need. "Need you."

"*Yes.*"

The word was low, throaty, and caused my blood to pump harder in my veins. She turned her head and kissed me again. And again, her fingers in my hair, our lips rubbing, her tongue dueling with mine.

My fingers found the edge of her panties. I slid my fingers inside, past her soft outer lips to her wet, warm, center. She ground down on me and I slipped a finger into her warmth.

Desire exploded in my veins much like champagne going to my head. I dragged my finger out, shaking with the need to replace it with my dick. She was soft and warm, tight and perfect.

"Em..."

"I want you, Knox. I need this."

"I'll give you anything. Everything."

I kissed her again. This time, when I pushed my finger into her, I added my thumb to her clit, rubbing in gentle circles. She pressed harder against my hand, which added pressure to my throbbing erection.

That friction...amazing. I needed to be inside of her.

I rubbed her clit harder. She tugged my hair, her eyes glassy. I added a second finger. She met my gaze, her eyes as desperate as I felt.

With gentle pressure, I maneuvered us so her back was against the headboard. I needed to free myself from the constraints of my dress pants. She batted my hands away and slid down my zipper.

She rubbed her soft palm against my dick, and I gritted my teeth, trying hard not to curse or even move. I needed her hand there. I would always need her warm skin on me. But my body screamed to connect with hers. Tingles built in the base of my spine, wrapping around and pulsing through my balls.

"Em..."

She climbed back into my lap and rose up, slipped her panties to the side and lowered herself on my dick.

My wide eyes met hers.

"Condom," I managed to choke out.

"Where?" she asked as she lifted herself off me. I groaned at the loss of her warm heat, and she bit her lip, two spots of color blooming over those rounded cheekbones.

I fumbled up onto my hip so I could reach my pants. I pulled out my wallet, and I grabbed the condom I kept there. I rolled it on. She hesitated for a moment, her soft lips hovering just over my tip. My hips jerked, and I slid an inch or so into her warmth. We both gasped. She ground down, I pressed up into her welcoming silky clutch.

I needed to stop. I couldn't. She felt too good.

I was halfway inside her. I pulled back, halted, and my hips jerked forward. She dropped her knees on either side of my hips and I slid home.

Home.

I couldn't catch my breath. My thoughts turned fuzzy. Em's body snuggled around mine but it was more than that—she felt right in my arms. Her weight, her scent, the tickle of her head against my cheek were perfection.

Em undulated, her head falling back, her neck exposed. I gathered her closer to me and pressed open-mouthed kisses on her neck. My hips pressed against hers. She swiveled her hips. I pulled out about halfway and slid back in. Her mouth stayed open in a silent moan as she rose and fell over me.

The tingles bubbled together headier than any champagne.

I gripped her hips and ground her tight against my base, causing my balls to tighten further. This...she...amazing.

"I should stop."

"No. Don't. Please don't stop. Knox."

The way she moaned my name slammed pleasure through my abdomen and curled around my spine.

"More," she whispered, seeming to read my mind. "More, harder."

I lifted her and then slammed her back down.

She whimpered out the word again. She was so wet, so tight. No way I'd ever get enough.

Again and again, I lifted her almost off me before filling her up. Sweat dripped from my forehead and shone at her temples. Her breathing was erratic, her whimpers egging me on. No way to hold this off. I'd pull out before I came—after I brought her to the peak.

I pushed her forward against my abs as I shoved in, trying to stimulate her clit. On the fourth brush, her eyes rolled back, and she shuddered. The tight ripples slid over my sensitized flesh and I orgasmed with her.

It went on and on, both of us shuddering and gasping from the pleasure.

Chapter Twenty-Eight
Emmaline

I woke, wrapped in Knox's arms. I snuggled back, enjoying the warmth from his body. For the first time in years, I felt content. No. I was happy. Except, as far as I knew, Knox still hadn't spoken to Nico.

I didn't want to lie to Nico about my relationship with Knox—not that Knox had asked me to, but he didn't answer my question as to whether he'd told Nico about us.

I lifted my head, pushing my tangled hair from my cheek. Knox lay on his side, lips slightly parted, breathing deep. *What he did to me.*

I was falling for him. Hard.

I sucked on my lower lip, considering my options. I'd broken the guidelines. As a rule-follower, that bothered me, deeply. I finally rose before the sun, unable to untangle the mess of the situation.

I rose, careful not to wake him, and slipped into a robe, heading down the stairs and into the kitchen. Coffee would help me think.

I settled at my kitchen table with a mug of coffee that I didn't sip. My eyes burned and my head pounded, but I gamely pulled out a pad and pen, deciding my best course of action was to make a list.

I had to come clean to Nico. That was first.

No, I needed to explain why I hadn't told Knox from the get-go that I'd been engaged to Sebastian Giovanni. Maybe that should be first. Doubt pooled in my belly, making my stomach roil.

I turned toward the sound of feet on the stairs. My breath hissed from my lungs. Knox stood there in a gray T-shirt and black gym shorts.

I tightened my short bathrobe and rose. His eyes burned as he took me. Then, in what seemed like a single bound, he was in front of me, his arm snaked around me. He tugged me flush against him.

"I hope that outfit is for me," he rumbled. His lips slammed down on mine, and I kissed him back with the same passion. Oh, this felt good. So right.

Perfect.

Within moments, our clothes were flying and then I was on the counter, the coolness of the granite beneath my butt a counterpoint to his hot, hard flesh between my thighs. And then he was inside me. We kissed, sharing breath, our hands touching, entwining. I moaned and threw my head back, bringing up my pelvis to meet his thrusts.

Nirvana hit like a sledgehammer and we both cried out, convulsing.

I tried to catch my breath.

"That was…unexpected," I murmured. The rawness of my thoughts from earlier returned, chafing at my emotions. I'd never reacted this strongly to Sebastian.

Wait…

"I told Nico you weren't interested in our secrets," he muttered.

Everything seemed to still. I wasn't sure my heart beat. "What?" I asked.

Nico...what did he have to do with this?

"He saw us out together, I guess, and isn't happy about it. He seems to think because you lied about Sebastian, you must have other ulterior motives."

I stiffened.

"Ulterior motives."

Knox hugged me tighter. "But that's bullshit. We can't keep our hands off each other. Last night...now...it's instinctive. Our sexual attraction is off the charts. Plus, it's not like you've been in my study, at my house, or even my office unattended."

"And that's a good thing?" I asked, wondering why I wouldn't be allowed in his office.

"It must be. I mean, sex has never been this combustible." I felt him smile into my hair. "I do it for you, Em. You're so hot for me. No way you can feel *that* level of attraction for anyone else."

Something dirty seeped into my belly. "What did you say?"

He pulled back enough to see my face. Whatever he saw must have caused him to realize my anger was deep. And it was—but it was built on hurt.

"I...I..."

I shoved on his shoulders, pushing until he stumbled back, out of my formerly willing body. His cum slid down my thighs, further embarrassing and enraging me.

I scrambled off the counter and grabbed the first item from the floor—my robe—and slid my arms into the sleeves. My hands shook so hard, I struggled to tie the belt.

Knox leaned forward. "I just meant that Nico was wrong. The moment you saw that file he placed on your desk, you called to make it right."

My eyes widened so far, I felt like they might pop out of my head. "You *planted* that file on my desk to test my loyalty?"

"I didn't."

I bent down, picking up his clothes. I handed them to him by slamming them into his chest. He had no choice but to take them.

"Explain this to me."

"The file was Nico's idea. He texted me, asking me to have you come in. He was watching you."

"Why?" I asked. I felt numb. I hadn't realized it was possible for my entire body to simply shut down.

"He was pissed when he found out you were engaged to Sebastian. He thought you were keeping details from him on purpose. And that you were only with me to steal our designs."

"I was." My chest rose and fell. "Because losing Sebastian broke me, and I don't like to be reminded of that low point."

"I get what you're saying, I really do, but Nico fixated on what he considered your omissions. He assumed if you'd left out details about that, then you might have lied about other things..."

After another glimpse of my face, he slid into his boxer-briefs and pulled on his shirt.

"Look, Em, it wasn't a big deal. You passed his test."

I crossed my arms over my chest. "*This* time. But what about the next time he decides I must be hiding something? And it might not be a big deal to you, but it's my integrity he questioned. *Mine.*"

"There won't be a next time. You're nothing like Melinda—"

"That is the second time you've compared me to your ex-girl-friend. I find it just as distasteful as when you compared yourself to Sebastian."

"I'm sorry. I'm not trying to be a dick. It's just that Melinda—"

"Isn't me," I snapped. Then, I gasped. "*That's* why you never invited me to your place." My hands balled into fists. "You're just as bad as Nico. You lumped me in with the women of your past."

He scowled. "And you've been waiting for a reason to get mad at me. You wanted us to end before we even had a chance to start."

I looked away but not before I saw the hurt seep into his eyes, obliterating the anger. "No, Knox. I didn't. I wanted to take us slow so that there weren't secrets and half-truths between us."

"Well, you did a poor job of that, didn't you?" he said, his tone sarcastic.

"Oh, and you've been so honest with me," I snapped.

"I was a hockey player, expected to be a first-round draft pick. Do you have *any* idea the kind of attention I garnered? Any idea what it's like to question everyone's motives—you never know if people like you or the fame that surrounds you."

"Yes. I do know." My shoulders dropped, and I turned away. "I'm exhausted, Knox. Please leave. I just can't do this with you now."

"Fine."

I heard him slide into his shorts and pick up his shoes.

"You know, it doesn't have to be this way," he said.

"Maybe you should have thought of that before you pushed past all my barriers and hurt me more than anyone else ever has."

"Em..."

He moved closer. I shook my head. He reached out anyway, and I knocked off his hand.

I turned and faced him. All the anger and stress and fear rose up. "You hurt me." I shoved at his chest. "*You*. You said I was precious but You. Hurt. Me."

I shoved him one last time and then he was out the door. I slammed it and turned the lock.

Then, I slid down the wood and burst into tears.

Chapter Twenty-Nine
Knox

Unsure how to proceed after Em kicked me out, I stood at her door. When I heard her sobbing, I leaned in, wanting to comfort her.

"Em, please," I said.

Either she didn't hear me, or she refused to answer.

I leaned my forehead against the wood panel next to the glass and caught sight of her huddled into a ball, her long, bare legs shaking as much as her shoulders.

I replayed the conversation in my head, wincing at my comments. She was correct to have called me out on turning my relationship with her into a competition with Sebastian. That's how I viewed most of my relationships, but, by doing so, I'd caused Em pain.

I pressed my hand to the glass. "Please, Em. Let me in."

I wasn't sure if I meant into her house or into her heart. With a pang, I realized I wanted both. What I wouldn't give to talk to my father or my mother now. Someone who could offer solace and advice.

That person definitely wasn't Nico. My brother was deeply damaged by his experiences and getting worse. Going along with his plan to prove Em wasn't a liar or a thief had felt wrong at the time, but I did it because I needed to prove to Nico, and to myself, that I could trust my instincts. That Em wasn't like Melinda or Amanda.

But the cost of my choice was Em sobbing into her knees. Finally, she rested her cheek on her thighs, her eyes shut, her face blotchy. She blew out a soft breath. And still I watched her, unable to leave while she was clearly so broken-hearted. Eventually, she slid down to the floor, and I realized she'd cried herself to sleep. My hands itched with the need to lift her up, but I didn't have a key to enter. So, I headed home.

I'd go back to see her this afternoon, once she was better rested. We'd talk—work out our differences. I'd tell her how much she meant to me, and that I wanted a life together. That I shouldn't have agreed to Nico's stupid plan.

Restless, unhappy to have to wait to execute my plan, I showered, then drove to Aidy's condo.

She opened the door, bleary-eyed, her hair half tumbling out of a ponytail, and the baby in a carrier on her chest.

"What the hell, Knox. It's barely seven in the morning."

"You're up," I noted. "You don't ever sleep."

"I was," she mumbled. "In the rocking chair. Best thirty minutes of my life."

I ignored her muttering and began to pace around her living room.

"What do you know about Emmaline? All of it. Don't leave anything out."

Aidy sank back into the chair, a hand on the back of Lilia's fuzzy head.

"She's getting hair," I said with a smile.

Aidy sighed as she set the glider in motion. "And it appears to be red."

I grinned. "She's going to be a ginger, like her mama."

Aidy groaned. "That's such a curse."

"A beautiful curse."

She chuckled, but then met my gaze. "What's going on?" she asked.

I collapsed onto her couch, my hands linked, elbows on my thighs. "I fucked up. Bad."

She remained silent, so I let the whole story spew out of me. Aidy winced when I got to the part where Nico planted a fake file on her desk.

"Oh, Knox." Aidy shook her head, eyes filled with sadness.

"I know. I know."

Lilia woke and started to fidget. Aidy held up her finger to me and left the room. I sat there, staring at the wall until I realized I was woolgathering. I rose and entered Aidy's kitchen. I made coffee—well, decaf, which was pretty much dirt with a faint coffee flavor that required both cream and sugar to taste halfway drinkable. I fixed Aidy a cup once I perfected my ratio and brought it over to her as she returned.

"She needs to nurse."

I glanced away, not wanting to make my sister uncomfortable.

"I'm assuming the situation gets worse," Aidy said.

I chanced a glance in her direction, my gaze locked on hers. "Why would you think that?"

"Because you've been trusting *Nico* for relationship advice up to this point. Now, you're here at the butt crack of dawn, looking like someone kicked you in the nuts."

"You really have a way with words, Aidy-pie."

"And you have a real knack for screwing up good things, Knox."

I frowned but decided not to pursue that comment further—the answer would either bash me in the head or tick me off.

"I might have told her that she must care about me more than Sebastian since it was obvious she couldn't resist me."

I braced myself for her shriek; Aidy didn't respond. She was stroking Lilia's cheek, her eyes filled with softness.

"That was...that was bad," I ventured.

"You're a total moron," Aidy agreed.

"Why aren't you yelling at me?"

She raised her gaze and an eyebrow. "That would upset Lilia and then this milk I've been working hard to make would shoot all over the room."

I paled. "Has that happened before?"

"Yep, but not because I yelled. I won't do that to my daughter, Knox. Even if you do deserve both a yelling and a thrashing." She shook her head. "But nothing I do to you is as bad as what you've done to yourself."

"You have to help me fix it," I said, panic shooting through my limbs, making them heavy.

"I can't," she said. "You messed up. You're going to have to wait for her to signal that she wants to talk."

"And then?" I asked, grasping at the thinnest thread of possible reconciliation.

"You grovel, apologize. Tell her how you feel."

I nodded. "I can do that. I love her, Aidy."

"I know you do, Knox. Unfortunately, you didn't show her that. In fact, you made her feel small, which is the opposite of showing love."

Lilia let out a little grunt before she filled her pants.

I guess I knew what she thought of me—and the situation.

— Å —

I rose from my seat, smile brimming when Em walked into my office close to nine on Monday. She'd come in, dressed for work, so even though she hadn't responded to my messages, that had to mean she was going to give me a chance to fix the mess I'd made over the weekend.

Relief and hope coursed through me as I took her in, drinking in her beauty. She was dressed in a teal silk blouse and a slim black skirt that slid over her curves and made me about swallow my tongue.

"I'm so glad you're here," I said.

Her mouth flattened from its normal lush curve and her chin quivered. She settled in the chair opposite me, knees pressed together, and ankles crossed. She appeared prim but stiff. The primness was hot; the stiffness caused my temples to slick with sweat.

"What's going on?" I asked, leaning against the edge of my desk. She huffed a breath and pulled out an envelope from her purse. She placed it next to my hip, her fingers lingering for a moment before she pulled back and dropped her hands into her lap.

"I broke your code of conduct, which means you have to let me go."

"What if I don't want to?" I asked, shock reverberating up my spine and down into my belly like a black oily slick.

My gaze bore into hers, searching for...something, but she remained silent as she tucked her hands between her knees, clasped tightly. Why? So that she didn't give in to the urge to grab me and pull me into her embrace. While a nice thought, that seemed deeply unlikely.

"I realize that I haven't been honest with my employer, and my ethics won't allow that to continue." She trailed off, shook her head. "If that's all." Em rose from the chair where she'd sat across from me, her skirt flirting with her knees.

"What the hell is going on?" I asked. My hungry gaze devoured her trim calves and slim ankles above her fanciful teal blue heel. It wasn't a stiletto—the heal was too chunky, but, damn, did the lift do amazing things to her already amazing legs.

"If this is about Saturday…"

"This is for the best, Knox." She smoothed her skirt and turned away from my desk—from me.

"You'd just walk away? What we've shared isn't casual, Em. It was deep and meaningful, and I know you felt it, too."

She stiffened so much I worried her spine would snap. But she kept walking.

Fuck.

"What we did was wrong," she said. "The employee handbook—"

"You're not really going to use that as an excuse," I snapped. "Us, together, was *magic*. And I've been working on options for you. Either to remain here or to move to another firm, if that's what you prefer."

"I'll approach other firms when I'm ready," she said.

Frustration mixed with anger, causing my tone to be biting when I asked, "But you're not willing to trust me to give you a recommendation? Or you're not willing to trust that I'll ensure your position here—as I promised to do?"

She narrowed her eyes too much for me to read the emotions there. "I can't believe you won't let this go. You. How many women have you been linked to over the years?" she asked.

"I don't know, and I don't care. None of them was you."

I walked around the desk and gripped her shoulders. My heart ached even as it sped up again. "Don't do this to us, Em. We're just—"

"My name is Emmaline. And I don't have a choice. I have to comply with the guidelines set by my employment. If I don't, Nico will find out—or find another excuse to fire me."

Her steadfast determination covered deeper emotion— which seethed in faint tremors of her body. Out of desperation, I covered her lips with mine, showing her with my mouth and tongue, with the passion that flared desperately between us.

She held stiff for a long moment—so long I worried she didn't feel the same. But then she melted against me, her arms enfolding me. Hope flared as hot as my desire. If I had to kiss her into submission, I would. Better, I'd fuck it into her. I pulled her blouse from her skirt, my hand snaking up her abdomen to cup the weighty heaven of her breast. I tilted my head, licking deeper into her mouth as her hips undulated against mine.

Yes. Yes. This was what we needed.

My door opened.

"I'm not sure what you needed to see me..."

Nico's words trailed off. I lifted my head, still dazed with the passion from the kiss. Em stumbled back, out of my arms, head bowed, cheeks burning.

She took a great shuddering breath.

"Knox," Nico said, his tone filled with reproach. "No wonder Emmaline requested I attend this private meeting."

A tear dripped onto her blouse. She'd set this up, made sure Nico found us together—knowing Nico would insist on terminating her employment.

"Goodbye," she whispered.

"No." The word tore from my throat.

She walked out the door, her shoulders pulled in, her arms around her waist. I moved toward her, but Nico blocked my exit. I shoved at him, but being my older brother, he knew all my moves and managed to restrain me. We were both breathing hard and my anger brimmed over.

"You asshole," I snarled, shoving him as hard as I could. "This is all your fault."

He stumbled back, arms flailing. I craned my neck but Em was no longer in the building.

"You need to remember this is a place of business. We're professionals who happen to be expecting a client—an important one in an hour."

I tugged at my hair, wishing I could yank out the pain in my head and heart with the hair follicles.

"Why would she cut me out like that?" I asked.

That wasn't like Em. She was considerate. She was loyal. She was...

Fuck.

I'd had sex with her Friday. Her first sexual experience since her relationship began with Sebastian. She'd been confused about that—and how good we were together. And I slapped her in the face with what she'd lost Saturday morning. And that I'd been expecting her to fail me, to lie to me again.

Now, as I thought about what we'd shared, I hated the idea of her comparing my performance to his, but it wasn't all that different from what I'd thought from the first moment I'd touched Em: her touch, her scent, her focus was the most important of my life.

But I'd done that.

"You set her up, and she passed that test. But you set me up, too." I swung around and stared at him. "I quit."

"You can't," Nico said. "And her leaving is good. It eliminates the probability of a sexual harassment suit since you went and fucked her."

And everything with Nico clicked.

"Amanda sued you?" I gasped.

Nico turned away, a dull red seeping up his neck and over his cheeks.

"Yes. My boss believed her and refused to settle. I didn't quit. I was fired. The only reason it didn't come out was because two other men stepped forward and said she'd done the same to them. So, I got to leave with a severance I spent on your fuck-up and an iron-clad NDA shoved up my ass."

He glared at me, the anger black and cloaking him, even as it clearly gutted him.

"I refuse to allow you to take us down into that place, Knox. You already took us far enough into the red with Melinda."

I drew myself up. "All the more reason for me to leave."

"You can't leave me here to do this alone," he said again. For the first time since my parents' memorial service, he looked scared.

"I've worried I fucked up, and I did. But you fucked up even worse. You know why? I had my head on right—I *saw* Em from the beginning. It was your toxic bullshit that clouded my vision."

I shoved him again. "I gave up my hockey career for you. I gave up the future *Dad* wanted for me. And you repaid me by undermining a relationship I told you mattered to me."

He gripped my tie as I attempted to storm past. He studied my face. "You actually love her."

I clenched my jaw. I wanted Em more than I'd ever wanted another woman. And to have her, to really know she felt the same way, loved me as I did her, I had to let her go. Had to give her time.

But that was antithetical to everything inside me. I was a doer—I powered through, I scored goals, won games. I'd fought to protect my teammates.

Except I hadn't protected Em.

I'd wanted her to prove herself because I was scared Nico was right.

Nico's expression turned as gloomy as mine must be.

"You're right; I fucked you over," he said. "I set you up to fail." He sucked in a long harsh breath. "I'm sorry, Knox. So, so sorry."

Chapter Thirty
Emmaline

I barreled out the door of the office and straight into Joshua, who teetered back on his heels but managed to stay upright. "Whoa, there. What's going on?"

I pressed my face into his chest, my arms encircling his waist and bawled. He stiffened.

"Are you hurt?"

Yes, I was hurt. My heart was breaking. Had broken. Whatever the stupid tense was, my chest hurt. Badly. But I couldn't let Joshua know. He cared for me, and he'd do something crazy, like pick a fight with Knox—even though I'd been the one to pull away.

I shook my head, desperate for a chance to pull myself together. "No, it's okay. I'm fine."

Joshua's concerned gaze filled my vision. "You're not fine. What happened?"

I felt his stare boring into my back. I stiffened. Joshua must have felt it because he raised his gaze.

"Ah. Knox. I see. Come on, I'll see you home."

He shifted, his gait a little off as he led me to his vehicle. I panicked. "I can't leave my car here," I shrieked. "I can't come back..."

"Okay, Emmy. Okay. How about this? I'll drive your car and come back for mine later?"

I shuddered, needing to get away from Knox. No way I'd be able to look into his slate-colored eyes and remain strong. He'd hurt me, and I wasn't prepared for another emotional beating—I'd been beaten down too many times in my life, and I was so damn tired of standing up again.

Each time I looked at Knox I was reminded of how he'd loved my body so beautifully only to blow it all apart thereafter.

I leaned against Joshua as he led me to my vehicle. He settled me into the passenger seat, and I stared out the side window, unwilling to look back and search for the man I'd so foolishly given my heart.

Josh put on the blinker to exit onto the main road into my neighborhood, and I shook my head, my hands clutching at my skirt. "I'm not ready to go home. I won't stay there."

"All right, honey. Whatever you want."

Something had snapped inside me after I woke up on the kitchen floor. That wasn't the first time I'd laid down, tears flowing in a puddle of grief in that house, but I vowed it would be the last.

If I'd sold the house years before, perhaps then I would have been more capable of moving forward. And I would have met another man. Anyone but Knox Wright, who strung me along to prove a point.

Joshua patted my hand, but I didn't loosen my hold until he continued onto the highway. He exited on Hope Boulevard, heading toward Blackstone Boulevard. Once we'd pulled through the gate of the Giovanni home, I sighed.

"You going to tell me what happened?"

"Maybe I should go up and visit with Sebastian," I said.

Joshua hesitated for a moment before he met my gaze. "He's not here. Nana and I decided to give him some time in a facility in Boston."

"Wh-what?"

I felt like I was getting hit with too many changes at once.

Joshua must have realized I'd reached my limit because he tugged me into the kitchen. Once installed in my normal seat, he made a pot of coffee.

"Manny suggested it. The facility has advanced technology that helps rebuild muscle in the arms and legs. Sebastian likes some of the other people there. He's made a few friends."

"Wow. Why didn't you tell me?"

Joshua sighed. "I wanted to, but Nana said you weren't ready to let him go then."

I stared down into my coffee, seeing my image altered into a Picasso-esque version—staring back.

"I wasn't," I murmured. "Holding on to Sebastian meant I didn't have to move forward and live."

I felt the emotion press up against the back of my eyes and clog my throat. I took a sip of coffee and then choked as the liquid struggled past the knot. I closed my eyes.

"Moving forward, learning to live again, it's just caused more heartache," I said. "I trusted Knox."

That's what hurt the most. We'd shared enough of our pasts that I thought he'd take care with my emotions. Instead, he judged and tested me, then he used my body as soon as I'd offered it—used his body—as a weapon against my better judgment.

Embarrassment warred with anger, and I wrestled with how

he'd managed to betray me with such ease. And so deeply.

"Time to get out of your head and tell me what's going on. You made me wait and it's killing me."

I stared down into my mug. With a sigh, I dumped in more cream. "I quit this morning."

"Damn," Joshua said, shaking his head.

"About time," Ellie said, breezing into the space.

"Do you get off on eavesdropping?" I snapped.

She raised her eyebrows. "Someone's sassy. No, actually I don't. But I am happy that you're making that young man work for a relationship with you. I always said you capitulated to Sebastian too easily."

I scowled. "Sebastian was easy to love. He still is."

"Yes, I know," Ellie said, with a bright smile. She handed me a tissue, then set the box in front of me. "But that doesn't mean he wasn't—isn't—spoiled. Thankfully, I never quite made you boys rotten."

Ellie smiled at Joshua with warm affection. His return smile was equally as pleased.

"What happened between you two?" I asked.

"Mmm. Joshua can fill you in later. First, I want to hear about your break from Wright and Associates—specifically that delicious Knox."

I did, leaving nothing out, though I did edit the sexy times. Both Ellie and Joshua listened, intent, not interrupting. Like, really heard what I was saying and not judging me.

They sat back when I finished.

"Wow," Joshua said.

I rested my chin on my fists. "I know. He doesn't know me very well if he thinks I'd steal."

Joshua shook his head. His dark hair stayed in place, thanks to the product he used. Unlike Knox, who was a wash-and-go guy. I loved how his golden hair flopped toward his eyes.

"Not that," Joshua said.

I focused on his face, thankful to get out of my head. "What are you thinking?" I asked.

Ellie sniffed. "Your friend Bridget told us who threw the wine on you. But Josh is just assimilating that with the fact that Melinda boned Knox for a couple of months before she raced over to Collins and Miner—with Knox's designs."

I blinked at Ellie, shocked by her word choice. She'd always been blunt, but...*boned*? My cheeks heated with the same embarrassment I would feel if my mother had said something like that. And then it hit me, Ellie *was* my mother. I wrapped my arm around her shoulders and squeezed.

"I love you," I said.

"And I love you, Emmaline." She patted my hand. "Which is why I'm already taking care of the Melinda situation."

"Knox mentioned that she stole the Wrights' designs."

"And tried to pass them off as her own."

"What would you like us to do about Knox?" Joshua asked.

"Nothing."

He raised his eyebrows.

"The renovation for your place on Martha's Vineyard is basically finished, and I'm the one who quit."

Joshua shook his head, a small smile grazing his lips. "Such integrity. You've grown into an amazing woman, Emmaline Schooler."

I rolled my eyes. "Thanks."

"Now that we've settled those details, you'll need some work," Ellie said. "I'm assuming you want to finish your cottage? You are planning to sell your parents' house, aren't you? Not the cottage. I mean, they're both yours, but I've been on tenterhooks since you met with the agent weeks ago."

I shook my head. "Nothing gets by you. Yes, I want to sell my parents' house and move into the cottage."

"Not when it's the people I care about. So, that's settled. You'll oversee the renovations here. I'll give you a glowing recommendation and you'll have your pick of jobs." Her eyes laughed. "I do like being a real-life fairy godmother."

I snorted. "Am I your only victim?"

"Of course not." Ellie reached over and patted Joshua's cheek. "This cutie thought I had no clue he was planning to ask Will to marry him. They'll have a wedding at the Martha's Vineyard property, of course. That's why he's been so swoony over the designs for the kitchen, dining, and patio. It's just what he and Will dreamed about for their reception." She winked.

Joshua smiled back. "All true," he said, turning that smile toward me.

"I'm so happy for you," I said, taking his hand and squeezing. "Tell me about the proposal and the wedding," I said.

Joshua's eyes lit up and his smile broadened to the point his dimples popped. "My favorite subject."

Even though my heart hurt, I was thankful to see Joshua happy.

He deserved this.

"Will suggested that we include Sebastian in the wedding as the ring bearer," Joshua said. His gaze turned dreamy.

Well, at least one of us might get our happy ending.

———— A ————

Not having a job proved both a blessing and a curse. I spent most of Tuesday at Aidy's, catching her up on my failed love affair with her brother and going over the projects I'd been working on.

"Good thing I'm heading back in the office soon," she murmured. But tears formed in her eyes. "I'm going to miss working with you."

Not as much I was going to miss her, but I just smiled. "Ellie's project will take a few months. It's a fabulous addition to my portfolio."

"All true," Aidy said with a sigh. "And I get that my brothers suck big time, but I loved having you in the office."

I blinked. "Don't cry. Please. I can't…I'm going to miss you, too."

We sniffled together. After eating way too many cookies I'd picked up from the bakery on my way to her place, I got ready to leave.

"What should I tell Knox when he asks me about you?"

I shrugged. "I'd prefer you to tell him nothing."

She frowned. "I don't think I can do that."

"Then tell him I refuse to talk to him."

"Emmaline…"

My lower lip quivered. "I need time, Aidy. Just…just give me some time."

She sighed. "Okay. But you owe me."

I hugged her. "Forever."

The weeks fell into a nice routine. I spent a few hours each weekend at Bridget's, loving on her babies so that she and Simon could run errands and have time together before heading either to my cottage or to Ellie's.

"You're sure you don't mind?" Bridget asked.

I smiled at her. "They give me a purpose."

Her eyes softened. "You have plenty of purpose, Emmaline. But I really appreciate getting a shower before bedtime."

"Then, it's a win-win for us both. Knox doesn't know where you live, and I get my baby fix." Because I wasn't ever going to date a man again. Emotion, affection, love—those feelings caused too much pain. Nope, I'd fix up my cottage and focus on my career.

And change another diaper, thanks to the little poop machines rolling around so adorably on the floor.

—— Å ——

With the radio blaring, I lifted the sledgehammer, ignoring my shaking arms, and pounded through the two-by-fours that divided the dining room from the living room.

I rested the heavy tool on the ground, winded by the exertion, ignoring the sweat trickling down my back. If I stopped, I'd start thinking. I grunted as I lifted the handle again. But my muscles screamed.

The music shut off. I whirled toward the kitchen doorway.

"That is not good for your ears," Aidy said, scowling. She eyed me. "I haven't seen you in forever. And I'm so mad you quit before you got to see the Carringtons' place completed."

I slid down onto my butt right there in the wreckage of my living room. "I am, too."

She sighed. "Knox asks me about you every day."

I closed my eyes and tipped my head back. "I'm not ready to see him."

"He owes you an apology."

I brought my head forward and seared her with my best glare. "I do not want to see your brother. Ever again."

Aidy raised her hands.

"I'm not the enemy. But he's really worried."

"He doesn't have the right. Not after what he said. What he did."

She tilted her head. "No. He doesn't. What he did to you was shitty. But I know he feels really bad about it."

"I hope he does about that—and that his ex tossed a glass of wine all over me because she was a jealous cow."

Thanks to Bridget's eyewitness account, and the footage from a closed-circuit camera on The Mac's property, Melinda's involvement was indisputable. She lawyered up immediately, but word trickled out that John Miner ended their engagement, and Walter Collins fired her from the company. Ellie insisted on bringing in her Boston law firm to handle my legal case—the one I didn't want to pursue—and Ellie told me yesterday when I visited that she'd keep up the pressure until Melinda was forced to plea or go to trial.

"She needs to pay for her actions, Emmy. That's the problem with that woman—she's used her looks and cunning to get everything she wants. But now, she can't seduce me into forgiving her for her treatment of you or what she said about Sebastian. She'll plea soon so she doesn't have to go to jail. But, if she doesn't, she'll still have the assault charge on her record. That's nonnegotiable. I've made my expectations clear to my lawyers—and they, to hers."

Slowly, I'd let the realization that my Sebastian was gone permanently sink in. Much as I hated that truth, it didn't change. We'd held each other back, and Sebastian had been brave enough to forge forward.

I slumped my shoulders and lifted my knees, resting my cheek on them. My life lay in shambles, thanks to my choices. I hated that I'd let everything I'd tried to hold together for so long spin apart.

Aidy crouched down in front of me, meeting my gaze. "Do you really want to carry this bitterness inside you? I mean, really? I get that you're hurting. You have every right to be angry with Knox. He screwed up."

"But?" I asked, eyebrows raised.

"No buts, Emmaline. I get where you're coming from." She hesitated. "I *was* you after my parents died. I sank further and further into the worst of myself, unable to find a toehold to start pulling myself up. I messed up my relationship with Nico. I almost didn't go to college. Everyone says the first year is the hardest, but I found that to be true of years two through five. I was so angry—with them, with myself, with the world."

She paused. I ingested her words.

"I can tell you that all those emotions you're feeling are normal. But if you don't deal with them, they'll become toxic."

Much as I wanted to lash out at Aidy, I couldn't. "I... I just need some time. Everything changed. For a minute, it was perfect, but then it all fell apart. I don't want to relive that, Aidy. And I just sold my parents' house. I'm...it's so much."

Aidy squeezed my knees.

"Actually, having a conversation with him might heal part of your heart."

"I hear what you're saying. I'll think about it."

"Good. It's probably a good thing you quit."

At my shocked look, she held up her hands. "Don't even think I don't want you there. But you and Knox...the optics are bad. Some people will always see you as the woman who slept with her boss and never see your talent."

I considered her comments. She slid down to settle cross-legged on the floor, grunting a little. From looking at her now, you'd never know Aidy birthed a child not long ago.

I shifted, aching. I'd forced my body into extreme physical labor for weeks as a penance. From what, I wasn't sure. Just that I needed to pay it.

Maybe for moving on from Sebastian. Or for running away from Knox the moment we hit a rough patch. He'd said hurtful things, true, but I'd never considered myself a coward.

Melinda had screwed both him and Wright and Associates over. Trust would be difficult to manifest after that type of betrayal. But that had nothing to do with me, not really. And he should have trusted me without asking me to jump through hoops.

I also should have listened to him when he told me he was sorry. I should have shown the compassion I would have wanted him to show me earlier when he'd railroaded me and refused to let me say anything.

I hadn't behaved any better. Perhaps I'd behaved worse. I wasn't sure, and that felt...icky.

"I'm afraid to talk to him," I said. I kept my gaze on the smashed wall.

"Why?" Aidy asked.

"Because..." I swallowed. "Everyone I love leaves me. My parents, Sebastian..."

"Oh, honey."

Aidy pulled me into her arms. The tears I hadn't wanted to fall slid down my cheeks as she rocked me back and forth, much like my mother used to.

"Knox quit."

I jerked, the tears drying. "What?"

"He and Nico had an epic fallout the same day you left. Nico had to grovel to get Knox back." Aidy sniffed. "I guess I can't expect the return of the perfect big brother I remember, but I sure prefer nice Nico to his jerk mode." She shook her head.

"Is Knox back at the firm?" I asked. Worry gnawed at my belly. He belonged there.

"Yeah. But the situation is tense. Knox is frosty."

I swiped at the last of the tears on my cheeks. I closed my sore, tired eyes. "That's weird."

"He's hurting, too, Emmaline."

"I'm not sure I can be anything to or for Knox. I...I just hurt."

"I understand," Aidy said.

I knew she did.

"Thanks for coming by," I said. "I'm sure you need to get back to your baby."

"True. But first, you have to tell me what you're doing here."

I settled back on my hands and turned to face the half-destroyed wall. I explained, in detail, what I planned for the space. Aidy offered some suggestions and I tucked them away.

Eventually, she rose and dusted off her jeans. She winced. "Ugh. That's so gross. My boob is leaking."

She glanced down at her shirt as a small wet spot appeared.

"Hang on. I'll get you another shirt."

I headed to my room and hesitated. Finally, I came up with a camisole and one of my RISD shirts. I brought them to Aidy, who changed in the small, recently completed half-bath.

"Thanks," she said. "I get so embarrassed when that happens, but Ryder says it's natural, and that I'm lucky to produce enough milk."

"The grass is always greener argument," I said with a smile.

"Something like that." Aidy shrugged. "Might be worth remembering that for yourself."

I walked her to the door and hugged her, unwilling to remark on her gentle meddling. Knox and I were over. There wasn't any point trying to sugarcoat that truth.

Honestly, we'd never had a true chance to begin.

Chapter Thirty-One
Knox

Not one peep from Emmaline in five weeks. When the For Sale sign went up in her yard, I panicked, calling her and texting her without a response. Now, with the sold sign smeared across the front, that tenseness turned into a boulder of regret.

I'd thought she needed time. I'd been wrong to give it to her. I needed to find a way to prove to her how much I wanted her in my life.

Even Joshua Giovanni broke down to tell me that he was worried about her. The Martha's Vineyard beach house was my first stop. We ran the final punch list with Abe. I'd refused to work with Sarah after her treatment of Emmaline.

I commented on the ring on Joshua's left ring finger. His grin sparkled bright enough to remove my ever present low-cloud gloom momentarily.

"I'm engaged."

"Congratulations," I said.

"Will proposed the same night I had planned to," Joshua gushed, his entire face beaming with love and pride. "We're getting married here. It'll be perfect."

I stilled. "How long have you two been together?"

He shot me a sly look. "Nearly four years. I met him the night of Sebastian and Emmaline's accident. He's a surgeon."

"Oh."

Joshua's expression morphed into one of impatience. "I didn't start seeing him for months afterward—once I realize Seb wasn't going to be the brother I knew and remembered. Plus, Will annoyed me because each time I saw him, he wanted Ellie, Emmaline, and me to go into therapy." His jaw shifted. "I had to admit he was right about that one. Not getting help, not dealing with how all our lives had changed nearly broke Will and me."

"But you persisted," I said, annoyance at Em's quick tuck-tail-and-run strategy flaming through my belly. "You didn't just disappear…"

"Is that what you think Emmy did? Ghost you?" Joshua shook his head. "Seriously, man? You betrayed her trust on *every* level. You spied on her, tested her to make sure she wouldn't steal from you. You fucked her after she told you she hadn't been with anyone since my brother—that she needed to take the situation slow."

"She told you all that?" I asked. My cheeks turned cold, my lips numb.

"Emmaline's like my sister. We talk. And she's…" He blew out a breath. "She's really, really hurt. I thought she'd be feeling better by now, moving past your idiocy, but she's not."

"Then tell me where she is." My muscles tensed as adrenaline hit my system. "I'll talk to her."

"Nope. No way I'm betraying her trust."

"I want to fix us," I said, frustration causing me to vibrate.

"It would have been better not to break it in the first place," Joshua snapped.

"I didn't mean..." I inhaled through my nose and tried to find some calm. "I care about her. A lot. I don't like that she's hurting."

Joshua's eyes narrowed. "You have a sister. How would you respond to a guy treating her like that?"

"I nearly punched in his face," I muttered. "What do you want to do to me?"

"I want you to leave her alone."

"I can't."

"Why?"

I dug my fingers through my hair. "I just can't! She matters to me. I miss her. I think about her all the time. I want to share bits of my day with her. I want to hold her, hear her talk, share a meal."

Joshua's shove on my shoulder made me blink away the haze of my past inter-spliced with the possibility of a future.

"Don't you get it?" he said, his voice as taut as his shoulders and arms. "She has severe trust issues, and you proved the reason for them existing *again*."

I stared back at him, dumbstruck. "What are you talking about?" I understood—well, I sort of understood. "I never thought she'd steal from us, but Nico wasn't sure. And after the Melinda incident, we couldn't be too careful."

His gaze turned hotter, angrier. "That was an asshole move, but I'm not talking about that." Joshua raised a brow. "Her father, mother, and Sebastian."

I hunched my shoulders. "I know she's afraid. Afraid I'll leave her. I figured that out. That's why I'm trying so hard to find her, to get her back."

He flattened his lips, and his eyes filled with pity. "I wish I could help you. You have no idea how much."

———— Å ————

I thanked Joshua and drove back from Martha's Vineyard in a daze. I handled my next site stop, barely functional.

"I need you to go check on the Carrington residence," Nico said after I answered my cell using my hands-free Bluetooth.

I'd promised Em I'd always give driving my full attention, and while I couldn't find her, I could keep that promise. So I did.

I groaned. The weather had shifted during the day, turning the brief warm spell back into a wintery mix. The clouds were low, leaden, and the air smelled of snow. In May. I fucking hated these late blizzards almost as much as I hated talking to Nico.

My irritability spiked with my exhaustion. Nico and I circled around each other, but I was still angry with him.

"Fine. Why?"

"Because the weather's crap, and I'm concerned about whether the contractor actually covered the equipment and supplies."

"Fine."

"I saw that a neighbor moved in, and she might not know how dangerous the place is. She has quite the fascination with cantilevered decks. I suggest you stop in, have a chat with her."

"Why do I care about the neighbor?" I asked. More like growled. I didn't want to deal with a woman—any woman other than Emmaline. My heart hurt from how we'd left us, and no matter how many times I called, Em refused to answer. She ignored my texts, emails, letters, the flowers I'd sent...nothing. In fact, the flowers had sat, droopy and pathetic, on her porch three days after I sent them.

I considered stealing Aidy's phone to call, send texts, whatever I needed to do to get in touch with Em. I *had* to talk to her. Before, the need to fix the situation between us stemmed from my desire to get back into her life and, hopefully, her bed. Now, I realized how selfish that was. Em's hurt and fear slashed through her, no doubt causing paralysis. And yet, she'd interviewed with us, driven with me to Martha's Vineyard, she'd opened up about her history.

I just hadn't paid close enough attention to what she was saying. I hadn't read between her words, listened to the gaps in what she was saying, to understand how scarred she was by the trauma. She'd lost her entire family—and I'd expected her to simply stroll into a relationship with me. Making new emotional connections must have been a Herculean effort.

Nico's reason for sending me out to the site appeared before my eyes like an apparition. At first, I assumed the thickening fog had played tricks on my eyes. But her voice carried over the clanging.

That was Em's voice, and she was pissed.

I canted my head as she banged and yelled. I followed the sounds, walking as close to the fence line between the properties as possible. As her voice became louder, I broke into a jog, desperate for a glimpse of my woman.

No. My *love*.

The thought settled over me, as right as a warm shower at the end of a long day. She was my woman, my love, and if I could talk her into it, my future wife.

But first, I wanted to help her out of whatever situation caused her this level of distress. After I kissed her senseless and assured myself she was well.

"Come on," she yelled. I could just make her out at this distance, and she was shivering with cold. With a frustrated grunt, she threw the wrench at the cause of her angst, a piece of equipment. She cupped her hands to her mouth and blew, trying to warm her numbed fingers.

Cold, humid air swirled around us. Temperatures were dropping faster than the New Year's Eve ball in New York. I wiggled my chilled toes in my winter boots, clamping my jaw at the tingles burning there. Fuck, it was cold. Whatever Em worked on, now wasn't the best time. Ah hell, if she didn't have heat, I was going to be pissed—not the most conducive scenario for a heart-to-heart.

"I should've added another pair of socks," she muttered. "I'll check the fuses. Maybe that's the problem, in which case, I'll be fine."

I watched as she used her phone as a flashlight and headed toward the garage. If all the fuses were on, that meant her only other option was checking the electrical line. Maybe the workers cut it when they were working on the place yesterday. That brought her in closer proximity to me, where I stood at the fence. My chilled fingers pushed through the chain link, desperate to grab her.

I caught my first look at her in what had to be forever: Her brows furrowed, and she scowled. She hunched her back and trotted toward the property line, gaze low. She bent down at the edge of the electrical box.

"Frayed wires," she shrieked. "They cut my power. Dammit."

She slammed her fist into the frozen ground and winced, cradling her fist against her soft belly. She muttered about keys and calling the power company, and her need for a shower.

She glanced up, eyes widening. She gasped out a negative sound. Her gaze hovered around my chest. I clenched the chain-link harder, my fingers numb with cold and pressure.

Her long, dark hair half out of a braid, framing her smudged face. Her clothing was old, ripped, and covered in dirt. She looked so beautiful.

"Hello, Emmaline."

My chest ached as I drank her in.

"What are you doing here?" she asked. Her eyes darted up to mine and they were too dark. She looked away, skittish.

"I came to check out the lack of power," I said, gesturing toward the cut wires.

"Oh. Well, good luck with that."

Chapter Thirty-Two
Emmaline

Everything hurt—my muscles screamed with exhaustion and cold while my heart and head pounded in tandem as the realization I'd been fighting for weeks slammed into my consciousness with more force than I wielded my sledgehammer.

I was in love with Knox Wright.

I gritted my teeth, annoyed that my sanctuary had been discovered. I ignored his voice, calling my name as I beelined for my cold little bungalow. I slammed the door shut and locked it. I shivered, trying to remember where I'd left my purse. The kitchen? Nope, it wasn't there. The bedroom, maybe.

I started down the hall, planning to grab it and get in my car before Knox managed to trek from that property to mine. The good news was the Carringtons' lot was three times the size of mine, so Knox would have to return to his vehicle on the far side of the house and then drive the quarter-mile between our homes.

"Em!" He pounded on the door.

Or...damn athlete that he was, he probably ran back to his car or maybe even jumped the fence.

"Come on, Em, we need to talk."

Much as I didn't want to, he was correct. I'd decided after Aidy's last visit that I was going to have to respond to his continued efforts to get in touch. I just hadn't expected to do so this soon.

But life wasn't about me being ready for the situation; what mattered was how I handled the problem in front of me. I'd give him the courtesy of hearing him out—even if I didn't like or agree with anything he had to say.

I was pretty sure I wouldn't.

I sucked in a breath and fumbled with the lock. I opened the door and he caught the edge. He didn't step inside but somehow seemed to crowd my space. I froze as his fingers settled on my cheeks. I shuddered, wanting to burrow in closer to his heat and his smell. But that would be stupid. Wouldn't it?

"Don't shut me out, Em. *Please.*"

Dammit. I needed to be mad. I wanted to shut the door and never think of him again. How could I remain angry when he didn't even try to step into my home? He hovered at the door jamb, clearly fighting with himself.

I opened the door wider. He huffed as he stepped inside.

"I've been so worried about you," Knox said, exasperation and something akin to anger lashing through his words. Or was it reproach?

I flinched, not liking how his emotions made my skin feel taut and a bit itchy. Clearly, this wasn't going to be a sweet reunion after all.

"I'm not your responsibility."

"I want you to be," he said.

I crossed my arms over my chest to put even more distance between us. Nothing about our relationship, such as it was, made any sense. As soon as he'd kissed me, I'd melted into him, wanting more. I shifted further away, hating how needy he made me feel—how out of control within my own body. Just the sight of Knox's burnished hair glinting in the weak afternoon light as he strode toward me had my breathing changing and every nerve in my body tingling with awareness. I fought my reaction, trying to subdue my response.

I was losing, and I knew it, but I wouldn't stop trying. I couldn't—the alternative scared me too damn much.

"I've missed you, Em. So much. I hurt from it." His voice was gravelly.

It was my turn to blink in shock, my mouth dropping open in surprise because his eyes blasted the lust I'd worked so hard to control within my own body.

"I'm calling BS," I said.

"Your call doesn't change the facts."

I shivered harder.

"Why is it so fucking cold in here?" Knox asked.

He started to shiver, and his breath slid out of his mouth in a faint white plume.

"Your construction guys severed my wires last night, Mr. Wright," I said. "And, once again, I'm left with the consequences of your stupid actions."

He took a step back, his eyes wide at my snarky—no—nasty tone.

While he kind of deserved what I was saying, that didn't mean I liked how I felt—I sounded petulant, pathetic. I inhaled sharply and raised my eyelids to meet his gaze square on. No more hiding, no more childish responses.

"I'm sorry. That was mean. I'm upset with you," I said, my

voice growing stronger. "I'm upset that you meant so much to me and yet, you were just using me, playing a game."

My shivering increased until my teeth chattered so hard, I could barely hear Knox's gravelly voice.

This place, in its current form, was uninhabitable.

Knox wrapped his arms around me, his head coming down so that his cheek laid against my hair.

"Emmaline, you were never a game or a conquest or a simple fuck. I said it before, and I'll keep saying it: I'm so sorry. I handled this situation poorly, but I'm going to fix it. I want to fix it. I need you in my life."

For weeks, I'd fantasized about him saying such words to me, which was why I didn't trust them now. They were too good to be true. His slate-blue gaze bore into my eyes.

"You said—"

He pressed his fingers to my lips. "*Please* don't repeat it. I know what I said, and I finally get how much I hurt you. I wanted to apologize when you showed up that Monday. I wanted to come after you even after you set us up, but Nico got in my way, and then you were gone. And I couldn't find you."

He huffed out a breath. "Come back to my place. We can talk where it's warm."

I shook my head, exhaustion cutting deep. "I was trying to figure out how to let people in again, how to date a man who wasn't the one I'd always thought I'd marry." I swiped at angry tears. "You were so sweet at first, but then, you just took... You made me desperate for you, and then you made our relationship

into a game. You made me into a trophy. Not a person. A...
a possession."

Knox made a deep, guttural sound.

"That's not the kind of man I want in my life. I've seen too
much, felt too much to settle. So, I guess I should say thank you
for showing me what you're really like before we continued seeing
each other." I walked the few steps to my living room. I settled
my body, so weary, so cold and spent, on the edge of my couch.
I'd close my eyes, just for a moment.

"Oh, Em. You're at your edge."

"Pretty sure I've passed it," I mumbled. Didn't matter who I
was talking to. I just needed the sweet oblivion of sleep. Tomorrow, in the light and warmth of the day, the situation wouldn't
look as bleak.

I'd just rest here for a few moments before I managed to haul
myself to bed. My eyes flew open when my body lifted in a pair
of strong arms. "What are you doing?"

"I'm taking you to my place. Shit, why are your clothes wet?
You have to be freezing."

My teeth chattered again now that I was pressed against his
warmth. "I don't want to go with you."

"Tough cookies."

I snorted. "What did you say?"

"I'm working on my language. You know, so I don't curse in
front of baby Lilia."

I shook my head. The conversations I had with this man never
went the way I expected them to. He settled me into my bed,
surprising me. I thought he said he was taking me to his house.

I was too tired and cold to worry about it any longer. I curled up into a ball as he pulled a blanket over me.

If I'd had the energy I would have cried, but I was past all that. All I wanted was to forget.

So I did.

I woke in a strange bed in a strange room to the smell of coffee. I sat up too quickly and my head throbbed.

"What?"

"Glad you're awake."

I turned to face Knox, who sat on the edge of the bed, a little scruffy, his hair wild, in pajama pants and a black T-shirt.

"Where am I?"

He hesitated for a moment before he met my gaze. "My house."

I narrowed my eyes. "That wasn't your call to make."

"Your lips were blue," he said, as if that ended the argument.

I scrambled out of bed, my chest heaving. At least I was wearing my clothes. I frowned. He'd left me in my clothes, which were filthy.

I was disgusting, and he'd laid me in his sheets that way. He was a caring, thoughtful man.

I pressed my fists to the sides of my forehead and screamed. It felt good so I did it again. I tipped my head back and let out all the pain and confusion and fear at the ceiling.

Spent, I settled on the edge of the bed.

"Feel better?" Knox asked.

I turned in time to see him grimace, pulling his finger from his ear.

"Sadly, no." My voice was raspy now from the excessive use of my vocal cords. "My life is still as big of a wreck." I closed my eyes and dropped my forehead into my raised palms. On top of that, I'm sure I had crazy bed-head, and I needed to pee.

The bed shifted as Knox settled next to me. "I'd like to help you."

I rose, shrugging off the arm he laid across my shoulders. "I need the bathroom. And my toothbrush."

Knox's lips pressed flat before he rose and opened a door across the room. I brushed past him, ignoring how good he smelled—how warm and inviting his chest was. I couldn't lay my head against him and pretend like he was going to fix all my problems.

He wasn't. I needed to do that.

I shut the door and locked it.

My toothbrush was on the counter next to a tube of toothpaste, so I took care of my dental hygiene first. After taking care of my other needs, I stepped from the bathroom, fresh-faced and with my hair pulled back in a loose braid.

Knox rose from the now-made bed and handed me a cup of coffee, the top dotted with cinnamon. The sweetness of the gesture warmed me.

"Thanks," I said, staring down into the mug instead of meeting his gaze. I could feel it boring into the top of my head, but I wasn't ready to deal with him.

After a few sips, nerves got the better of me and I raised my head. "I want to go home."

Knox shook his head. "Bad idea. You don't have any heat and we're in the middle of a blizzard."

"Well, I can't stay here."

"Of course you can. I want you here."

I shook my head. He grabbed my free hand and led me to the window. It was an absolute white-out. My shoulders sagged. No way I could leave in these conditions.

"Why is being with me so bad?" he asked.

"Do I have any clothes here? I'd like to take a shower."

"Em…"

"What Knox? *What?*"

I blinked rapidly, pushed beyond my capabilities once more. "What else can you possibly want from me?"

He studied my face, his impassive. The moment spiraled out as the silence grew. He said nothing, just continued to watch me.

When I couldn't stand it anymore, I started to turn away.

"Everything," he whispered. "I want everything."

"Pretty sure you already took that," I said, looking directly at him.

He winced, his eyes darkening with hurt. He shoved his fingers through his hair and stepped back.

"Your clothes are in the closet," he said over his shoulder as he stalked from the room.

I tried not to feel bad about the encounter, but, really, what did he expect from me?

I finished the now-cool coffee and gathered up some clean clothes from my small black carry-on that was pushed to the back wall of the walk-in closet. I headed into the bathroom and turned on the tap, setting it as hot as possible. I hadn't had the luxury of a steaming-hot shower in a couple of days, thanks to my frayed electrical line.

As I rinsed the soap from my hair the guilt started to kick in. Sure, Knox was the one to compare my relationship with him to my relationship with Sebastian, but he'd also apologized many times.

Maybe I should forgive him. At least then I could find closure from our short-lived affair. We could both move on with the past behind us.

Chapter Thirty-Three
Knox

I faced the very real possibility that Emmaline wasn't going to give me another chance. In her mind, she saw me as the villain—someone who took advantage of her work ethic and then her body.

I saw my decision to go along with Nico's scheme to test her loyalty as smart business and my mouthiness after the best sex of my life as jealousy about her relationship with Sebastian. I messed up. I readily admitted that, but I wasn't ready to give up yet. I was a stubborn-as-hell hockey player.

I'd dreamed about her, here, in my home, for too long to quit now.

Except...except the hurt in her eyes each time she looked at me spoke of something soul-deep—as if she hadn't had any faith in me staying to begin with.

I banged around in the kitchen, more frustrated than I'd been since she'd locked me out of her house. Then, I'd assumed I could simply talk to her. Now, I was learning that Em's stubborn streak might well be wider than the Mississippi River. How I'd missed this frustrated me. Until I remembered she'd been my employee before—and apparently adhered to the hierarchy of command. Now that I'd dismissed her from my company, she no longer felt the need to look at me as a person of authority.

Well, at least that made sense.

But I was unsure how best to approach the situation. I considered my choices as I whisked together eggs for omelets, which was one of Em's favorite breakfasts. I had all of them here. After I had put Em in her bed, I headed over to get my car and drove her here, settling her in my guest room; I'd braved the growing storm last night after I put her to bed to make a grocery run so that she'd be comfortable as we waited out the blizzard. I simply hadn't considered the possibility that my presence would keep her so unhappy.

I tensed at the first tentative step I heard on the wide wood planks of my hall. I poured the whisked eggs into the pan and sprinkled the top with cheese, chives, sun-dried tomatoes and bell peppers.

"Thank you for the coffee. And the bed," she said. "And the shower."

I nodded.

"I'm making you an omelet."

Her gaze darted to the window, no doubt checking the weather once again. My shoulders stiffened. Would we be able to have an actual conversation that didn't devolve immediately into my defensiveness over her unwillingness to see the situation from a different point of view?

"Yum," she said, moving toward the table.

I sighed with relief.

She ambled further into the kitchen and refilled her coffee cup to the brim as if our conversation required greater levels of caffeine. I plated the omelet, cutting it in half and adding a piece of toast.

"I realized something in the shower," she said, staring at her plate. "I keep throwing up walls, deflecting, unwilling to talk to you. That's because I don't want you to know how much you hurt me. But, in trying to protect myself, I'm hurting us both more."

"All right." I cut a bite of the omelet even though my heart pounded hard against my ribs. Was I being too nonchalant? I needed Em to talk to me, but I worried she'd clam up if I pushed again. Getting her here, at my table, in my home, probably used up all the goodwill she had—if she'd had any.

Steam drifted from the fluffy concoction dotted with sharp feta and sun-dried tomatoes. This was good; I'd make it again.

She took a tentative bite, savoring it. Then another. She managed half of the omelet before she pushed her plate back, surprising me. I'd expected her to draw out the meal.

She met my gaze over the rim. I lowered the cup, my chest tight.

"You hurt me." Her lip quivered.

I watched it, sadness hitting me hard. "I know." I wanted so badly to touch her, but I didn't. "And I feel awful about that. I *never* meant to hurt you. I was so elated about us finally being together, and the words slid out before I considered them."

She frowned. After a moment, she dropped her gaze to her mug, running her finger around the edge.

"I thought I was worth your regard. And you snapped that connection as if it meant nothing."

I bit my cheek against the denial that built on my lips. She needed to talk. I needed to listen.

"Which is why I don't understand why I'm here now. Why you've tried to check in with me. Because the man who belittled my feelings after we made...after that bout of sex..." She dropped her gaze, her lashes fluttering. "Taking care of me, feeding me— they don't resolve in my head."

I splayed my hand on the table as she spoke; my knuckles whitened further. I couldn't feel my fingertips now.

"That's not how I see this at all."

She half rose from the chair and I reached forward, my fingers wrapping around her wrist as panic seized me.

"Don't leave," I said. "I'm trying to tell you that your perspective—your reality—isn't mine." I met her gaze. "Not that you're wrong, Em. Just that I didn't realize how you would perceive my actions."

I forced myself to keep the visual connection as I breathed in deep and slow. She planted her butt back in the padded leather high backed armless Parson chair. "Explain this to me, please."

"I'll try, but I don't think you're going to like what I have to say."

She tilted her head to the side. "Right now, I really can't stand to be near you."

I flinched.

"So, I doubt there's anything you can say or do to make that worse."

I laughed but it was pained. "Oh, I can probably make it worse. There doesn't seem to be a bottom to me fucking this whole situation up."

She folded her hands in her lap but seemed half a second from darting away. "Spill it, Knox."

I grunted. "You've gotten bossier."

"Nope. I just no longer need to be deferential."

She raised her coffee to her lips in an effort to cover the trembling seizing her body. I reached across the table and clasped her free hand. My fingers trembled against hers. We stayed like that for a long moment, staring at where our skin connects.

"Will you...will you tell me why you felt the need to test my loyalty?"

I blew out a breath. Okay. She wanted to start there. In some ways, that was easier.

"Melinda took some of my designs with her to Collins and Miner. We had to get lawyers involved, and the legal fees to enforce the NDAs nearly bankrupted us." My shoulders slumped. "*I* nearly cost us our business—all because I chose to date our intern." I met her gaze. "For the record, I never thought you were anything like her. Testing you was Nico's idea. He and I fought about it."

I considered my choices. Time to put my emotions on the line.

I met her gaze. "I'm in love with you, Emmaline."

Shock settled over her face, her eyes widening, and then she shook her head once.

I leaned forward and cupped her cool cheeks in my palms. "It's true. Falling for you scared the shit out of me—because of what you were to me. An employee." I swallowed hard. "You ever been in rapids?"

She nodded.

"You know how the first drops are a rush—best feeling ever."

Another nod.

"When I took you to the Giovannis' Martha's Vineyard residence, that's how I felt: exhilarated. Like winning the Frozen Four."

I smiled and she continued to stare, almost as if she couldn't believe the words I spoke.

"When we got back, I freaked out. If Nico knew about how deep my feelings were for you, he would have fired you because of me, and I couldn't let that happen. Well, you get it. I told you about that already."

She nodded.

I scrubbed my fingers through my hair. "I also couldn't stop spending time with you, but if I didn't, you would lose your job. I hated being in that position, putting you in that position."

She snorted.

Much as I wanted to bolt from my seat and pace, I kept my ass in the chair. She needed to see this. Because of my actions in her kitchen, I'd made her vulnerable, and I had to give that back. Even though it felt as though I was about to dive over those rapids and there wasn't going to be a river below to catch me.

"The night at The Mac." I sighed. "I wanted nothing more than to draw you to my side, introduce you as my date." I swallowed. "When Nannette told me you were attacked, that you needed me, I couldn't get there fast enough. I had to help you. I *had* to comfort you." I kept my gaze steady. "I'll always want you, Em. Any way I can get you. Always. I've thought about you every day, every hour, since you sent me away. I can't tell you how many times."

"What I don't understand," she said, voice soft, "is why you weren't honest with me about Nico's concerns. Or that you knew about Sebastian."

"I was jealous," I said. "That sounds stupid, but I was so fucking jealous that he had you first."

She closed her eyes. "That's what hurt the most. I loved Sebastian. Part of me always will, and I need to be with someone who can love me enough to understand that relationship—to support it."

She pressed her lips together so tightly, I worried she'd bite through them.

"I've never had to deal with exes before. It's uncomfortable for me," I said. "And this is unique. I get that he's special to you, as are Josh and Ellie."

Emmaline's lips turned up the briefest amount. "They are. They're my family."

"I've thought about that a lot. About what they mean to you, and what they mean to me because they matter to you."

"And?"

"And I care about your happiness. So, if they make you happy, I'll learn to deal."

She inhaled hard. "Can you? I mean, really? Because I can't go through breaking up with you again. Some things shatter and there's no putting them back. That would be me next time."

"It's a big thing for Sebastian to be a part of your life."

She met my gaze. "Yes, it is. That's why I wanted to take us slowly. And why I fought us at the beginning."

Hope pressed hard against my chest. "Oh?"

"I think my fear of you leaving me, of you hurting me, made our situation worse."

Much as I wanted to touch her I stayed still, giving her the space she needed. "I worried about you, Em. I'll always worry about you because I love you."

Her tongue darted out to touch her lower lip. "I get that now. And I'm sorry for not respecting your feelings enough. I was caught up in my head." She sucked in a breath. "I want to give us a try, Knox, if you're willing."

The hope exploded, causing my chest to squeeze. "I am."

Her eyes brightened at the speed of my answer. Like I was going to say anything else.

"I saw the hurt on your face earlier when I didn't reciprocate and tell you that I'm in love with you, too," she murmured.

I crossed the space and pulled her upright. I cupped my hand around the back of her neck. "I love you, Em. I've never been in love before. And...it's scary. Our connection seems so fragile, and all I want to do is strengthen it."

Her eyes danced. "You mean with a physical display?"

A deep, needy groan rose out of my chest. "Yes."

"That requires orgasms?" she asked.

"Definitely. Yes. If that's what you want."

"Okay."

I swooped my arms around her, and she pressed her hand to my chest. I scooted back.

She met my gaze. "My heart is still fragile, Knox." Her voice wavered. "I love you, but, please be careful with it. With me."

I bent my head and touched my lips to hers with as much tenderness as I could manage.

"I want to make you happy."

"Start now. With naked time and orgasms."

"There's no better way to spend my day."

She raised her eyebrows. "Because of the storm?"

I swept her up in my arms and kissed her again—this time with weeks' worth of passion.

I carried her to my bed, lying her down gently, right where she belonged.

I smoothed her hair back from her brow.

"Because I love you."

Chapter Thirty-Four
Emmaline

Knox and I spent every night together—sometimes at his house and sometimes at my beach house, which now looked like something out of *Town and Country* magazine. It might be small, but the finishes were all high end and every detail considered. Both Knox and I loved the space and planned to spend our summers there on the beach. I'd started overseeing the renovations at Ellie's mansion as she'd requested and enjoyed spending more time with her. Sebastian still remained at the facility in Boston, and I hadn't seen him since the night he told me not to come back.

During long walks on the beach, I'd told him about my last conversation with Sebastian, about forcing myself to go to class and focusing on the goal of a degree, taking full loads during the summer to finish more quickly, then on landing the position at Wright and Associates. He'd told me more about his parents' relationship—how close they'd been to the very end. He'd talked about the pressures of being an elite college athlete, of feeling pressured to give up his dream to help out his family. We'd had fits and starts, but overall, we'd learned to communicate and to listen. We'd learned how to read each other better and how to support each other.

We were happy. No, we were blissful.

I didn't want anything to mess that up, which was why I'd considered skipping Joshua's wedding.

But when I told Knox that—and my reason—he'd pressed a kiss to my knuckles and said, "We have to know we're strong enough for any challenge, Em. If we're not willing to face tough situations, together, then we're not as *together* as I want us to be."

Those words cost him—his hands shook, and fear darkened his eyes. But he'd been strong and steadfast with me since I'd offered him the chance he asked for, and I could do no less for him.

So, we drove up to Martha's Vineyard for the rehearsal dinner. My only stipulation was that we stay at a bed and breakfast down the coast so we'd have an escape.

Knox slid his hand into mine as we stopped in front of the Giovannis' Martha's Vineyard beach house. Now, it belonged to Joshua—a wedding gift from Ellie. His fingers trembled.

"What if he doesn't like me?" Knox asked.

I shivered a little.

I squeezed his hand. "I love you."

"What if he wants to...I don't know...fight for your honor or something."

"I'm nervous, too," I admitted. At Knox's wide-eyed look, I shook my head. "No, you aren't going to have to duel or anything." I giggled at the image.

"Thank fuck," he muttered.

"I haven't seen Sebastian in months, and the last time wasn't great."

I leaned over the console and kissed him. "Do you know what?" I asked.

His lips lingered on mine. "What?"

"I love you. You're my future."

He smiled, his eyes alight with pleasure. "Let's do this."

I laughed.

We strolled into the great room, hand-in-hand. Ellie detached herself from a small group and pulled me into her arms.

"You brought that handsome devil with you," she said loud enough for Knox to hear.

He chuckled, his hand still threaded through mine.

"Good to see you, Ellie," I said.

"I'm glad you're here. Sebastian's been asking about you."

Knox stiffened, and I gave his hand a gentle squeeze.

"Well, then, by all means, we should say hello," I said.

Ellie's face held a secretive smile as she led us through the kitchen, past Joshua and Will, and out onto the patio. Sebastian sat in an Adirondack chair next to an Asian woman. He turned when Ellie said his name.

His eyes lit up when he saw me. "Emmy! I missed you."

I felt a pang, realizing that Sebastian had greeted me this way nearly every time I saw him.

Knox let go of my hand and I stepped forward, wrapping Sebastian in a brief hug. "I missed you, too."

I stepped back, next to Knox, and retained my fingers through his hand. "This is Knox. My boyfriend."

"Hi, Knox," Sebastian said, garbling Knox's unfamiliar name a little. Tension remained in Knox's arm, as if he weren't sure if Sebastian messed up his name on purpose or if he simply couldn't get the sounds out.

Sebastian, unaware of the larger drama, grinned first at Knox, then at me, then at the woman sitting beside him.

"This is Lisa," he said her name carefully, and I had the impression he'd worked hard to get the sounds correct.

"She is my friend," Sebastian said. He beamed.

"Hi, Lisa."

"Hello," she said. Her voice was as soft and serene as her face. "Sebastian's told me all about you. He was very excited to meet Knox."

"Yes. I'm happy because I get to spend time with Lisa. And Emmy is happy with Knox," Sebastian said.

Knox relaxed, which allowed the tension to drain out of me.

We chatted for another ten minutes until Joshua and Will joined us. I hugged them both and Knox shook their hands. I was glad they slid back into the easy rapport I'd noted at The Mac's reception.

Soon, dinner was announced, and we all settled in at the table. Lisa sat next to Sebastian, helping him. I slid my hand up Knox's thigh and squeezed.

"You made a good call with us staying at the B&B," he whispered into my ear.

"Oh?" I asked, blinking up at him with a wide, innocent expression.

"I'm going to tie you to the bed frame and fuck you from behind until you scream. Twice." He passed me a platter. "Bread?"

I shook my head, too turned-on to speak. He winked.

I slid my hand up so that my hand sat at the juncture of his thigh, under his napkin. He continued to chat with Will's father, who was an engineer—and, surprise, surprise, a big hockey fan.

Once the meal ended, Lisa led Sebastian up to his room. I watched him, affection warming my heart along with a tender concern as I noted the exhaustion in his frame.

Joshua slid his arm around my waist and squeezed. "He's as good as he's going to get."

"Yes, I understand that." I hesitated. "Is Lisa his…" I trailed off.

Joshua smiled. "His nurse. And friend, though we all see that Sebastian is interested in more than that."

I nodded.

"Are you happy, Emmy?" Josh asked.

I glanced over at Knox, who was laughing at something Ellie said to him.

"I am. For Sebastian and for me."

Joshua pressed a kiss to my temple. "Then, so am I."

———— Å ————

I told Knox about the conversation as he drove us back to our room. Knox stared forward and then nodded.

"He was worried about you getting stuck. Of being unwilling to live again because of your fear of losing someone you loved."

"I almost did. I almost lost you." Tears welled in my eyes. "I'm so sorry, Knox. I couldn't see this bright, beautiful future."

He turned into the driveway and parked the car before he picked up my hand and kissed my palm.

"I was afraid that Sebastian still had a hold over you. That you'd always love him best."

I shook my head, my throat tight. "You're exactly the man I need."

He smiled, leaning forward to kiss me. His tongue touched mine, rubbing with seductive power. An idea flitted through my mind, and I slid my hand down his chest. Once I reached his seat belt, I unclipped his, then I unclipped mine. I slid over the center console as Knox's eyes began to burn with lust. He re-situated his seat while I lifted my skirt and straddled him. I rubbed my center against his impressive erection and we both moaned.

"I'd like you to take me, here in the car."

He cupped the back of my neck and pulled me down until my lips hovered a breath above his. "Thank fuck for dark windows and no street lamps. And it would be my absolute pleasure."

He kissed me again, and I slid one hand into the hair at his nape while I smoothed the other down his chest; the whole time I slid back and forth in his lap, amping up the friction that caused us both to gasp and moan.

He palmed my breasts, and I flicked his nipple through his shirt with my thumbnail, causing his hips to snap up between my thighs. I hissed in pleasure as he bumped my clit.

"I love you, Knox."

"I love you, Em. So damn much."

I levered upward and unzipped his pants and tugged his thick, warm flesh from his boxer briefs. He groaned.

"Slow down." He gasped as I squeezed him right below the head, circling my thumb on the plump, warm flesh.

"I don't think I will." I used my free hand to slide the gusset of my thong to the side and then maneuvered myself over his big, hard dick before sinking down onto him.

He muttered something unintelligible and I moaned. I placed

my lips over his, drifting them back and forth as I swirled my hips, so full of Knox.

We moved together in a perfect rhythm, our tongues mimicking our bodies' connection. We peaked together in a shuddering rush of pleasure. I leaned my flushed cheek against his racing heart.

"This might need to be our thing," I murmured.

"What's that, darling?"

"Car sex. It's our thing."

He brushed the few tendrils that had escaped my updo off my cheek.

"If you want it to be, sure. But I'm still tying you up in that big bed upstairs."

I pulled back, and the change in our position made us both gasp. I smiled.

"Promise?"

He cupped my cheek, rubbing his thumb over my lower lip. "For you, darling, I promise everything."

Chapter Thirty-Five
Knox

My hands sweat and my heart thumped faster than after a series of sprinting drills across the ice. Nothing in my life prepared me for this moment...or the possibility of failure. But that wasn't an option I was willing to accept.

I rehearsed the speech I planned to deliver tomorrow again—and again—as I waited for Em to open the bathroom door. She'd locked herself in there more than an hour ago, and I admitted to getting antsy. Will had texted her late last night, asking her if she'd mind saying a few words at the wedding. She'd accepted and then freaked out. Much as I hated seeing her frazzled, she'd discussed her feelings before allowing me to fuck her into purring oblivion, so the night had gone along with my plan after all.

I liked both the sharing and the fucking, equally. I assumed that showed my emotional growth, and pride swelled my chest as I realized just how far Em and I had come together in the past few months.

She was my moon, my stars, my entire universe. I made a mental note to apologize for giving Ryder such shit when he'd said something similar about Aidy all those months ago. I wanted a man with my sister who treated her like the treasure she was.

The bathroom door opened with the faint creak I couldn't quite remove. I turned and the glass of water in my hand slid out.

The splash of water in my face caused me to step back, glancing down to find my tie and dress shirt splotchy with wetness before the glass hit the ground with a soft thunk.

"I'm going to take that to mean you like the dress."

"If I liked it any more I would have come in my pants and really embarrassed myself."

She walked forward, her smile widening to a grin. She laid her hand on my wet chest and rose up to kiss me.

"I guess I shouldn't show you the back then."

"Turn," I said, my tone stern. "Now."

She did, glancing at me over her shoulder.

I took in the long, elegant line of her spine. Two faint dimples flirted with the turquoise silk—a color I was quickly coming to associate with Em.

"Fuck," I whispered and drew out the word.

"You like it?"

"I...yes."

She turned around and ran her finger down to my navel, cupping my rock hard dick resting there in her warm hand. I inhaled sharply. My control cratering as she licked her red, slicked lips. "I thought of you when I saw it. Thought of how you'd slide it off me, kissing down my neck, licking across my collarbones."

I groaned. She squeezed me. My dick throbbed.

"I hoped you'd want me to drop to my knees and take you in my mouth."

I closed my eyes and tried to breathe through my excitement at the image. I was so close to losing control, but I wouldn't. I prided myself on...

She gave my dick a gentle tug with a squeeze, then again, and again. Fuck. Em was giving me a hand job while wearing a fuck-me dress. She turned and looked at me over her shoulder, biting her lip. That, her hand rubbing me, and her nude back caused my so-called control to fizzle. I groaned, pressing myself into her hand, knees weakened and dizzy with release. I sought one of the bedposts.

"I need to change."

She smirked. The minx. "Because your shirt's wet?"

I laughed. I loved this woman. "Because you turned me on too much." I caged her with my arms on either side of one of the posters on the B&B's bed, careful not to touch her beautiful dress with my wet front.

"I love you, Emmaline. I love how sexy you are. I love how caring you are. I love how thoughtful you are by wearing clothes that seduce me—and then actually seducing me. But mainly I love you because you're you and I'm me, and I couldn't have stopped my feelings for you for the world."

She blinked up at me, eyes shimmering. She cupped my cheek. Her thumb pressed to the center of my lower lip. "That was, without a doubt, the sweetest thing anyone has ever said to me."

I pressed a kiss to her thumb. "I meant every word, darling."

Her smile was soft. "I know. And I love you, too." She tipped her head further back and sighed. "I used to think that was wrong—that I shouldn't be able to love two men. That I was fundamentally flawed. But I realized something last night as I saw you with Sebastian."

I waited, breath hitching and heart once again thumping like I'd played an entire championship game.

Her hand remained on my cheek, her gaze steady. "I realized that I had to love Sebastian then in order to realize just how special what I have with you is now. I realized that Sebastian will own that first blossom, that youthful love that was so full of dreams and possibilities, but you have the love of maturity." She leaned in closer, her breast grazing the front of my damp and messy chest.

"I'd fight my demons for you all over again," she murmured. "I'd defy odds for you. I'd give up all my former dreams to have just one more day with you."

This time my eyes grew misty. I clenched the bedpost so that I didn't pull her tight against me, crushing her to my chest and ruining her beautiful gown.

She slid her arm around my neck and molded her body to mine, and I loved that even more.

"I want to spend every minute I have with you, Knox. I want to be with you through the highs of getting another big contract, of holding our first child, of sharing our first married kiss."

Her eyes sparkled, and her lips quirked up into a soft, sensual smile that stole my breath. Or maybe that was her words. Whatever the reason, Em's held me spellbound.

"I want to have quiet nights together on the couch, your arm around my shoulders and chest as we snuggle together. I want to cook with you in our amazing kitchen, trying first bites of new, interesting recipes. I want to drive through little towns and have you tell me about the architectural history. I want to love you with my mouth and my hands and body every night in our big bed."

She pressed even tighter against me; neither of us worried any more about clothing. I wrapped my arms around her waist, one hand moving upward to hold her between her shoulders, just below her nape.

"I want all that with you—and I never knew how much I could want that until we came here all those months ago. That was my *a-ha*! moment. I fought it, sure I was being unfaithful to Sebastian. But you know what, Knox? By doing so, I was unfaithful to *your* love, to us, and I'm so, so sorry."

Her voice cracked and her eyes filled further. Overcome, I pressed another kiss to her lips. It was soft, more of a question. She opened under my mouth, her tongue teasing the seam of my lips.

"Be mine," I whispered against her petal-soft skin. "Always. Forever. Starting now. Be my lover, my fiancée, and soon my wife. *Be mine.*"

She pulled back enough to cup both my cheeks in her small palms. "I already am."

I gathered her closer and kissed her again. And I kept kissing her and kept doing so until my phone chimed in my pocket and hers went off in her little clutch.

"We need to go," I said against her mouth.

"I need to freshen up," she said.

I chuckled, glancing down at my rumpled dress shirt. I sighed. "I guess that means I'm wearing the clothes I wore last night."

"Nope," Em said. "I brought you another suit and packed a couple extra sets of undergarments for us both. They're in the closet."

"You minx," I said.

"Hey, it was worth it," she said her tone haughty.

I snagged her hand and pulled her into the small walk-in closet.

"I have something for you—if you're willing to put it on."

"Well, if it's a new dress, I am," Em said. "This one is a bit wrinkled."

I turned to look her over. The moisture had left faint, darker stains on her rib cage and abdomen. I licked my lips.

"You look good enough to lick, top to bottom."

Her laugh peeled through the space, clarion clear and full of pleasure. "Let's do that later, for sure. Good thing I brought another gown."

"You did? Then why'd you put on that one?" I asked.

I tugged off my tie and began unbuttoning my shirt. I tossed both into the open suitcase and then undid my belt.

"You weren't kidding about needing to change," she said, amusement and satisfaction settling in her eyes. She raised her gaze as I stripped out of my damp boxer briefs. I wiped myself to get off as much of the sticky residue as possible.

"That's why I wore it." She tipped her head toward my semi-hard dick. "To see how far I could push you—to get you in a haze so that you *had* to agree to marry me."

I stopped, my second leg just about to settle into my new underwear. I stumbled a little but managed to pull them up. "Wait. What?"

She shrugged as she slid down the side zipper of her dress. With another gentle shrug, the dress pooled at her feet. She wasn't wearing a bra. Her panties were barely more than the thinnest, finest strips of silk. I pulled a play from her book and raised my gaze to her face.

"You were dilly-dallying about asking me, and I decided weeks ago it was time for us to start planning our wedding." She drew in a deep breath, her gaze serious when she met mine. "Life is short, Knox. I don't want to miss a minute of our time together."

She slid into a more modest lavender silk gown that matched her heels.

"You tricked me?" I asked. But the thought amused me. I hadn't been dilly-dallying; I'd been worried it was too soon.

I frowned. Damn, that sounded a lot like dilly-dallying.

I grabbed a new white dress shirt from a hanger and slid it on. I pulled on my new suit pants and took the tie she handed me. It was new—and matched her dress, exactly.

The little schemer.

"No, *I* seduced you. You know, like you did during the blizzard. Fair's fair, Knox. I'm playing for keeps."

I finished buttoning my shirt and slid the tails into the waistband of my pants. We moved together to the bathroom, and I turned up the collar of my shirt and started tying my tie in the double Windsor knot I preferred.

"What if I don't want to be seduced into agreeing?" I asked, side-eyeing her. She paused in the act of repainting her lips, her tube of lipstick almost to her lips.

"You don't want to marry me?"

A note of uncertainty flitted through her words. She set down her lipstick, devastation written all over her face.

"Okay. Well. Um. Sure. My...my mistake."

"Em, would you look at me?" I coaxed.

Tears once again swam in her eyes. Behind the moisture I saw such disappointment, it stole my breath.

"I want to marry you more than I want my next breath. But...I want to ask you."

"You did. A few minutes ago. And I said yes."

"And you want to wear my ring tonight, when we're at Joshua's wedding? With Sebastian there?"

She beamed up at me. "Of course. Nothing would make me happier."

"All right."

I retreated to the closet and pulled the black leather belt through my slacks before shoving my feet into my sleek black dress shoes. I palmed the small, understated box from Cynthia Britt I'd picked up a few weeks ago after a meeting in Boston that I'd shoved into the bottom of my suitcase. I met her in the bedroom, dropping down on my knee.

Without a word, I opened the box, smiling at her gasp as I took the ring out and slid it onto her trembling finger. It was a round-cut diamond with a halo of small sapphires around it, all set in platinum, which shone against her pale skin.

I pressed a kiss to her finger.

"It looks good on you."

"It's beautiful," she breathed.

"You're beautiful. And you're perfect for me."

I kissed her hard and deep. She pulled back, breathless as our phones chimed again.

"Better get going, darling," I said with a wink.

She pouted. "I didn't plan this well." I took her hand, playing with my ring on her finger. "I don't want to go to Josh's wedding. I want to take you to bed."

"That's why I planned to ask you tomorrow so we could have a nice, leisurely bout of lovemaking afterward."

She nibbled her lower lip, which was swollen thanks to our hot make-out session earlier. "I jumped the gun."

"Not the first time," I said cheerfully.

"And I'm horny."

"I am, too, but not as bad as I thought I'd be when I claimed you. Must be the orgasm you gave me from that ridiculously sexy dress and hand job."

I led her down the stairs of the large house and out the front door. I opened her car door. She slid inside, a slight pout making her even more adorable.

"Bet you wish you'd had one of those," I said with a chuckle.

"I do still own that dress," she mused. "Next time, I'll wear it out in public."

I shook my head. "If you don't, I'll give you the best orgasm of your life," I whispered as I leaned down to nip her ear. "A deep, long pull of pleasure that'll leave you breathless and wanting more."

"Oh."

I shut her car door and hurried around to the other side, entering quickly.

"By the way, that ring's part of the no-take-backsies rule. You're mine, darling. Even if you did mess up my epic proposal."

"Epic, huh?"

"*Epic.*"

"Now, I'm curious."

"Too bad. You wanted the ring now. You're mine." I said the word again because I could—and she was.

"I sure am," she said in a chipper voice. "Which is why you're going to meet me in the bathroom before my speech, and make sure you take away all my nervous energy."

I nodded solemnly. "That's the least I can do."

Her smile overflowed with emotion. "The bare minimum."

"I'll bare you later and you won't be leaving that bed for a long, long time."

"Only fair," she said, voice husky with need.

I pulled up to a light and glanced over at her. "By the way, there's nothing in the handbook about married couples working at Wright and Associates. And, seeing how you'll be a Wright soon, I believe you really need to reclaim your desk."

She crossed her legs, exposing a long slit that I had to ignore. I'd given her my word to pay attention to the road with my full focus, and I planned to always keep that vow. Em deserved my promises and my best—in all things.

"That could be arranged," she said. "After I finish Ellie's renovations, of course."

"Of course."

She was quiet for the last few minutes of the ride. As I helped her from the car, she said, "I don't want a desk in the middle of the open space." She wrinkled her nose. "I want an office. With a door. So I can fuck you when the mood strikes."

I shifted, my pants constricting in the crotch. This woman. I shook my head. "I have an office. With a door."

"But *I* don't. And everyone would know you were calling me in for a booty call." She *tsked*. "Where's your professionalism, Knox?"

"Flew out the window the moment I laid eyes on you, darling." I helped her up the steps to the front door now festooned with a large monogram of Josh and Will's new initials.

"I'll work on the office," I said.

I turned and leered at her as I led her toward the patio where Josh and Will planned to exchange their vows. The space boasted an arbor of white roses and plush white chairs. Blue peonies added a splash of color.

"Or we could share one."

"I'll consider that," she said, her tone prim as we walked to our seats on the groom's side. And she settled into her chair. "I have another request."

"What's that?" I asked.

She leaned in close and murmured in a low voice. "I'll consider sharing your office and working for you if you really do give me the best orgasm of my life before I have to give this speech later." She shifted, her eyes dropping to her clasped hands. "I'm nervous."

"You got yourself a deal. I'll leave you so satisfied, you won't be able to feel any nerves."

I caught her smirk in my peripheral vision. "There's that arrogance I love so much. I'm glad I found you, Knox."

I pressed a kiss to her temple and placed her hand on my thigh, pride swirling through me as her ring—my promise for our future—sparkled in the afternoon sunlight.

"So am I, darling. So am I."

Want to keep up with all of the new releases in Vi Keeland and Penelope Ward's Cocky Hero Club world? Make sure you sign up for the official Cocky Hero Club newsletter for all the latest on our upcoming books:
https://www.subscribepage.com/CockyHeroClub

Check out other books in the Cocky Hero Club series:
http://www.cockyheroclub.com

ACKNOWLEDGMENTS

Thank you, Deborah Nemeth, for bringing this rough diamond to a polished one.

Piper Lawson, I've so enjoyed our coffee chats and your thoughtful critiques. Both have made me a better indie writer. Many, many thanks for sharing your knowledge and expertise.

Thanks to Kathleen Page and Charity Chimni for their time and amazing proofreading skills. You ladies are the best nitpickers and I'm so thankful to have you on my team!

And, as always, to Chris. You help me in so many ways—like this rockin' cover! Thank you for all that you do for me professionally, but more, for putting up with my crazy all these years.

To my awesome PR team at The Next Step PR, you ladies rock! Working with you is pure joy.

And to my readers. Well, clearly, without you, none of this would be possible. The fact that you trust me with your time is the greatest compliment. Thank you so, so much.

ABOUT THE AUTHOR

USA Today bestseller Alexa Padgett's books have garnered accolades from prestigious organizations, including *Kirkus Reviews*, National Indie Excellence Awards, and *Publishers Weekly*.

Alexa spent a good part of her youth traveling. From Budapest to Belize, Calgary to Coober Pedy, she soaked in the myriad smells, sounds, and feels of these gorgeous places, wishing she could live in them all–at least for a while. And she does in her books.

She lives in New Mexico with her husband, children, and Great Pyrenees pup, Ash. When not writing, schlepping, or volunteering, she can be found in her tiny kitchen, channeling her inner Barefoot Contessa.